Euphemia MacFarrigle
and the Laughing Virgin

Euphemia MacFarrigle and the Laughing Virgin

CHRISTOPHER WHYTE

VICTOR GOLLANCZ

LONDON

First published in Great Britain 1995
by Victor Gollancz
An imprint of the Cassell Group
Wellington House, 125 Strand, London WC2R OBB

The poem reproduced on pages 157/8 is 'Requiem für Wolf
Graf von Kalckreuth' by Rainer Maria Rilke.

A catalogue record for this book is
available from the British Library.

ISBN 0 575 06065 4

Typeset at The Spartan Press Ltd,
Lymington, Hants
Printed in Great Britain by
St Edmundsbury Press Ltd, Bury St Edmunds, Suffolk

Euphemia MacFarrigle
and the Laughing Virgin

ONE

Cissie MacPhail was at a loss to explain why it was that every time she found herself in the vicinity of Euphemia MacFarrigle she became peculiarly conscious of her own private parts. It could have been a nervous reaction. But the tensing was a little too low down in the body for it to be her gut. And in any case, what reason had she to fear the woman?

An untutored eye would have judged them to be very much the same sort of person. Both dressed as respectably married women in their fifties are expected to do, carried sizeable handbags, and devoted considerable attention (Cissie, at any rate) to the choice of their hats. Euphemia, she remembered, had even complimented her on her taste, on one of those rare occasions when a knot of worshippers lingered at the convent door after Lenten morning mass, until the chill wind of early spring sent them scuttling with its cold, piercing tongue.

The strange sensation produced a frown of displeasure on Cissie's brow. The reaction was also provoked by disappointment at sharing the privilege, accorded her only at infrequent intervals, of afternoon tea in Mother Genevieve's sitting room. Euphemia was ensconced there already when Cissie arrived. She had taken the warmest seat by the one-bar electric fire. Smoothing her yellow skirt primly over her hidden kneecaps, she was indicating that yes, she would take three cubes of sugar in her extremely milky tea.

Their paths had crossed earlier that day. It was the third week of Lent and Cissie was proud that she had attended seven o'clock mass every morning since the season of penitence began. Euphemia was nothing like so assiduous in her attendance. Getting out of bed on these chill, dark mornings was no small sacrifice, particularly since Cissie left Rob curled up comfortably under the blankets while she shivered in the unheated bedroom. As she hurriedly encased her meagre curves in various articles of pale beige lingerie, she would watch him turn over and settle in the centre of the mattress, not even opening an eye to acknowledge her departure.

Neither food nor drink must pass her lips if she was to partake of the sacrament. Consequently, she could be out of the house barely ten minutes after the alarm clock's speedily suppressed tinkling. If she was lucky, she would be among the first to push open the heavy wooden door of the Oratory of St Bridget and could take her place at the very front of the pews.

That morning she had arrived before the nuns filed in. A black metal grille separated them from the rest of the congregation. Cissie had pressed her nose against its coldness while a shadowy, veiled figure lit the altar candles and placed the wine and water cruets on a small table to one side.

Only dim echoes of the joys and discontents of this mysterious community of women ever reached her. As a result they had lost nothing of the glamour which had attracted her as long as she could remember. Married early, the mother of a grown-up son, she had had to abandon any idea of becoming a bride of Christ. But if she could have lived her life again, perhaps that was the path she would have chosen.

At least she would have known a little more of what was now afoot. A glance at Mother Genevieve's troubled face confirmed her suspicions that at present all was not well with the community. It comprised, alongside the Mother Superior, eleven nuns, three of whom were novices. On the first Wednesday in Lent one of them had entered the chapel with tears streaming down her cheeks and had continued sobbing, supported on either side by her two sisters, throughout the ceremony. Two days later another had rushed from her pew just before the consecration. Soon she could be heard retching from a nearby chamber. She had not returned, and the incident had been repeated with the third novice.

Cissie noted how the three took on heightened colour from day to day, sometimes pale, sometimes flushed with a sultry, excited look. Strangest of all had been this morning's novelty. There could be no doubt about it, for she had a privileged view and could have reached through the grille with her hand and brushed the sisters' crisply starched wimples as they passed. All but the three youngest were wearing earplugs, not just in one, but in both ears. She had been able to check this when they filed out at the end of mass, heading in the opposite direction.

Was Mother Genevieve now going to enlighten them? Cissie mumbled her thanks as she took her cup of tea and looked round for a suitable place to park her handbag. A horrid thought struck her. What if Euphemia was on to her? What if she had got word of the secret sodality of Blessed Maria Alfocorado and its work? And to think that it had crossed her mind to divulge the great plan to Mother Genevieve if they had been alone together that afternoon! Mentally she gave herself a severe scolding. But one look at Euphemia reassured her. The woman had other preoccupations.

Euphemia had produced a moderately sized Quality Street chocolates tin from her handbag. She placed it on the table and opened it. It contained a decorated plate wrapped in paper napkins and three fairy cakes in clingfilm. Cissie was rather offended at the implication that Euphemia, at any rate, had been informed she would be coming.

The fairy cakes had pleated paper cup cases. Each had a splurge of white icing at its crown. The one she was pressing on Mother Genevieve undoubtedly had the most tasteless decoration. Two rows of little blue globules formed a Greek cross, with a surprisingly large red globule at the point where the arms intersected.

Mother Genevieve was protesting. During Lent she would only accept weak tea without milk or sugar. How could she possibly agree to eat a cake?

All at once her protestations struck Cissie as preposterous. She was liable to forget that she and Mother Genevieve went back a long way. They had been brought up on the same stair in one of the quieter streets in Glasgow's West End, no more than five minutes' walk from the tea party they were at present engaged in, and had gone to the same secondary school. At that time Mother Genevieve was simple Brenda MacCafferty, notorious among her schoolmates for allowing boys to feel her up in a shack at a murky spot along the banks of the River Kelvin. Cissie was well aware of the location of the shack and the times of the rendezvous. Nevertheless she had not taken part, more through fear than for any considerations of piety.

A scandal broke when the whole thing came out and, branded as the ringleader, Brenda was packed off to board at a convent school, a transition which launched her in her ecclesiastical career. Her father was a lawyer and her family could easily afford that kind of thing. Cissie's parents had had to struggle to meet the admittedly very reasonable fees of the private day school which still operated on the other side of the Botanic Gardens.

After further coaxing, Mother Genevieve at last agreed and tucked the fairy cake into her small mouth with much munching and complacent salivation. Cissie noticed the moustache that graced her upper lip, its hairs so pale they could only be made out when they caught the light and glinted against her puffy skin.

Euphemia, who had shown considerable anxiety that Mother Genevieve should consume that particular cake, adjusted her hat contentedly and shook the crumbs from her lap. The talk could now begin.

☆

The archbishop's palace occupies three floors and the basement of an austere yet august tenement in one of Glasgow's prime real estate locations. The circus where it lies is perched at the top of a gentle hill which offers stupendous views westwards across the Kelvin valley to the tower of the university, eastwards to a horizon of high-rise flats and snaking motorways, and south-wards to the Renfrewshire hills past a river shorn of the cranes that once peopled it.

In the city's heyday, the coaches of industrial magnates and distinguished professionals would circle the hilltop, with its neatly groomed park at the centre, then pause in front of one of the splendid residences to collect a young lady bound for her French lessons, or a young man late for his lecture in the anatomy theatre just hidden by the neighbouring hill.

The ancestors of those who now finance the operations of the archdiocese and fill its churches not quite to overflowing were the lowest of the low. It took two generations for navvies, hawkers, factory workers, nannies, and girls who found prostitution the only profession open to them on disembarking at the Broomielaw, to amass money and respectability. Lawyers and surgeons, bookmakers, police inspectors and schoolteachers were numbered among their grandchildren.

Today the circus is a lugubrious haunt of insurance offices, architects' studios and cultural institutes, with only lively cacophonies from the student residences at its western end to break the uninterrupted silence of its decadence.

The consultant Dr Aloysius Quinn spent nearly fifteen minutes driving round in search of a parking place, enough to spoil his temper and inspire him with a distinct nervousness. The archbishop was a client who hated to be kept waiting. As it was, the doctor had to leave his sleek Mercedes saloon on a double yellow line. All he wanted now was to find it had been towed away when he emerged from his appointment. He was due in at the hospital before lunchtime.

A man of sterling Catholic descent with a Jesuit education, he derived a not insignificant part of his considerable income from private ministrations to the upper echelons of the city's ecclesiastical hierarchy. Neither unintelligent nor narrow-minded, he found it politic to speak of contraception and abortion as abominations, their practice a disgrace to the profession he had espoused with such idealism and devotion in his youth.

It wasn't just being late that made him nervous. The business he had been summoned about was rum stuff indeed. So far his Catholic faith and medical textbooks had been able to account for just about all the phenomena he encountered in his life. Excitement and the irrational were confined to the football field he visited on alternate Saturdays and occasionally on Wednesday evenings. There was no room for them in his professional life. And now he confronted a series of events for which there was no rational explanation.

The archbishop, too, had got the wind up. That must be why he was harrying Quinn with calls and confidential meetings. Yet this was a matter that as a doctor he could not resolve or tidy away. All he could do was allow nature, if indeed these things were natural, to take its course.

Money was not as plentiful in the archdiocese as it had once been. Staff cuts meant that he had to ring the doorbell several times before someone came to open. It was not Mrs Donnelly, the archbishop's housekeeper. Presumably she was out doing the shopping. Instead a nun appeared, clutching a knife and a half-peeled carrot in one hand while she wiped the other on a smutty apron and peered blearily at him. She had forgotten to put in her contact lenses that morning.

He muttered a greeting, shot past and was surprised to find the archbishop waiting for him at the head of the stairs. Instead of being taken into the private cabinet, he was ushered into a side room and told to sit down. The archbishop looked scared.

'Most kind of you to come, Dr Quinn,' he said. He was not a Glasgow man, but came from Connemara and his accent had lost none of its richness in the course of fifteen years spent in Scotland.

'There have been unexpected developments,' he said, almost in a whisper.

'As you know, we had to inform Rome of this most regrettable affair. It has been extremely embarrassing to be incapable of accounting in any way for what is going on. You would think someone was playing a practical joke on us were it not obvious that those poor distressed girls are perfectly blameless. I suspect the Vatican may even have doubted our words. They demanded confirmation of the facts no less than three times. And now they have decided to send an investigator.'

He looked at Quinn with raised, expressive eyebrows, flexing his hands on the table between them. Quinn could not quite see the reasons for his alarm.

'An envoy of the Black Pope, Dr Quinn! One of his men! This is serious!'

Quinn's expression was blank. Then he remembered an overweight and rather sinister Italian who had visited the school when he was a boy.

'The Black Pope? You mean the head of the Jesuit order?'

'Yes, I do!' The archbishop's eyes gleamed in triumph. Now the consultant would appreciate the gravity of his predicament.

'These are the people they put on to heretics, the ones they set to ferret out false miracles. They've been very busy in Yugoslavia, or Croatia, or wherever it is now, that bare mountainside the madonna keeps appearing on.'

He got up and went over to the window.

'I'm not at all happy about this. You know my brother, the one who was at Galway, was made a cardinal last year. I presumed it was only a matter of time before my turn came to be elevated. But if things are seen to be haywire in the archdiocese, who knows how long it may take! As if it wasn't enough with all the financial worries I have!'

The priest came and sat down again.

'I want all of this cleared up before the man gets here.'

He took a sheet of paper from his breast pocket and scrutinized it through his bifocals.

'Feli—, Felipe Gu . . . tierr . . . ez. A Basque, to boot! Good Lord, they're real fanatics! There'll be no peace to be had once he arrives.'

He took the consultant's hand in a grasp that was intended to be friendly but came over as merely pleading.

'Dr Quinn, I have decided to call in a private detective. He's with my personal secretary next door. I want you to come through with me now and back me up as I fill him in on all the details of this incredible affair.'

☆

The priest called it nocturnal pollution. So that was what had happened. He thought he had burst something, thought it was a kind of wound inside him, though what came out was not blood but that white, sticky, almond-scented stuff. He'd found it on his pyjamas before, in the morning, or waking up halfway through the night with a damp feeling in his crotch. This was the first time he had actually made it happen.

There was no way it could be a sin when it happened like that during sleep. Surely he wasn't responsible for anything that came into his mind then. He wasn't even conscious, so how could there be a question of venial or mortal sin? But if he brought it upon himself, that had to be another matter. That kind of stuff took you to hell.

Confessing it hadn't been easy. Confessions were on Saturday afternoons in the parish church, from five till eight. The first Saturday afternoon he had sat for three hours motionless at home, unable to face going and unable to do anything but think about what might happen if he didn't go. His mother had put her head round the door of his room a couple of times to see what he was doing but hadn't asked any questions. He felt a sense of relief when she went out that night, leaving him on his own with his books and the television.

The night had been difficult to get through. All sorts of strange obsessions crowded into his head. The roof might collapse and crush him underneath rubble and broken rafters. Perhaps the gas fire in his bedroom had not been turned off properly and the escape would gradually poison the air, lulling him into unconsciousness before he woke with a start to judgement and the fires of hell.

It was in and out of his mind all during the week. When he went to the concert on Tuesday night he sat in the middle of a row with bodies tightly packed together on either side of him. The emergency exits were a long way away. If a fire were to break out suddenly it would be impossible for all of the audience to get out in time. He would be trapped in the burning inferno, stifled by the smoke, and then he would be for it. On Friday night he made it happen again. That decided him. At five past five on Saturday afternoon he was in his row in the church, head bowed, preparing his speech.

The priest was surprisingly unaffected by what he heard, and the penance he imposed was very lenient. But then, Gerald had kept back one crucial detail. Did it make a difference whether he had been thinking about a man or about a woman? Of course it did. Both were mortal sins, but even among mortal sins there are gradations and degrees.

He hadn't been able to bring himself to tell the priest how he made it happen, or what kind of pictures were in his head when it did.

Pictures of that kind had always been with him, almost as far back as he could remember. He could only have been about six when his parents took him to see *Babes in the Wood* at Christmas time. That was one of the first occasions when he had felt a sensation nothing else could quite match, a mixture of excitement and abandon, dangerous and invigorating at the same time. It came when the two babes lay asleep between the knotted roots of a great oak tree and round its bole peeped the young robber chief, wearing a three-cornered hat and a black Lone Ranger mask that concealed his eyes and perched on his finely modelled nose. The robber was an outlaw and you never knew what he might be capable of, but somehow you also knew he was not bad and would turn out to be the long-lost prince in the end. He would take off his mask and hat, and the abundant golden curls would burst free and jostle at his neckline as he offered the princess his hand.

Other images made the sensation come back. He imagined he was suffering from a mysterious illness, confined to bed, the object of unstinting attention from his mother and friends, and in particular from a young intern. This doctor measured his pulse, then sat at the bedside holding his hand, murmuring gently that Gerald was not to worry, they would come up with a cure before too long.

Another story was so ridiculous he was embarrassed to remind himself of it. Its incongruity did nothing to deprive it of power. The flat they stayed in was on the second floor, and from its windows you could see across the narrow street into the rooms of the houses opposite. At night, when he went to sleep, he would leave the middle sash of the three-bayed window slightly raised because his mother had told him the change of air while he slept would promote his health. During the night he would hear a soft tapping at the opened window. Getting up in his pyjamas, he pulled the curtains aside and noted without surprise a beautiful white horse parked at second-floor level in the cold air outside. Its rider had come to summon him. He pulled the sash up as high as he could and the rider clambered in. They embraced briefly (his head barely reached the man's shoulder), then mounted the steed and rode off together into the sky. Where were they bound? Who was the rider? Why did he feel no cold? Gerald knew the answer to none of these questions. All he had was the certainty that he was safe with this man and would come to no harm, and that the place he was being taken to was a happier one than the world in which he lived.

Everything about these imaginings was innocent, even chaste. Until the nocturnal pollution happened he had managed to convince himself that they were not sexual in any way. He had learned about the facts of life in furtive conversations with a school companion who had the *Encyclopaedia Britannica* at home. The idea had puzzled him at first, as if the man peed into the woman, although he soon realized that could not be the case. Nothing had prepared him for what his body did now, and he was at a loss to connect it with the feelings he was supposed to have for a woman, or with how his body and hers would eventually fit together.

☆

It had never brought him anything but trouble. Other men would have been overjoyed by a similar endowment, and at least some women must be hunting for it fruitlessly, jettisoning man after man in the process. Precious as it was reputed to be, it had dogged Cyril Braithwaite ever since his first girlfriend had remarked on it. In some strange way he blamed it for what was happening to his marriage. And he was absolutely furious with himself for letting one of the choirboys glimpse it in the showers.

Nobody could have objected to the cathedral prebendary supervising the Saturday afternoon football match. It was an institution he himself had introduced and it had done a lot to boost the morale and numbers of the choir that sang on Sundays. Showering with his team was a natural consequence. Players, reserves and referees showered together, adults and minors, pubescent and pre-pubescent. A lot of horseplay went on which he did nothing to prevent. It was perfectly natural and even beneficial. Just because the boys were Christians didn't mean they had to grow up with hang ups about their appendages.

Naturally Cyril did not take part. But that day he had been unable to resist playing with himself under the jet of warm water, briefly and deliciously. He was sweaty and muddy and the soap suds slid luxuriously over his skin. It was ten days since he had washed. Ten days, in fact, since Amanda had finally packed her bags and left. There had been no point in keeping himself clean since then, no point even in changing his clothes. Truly he had allowed himself to get into a dreadful state.

Showering naked was strictly forbidden. All he had done was to manoeuvre his shorts down over his hips and lather his

16

private parts. It reminded him of that glorious summer in the Greek islands the year before he qualified, when he had swum in the nude day after day with the ease and confidence of a pagan god. It was the first time he had felt good about himself in a long train of dreary weeks as things with Amanda deteriorated. And then he caught the lead treble watching him. Their eyes met straight on. Cyril froze and flushed. The boy did not look away at once but nodded knowingly and turned to one of his companions. Quickly Cyril flipped his shorts into place and turned his back, not daring to touch it although it had ended up in a rather uncomfortable position.

The damage was done. Word had in fact already got about. If only Amanda could have held her tongue! He attempted to calm the access of anger. It was not Christian and until he learned to control these impulses there was absolutely no chance of getting her back.

He had not been a controlling husband. He respected his wife's right to go where she wished and believe what she chose, even when her unconcealed scepticism made it more and more difficult for her to perform the duties expected of a clergyman's helpmate. The wives of the clergy fortnightly discussion group sounded innocent enough. Nevertheless his forebodings had proved to be entirely justified. God knows what those women talked about! They certainly didn't limit themselves to the management of a parish and points of doctrine.

He was convinced Amanda had let it slip about her husband's problem. To be fair, it was both their problem. If the sexual side of things had gone more smoothly he was sure they could have handled their other incompatibilities. After all, one did not expect marriage to be a bed of roses. She, too, had been very distressed at their increasing failure to get on. And she would naturally pour out her troubles to the other women in the group. This meant that not just the Episcopalians, but the Church of Scotland woman and the Wee Frees and even a Catholic nun or two now knew exactly what it was that made him just a little different from the ordinary run of men.

He cursed the day he had been sent to Scotland. In the United States they were infinitely more laid-back about matters sexual. He and Amanda would have gone to a clinic with the blessing of their bishop and sorted the whole mess out after one or two appointments. The Scots were so strait-laced! And he objected to them calling his congregation Piskies and the place they worshipped the English Church. Not only did it rain almost every day, with grey skies and lowering cloud even when it was dry, the attitudes in this godforsaken city had contributed directly to the break-up of his marriage. If Amanda hadn't been cut off from contact with her friends in Oxford she would have coped quite differently. And if she'd had some tutoring to do there would have been less time for her to brood on the things that made her so unhappy.

☆

O great commandress and chief mischief-maker!

You have entrusted an exceedingly strange task to myself and my minions. I am ready to swear by those ends which we all serve that never in the long history of my kind has such a request been made of us. Yet we are prompt to your every wish, and the laughter your plan provoked is surety that it conforms to our cherished ideals.

Nonetheless the practical aspect gives me pause. Far be it from me to boast! You know, however, that in the course of a long and distinguished career I have assumed almost all the shapes and sizes conceivable by a human, or other than human, imagination. Where the tools and weapons at my disposal were inappropriate for the task I faced, I did not hesitate to invent new ones whose efficacy has been put to the test time and again, in situations of great danger and great laughter.

Having said all this, you are the first to command that I should assemble a working party to penetrate the deepest mysteries of the human anatomy and to investigate the furthest recesses of the sex they call female. I foresee numerous problems. Consequently it may not be beyond my station to observe that I find your request to keep you regularly informed of our progress thoroughly appropriate.

To begin with, I am uncertain whether we can reach the area destined for our activities from the point of entry you propose. The passage of matter through the human body is rapid in the extreme. When all is in smooth working order they ingest,

18

absorb and eject within the space of twenty-four hours. I therefore fear that the energy of this progress may sweep my party out into the world again before we have the chance to get our bearings.

If we have to deviate from the digestive channel in order to enter the organs of generation it is of the utmost importance that we should make whatever incisions are necessary at precisely the right spot. If we are to adopt circuitous routes and hazard our steps in the body's more devious and labyrinthine passages, then we must be sure of coming out at the correct point. Imagine if we were to be trapped inside for ever, or at least until the natural process of decomposition released the body's constituents to the elements once more!

You will therefore, I make no doubt, be reassured to learn that our navigator is equipped with several works of anatomy whose diagrams are detailed in the extreme. These will serve as maps in the odyssey we are about to undertake. We have also accumulated, as per your explicit instructions, a wide range of cleaning instruments, namely brushes, sponge pads, dusters, mops, absorbent tissues, pincers, tweezers, syringes, suction tubes and probes, as well as a battery of fluids, solvents, jellies and powders and a discreet quantity of minor explosives.

Suitably shrunken, myself, my helpers and our equipment are now ready to enter the globule you have confected for our transportation. May your allseeing eyes watch over us on our perilous and, I sincerely hope, hilarious journey. My next report will reach you from a very different and novel location.

✳

Mick McFall had been working as a private detective for just over seven months. The first weeks were very lean indeed. Then, once he got his name into the *Yellow Pages*, a regular flow of clients began to enter his office. He regretted not being able to afford the West End. It would have been a classier location. Limited finances had led him to rent a flat on the other side of the road from the Tron Theatre near the Saltmarket, just above the tattoo artist's salon. He consoled himself that it was merely a question of exchange of styles. The West End was select and moneyed but rather effete, Argyle Street macho and intense with just a hint of hidden violence. The flat was two stairs up and had the big storm doors intact. He had a rippled glass panel cut into the inner door of the kind he had seen in Hollywood gangster films. 'Michael McFall MA – Private Investigations Agency' it read, in solid black capitals which formed the upper two thirds of a large circle.

Mick was in his early forties, a refugee from secondary-school teaching, which had got too much for his sorely frayed nerves after a dart hit the blackboard just six inches to the left of his ear during an afternoon English interpretation class. St Pius XXVII's was the third school he had worked in, amidst a downward spiral of collapsing discipline, crude sexual innuendo and spelling errors whose outrageousness pained his neat, clerkish soul.

Unfortunately he was also a romantic, inured to American detective fiction since adolescence. On Saturday afternoons he liked to loll in a coffee shop in Princes Square and, feet up on a vacant chair, survey the legs of the women who passed by, seeking out his Glaswegian Lauren Bacall. The torso and head were inevitably a disappointment.

Even more disillusioning were the cameos of human spite and wretchedness which constituted his first cases. Jealous husbands wished to have their wives stalked. Business partners sought details of each other's private lives that could come in useful in coercing assent to shady or downright illegal agreements which would otherwise have been laughed off with scorn. He was asked to disfigure, maim and, on one memorable occasion, to kill those who had incurred the anger of ex-lovers, step-parents, accomplices in crime and former employees. Mick drew the line at violence, and settled for more humdrum pursuits, such as chasing after missing persons he was reassuringly unlikely to find, or helping a stockbroker extract his youngest son from drug-infested parties.

When the archbishop called he could hardly contain his excitement. This was his first major assignment and, asked to name a fee, he hazarded a four-figure sum which was accepted with alacrity. Secrecy was of the highest order. Mick was a little afraid the archbishop would recognize him. After all, it was little more than three years since the high-ranking cleric had visited the school and called in on Mick's class, who sat simpering and supercilious with all hands on desks just for the occasion. The archbishop had been accompanied by a lesser priest in biretta and white surplice with a bowl of holy water. He sprinkled it over the front rows and blessed the classroom crucifix before continuing his tour.

Now, sitting in the Ubiquitous Chip pub just off Byres Road and recounting the interview to his young sidekick Craig Donaldson, he skipped details such as his own fear and trembling or dropping his hat as soon as he got in the door. His thumbnail verbal sketches of the archbishop, his chief secretary Fr Feenan and the consultant Dr Quinn were intended to be models of professional concision for his apprentice.

'When they got down to business, I couldn't believe my ears. There have been three immaculate conceptions in a Glasgow convent!'

Craig was a Protestant and failed to pick up on his employer's doctrinal inaccuracy. His eyes widened.

'What's an immaculate conception?'

Mick stopped the wheezing, which was his asthmatic's equivalent of hearty laughter, and wiped his eyes.

'Three of the young sisters are in the family way. And they've managed to convince the doctor they've never been near a man.'

'But that's impossible!'

Notions about the queer habits of Catholics that Craig had imbibed with his mother's milk in enlightened Govan received startling confirmation. He reflected that his boss was, or had been, one of them, and shifted inside his carefully laundered suit, which was a size or two too large. These people spoke a different language.

Hilarity had overwhelmed Mick again and he rocked back and forth, slapping his knee with an open palm. Craig sipped his Bacardi and Coke nervously.

'Can they really make such fools of an archbishop and a consultant?'

'If it happened once, why shouldn't it happen again three times over? After all, miracles are what the Church is all about! No, seriously, with the money they're offering us we can't afford to laugh too much. The problem is what we do to give them the impression we are earning it.'

Craig furrowed his brow and tried to look as if he was thinking. As usual in these cases, his mind was a blank. He had been unable to make use of his history degree since leaving university. After two and a half years of odd jobs, Mick's offer had looked like a big break. Now he was beginning to think that accountancy really did make more sense. At least his mother would be happier. Understandable perspiration and a determination to look smart led to constant changes of clothing. The quantity of laundry he brought home each Friday night aroused her suspicions. Not daring to reveal what his job involved, he fobbed her off with the vaguest of answers and staggered back to his Oakfield Avenue bedsit with a pile of neatly ironed intimates each Monday morning.

'Why not interview the women and try and get them to tell?'

'I'm afraid that's out. We can't get access to them. Anyway, why should they give anything away to you or me that they wouldn't tell the archbishop?'

'What did the consultant actually say?'

'He's no fool. He admitted that he was absolutely dumbfounded. He examined the women and found no sign they had engaged in sexual intercourse. The funniest thing of all is . . .'

Once more Mick could not control his mirth and found it impossible to speak. More and more uneasy, Craig waited for him to recover.

'. . . all the others have been ordered to wear earplugs. And not just in that convent! Everywhere in the diocese!'

'Earplugs?'

Craig was utterly out of his depth. Mick sobered up and tried to explain. He needed to share the joke with someone and, under present cirumstances, Craig was the only person he could tell.

'Have you ever seen an old painting of the Annunciation? One by an Italian, or a German master?'

Craig shook his head. His history course had taken no account of miracles and there were no altarpieces in the churches he had frequented. That there should be a connection between painting and religion struck him instinctively as rather unhealthy.

'Well, if you look closely, you'll see that there's usually a dove hovering above the angel who's telling Mary she's going to give birth. And a golden ray goes straight from its beak to the madonna's ear. The idea is to show how intently she's listening to the word of God. But some loony theologian in the Middle Ages got it into his head that that was how she was impregnated. The seed went in via the ear.'

It was perfectly clear to Mick. Craig was beginning to feel sick.

'So the archbishop's right-hand man Feenan decided that same effect – same cause. These women had been fecundated in an identical way. And to prevent an epidemic breaking out, all those poor nuns are going to have to keep their ears blocked up until the whole mess gets sorted.'

'What do you want me to do?'

Craig didn't want to hear any more. He would get his instructions and then scarper. The general madness had infected his boss as well, as far as he could see.

'I want you to watch the head of the convent, Mother Genevieve. Quinn and the archbishop think she knows more than she has let on. She's very involved in ecumenical committees and spends a lot of time with the Piskies. That makes her not quite kosher in their eyes. Every time this next week she steps out of that convent, I want you to be on her heels and keep a record of the places she goes and the people she speaks to.'

☆

The Orange Sun Café in Kelvinbridge is not a very exciting place on weekday afternoons. The lunchtime rush of leather queens and diesel dykes tails off about half past two, leaving stale cigarette smoke and a cocktail of ambivalent scent suspended in the atmosphere. The staff behind the counter then let rip with the stereo system and put on the kind of soulful, sentimental rubbish they would never dare listen to when the café is packed. Beyond the smutty windowpanes, sunlight plays listlessly in an ill-tended backyard, and in the brief intervals between tapes you can just hear the thunder of the River Kelvin as it passes under the bridge and is diverted through a wasteland before entering the silvan fastnesses of the park.

Tommy was finishing the washing-up, sobbing discreetly into the suds. The song they were playing had been his ex-boyfriend's favourite and, since they had only broken up four days ago, his wounds were still fresh.

Meanwhile Fred stood by the cash register, totting up the morning's takings and glancing from time to time at the few, morose clients scattered round the tables. He knew them all: a retired policeman working his way through the classified column in a gay magazine, an out-of-work plumber staring vacantly into space, and a girl from the nearby jeweller's shop on her afternoon off, immersed in yesterday's *Herald*.

Then an unusual personage entered. She was a woman in her mid-fifties, rather smartly turned out in dark blue. Her neatly permed hair had the most delicate of blue rinses and her hat was in a thirties style just coming back into vogue. She had a silver thistle brooch on her left lapel. The most striking thing about her was her outsize handbag.

She clutched it to her breast with both hands, like a shield. And Cissie MacPhail believed she needed a shield in those surroundings. She had ideas about homosexuality which were all the more outlandish for being vague and inarticulate. The aura of disease about these people dated back long before AIDS. After all, the very feelings that impelled them to seek one another out, that brought them to places like these, were a form of disease.

Who knows, maybe homosexual and lesbian germs hung in the atmosphere and, breathed in even in minimal quantities by an innocent believer like herself, might induce abominable desires and hallucinations in a very short space of time. It would be just a different kind of passive smoking.

Cissie had resolved to act inconspicuously. As it was, her movements could hardly have drawn more attention if they had been designed to do so. She paused in the midst of the empty tables, absorbed in the horrific speculations just detailed and, as they took shape in her mind, shot her handbag down from her breast to the level of her crotch, as if it could offer more adequate defence in that position.

Then she recalled the significance of the mission on which she was engaged. The vision of the sodality of Blessed Maria Alfocorado gathered round the kitchen table in the archbishop's palace came back to her. Those stern cohorts of Catholic matrons had assembled under the beetling gaze of their commander Mrs Donnelly the housekeeper. She felt heartened. Her fellow campaigners were with her in spirit as she willingly exposed her body to who knew what dangers.

She sat down abruptly in the nearest chair. As she slid her handbag on to the table in front of her it knocked off a full ashtray which fell to the floor with a clatter. Fred, who had been watching her every movement with fascination, hoping that she might be drag but not quite able to convince himself she was, sauntered over. With a courteous smile he picked up the miraculously undamaged article, polished it and put it back on the table. He then bent to scoop up its scattered contents with a brush and pail.

He hoped she would say something. Instead she pretended not to notice him, a difficult task when his bent head nearly brushed her elbow. She stared resolutely straight in front of her, once more clutching the handbag.

Fred sighed, then decided to have a go.

'No table service, missus. You have to come up to the counter, order what you want and pay for it.'

She nodded but did not dare look at him directly. As he vanished into the kitchen she calmed down and focused on the serving counter and the objects placed upon it. When they had told her, it had seemed incredible. Now she had to accept the evidence of her eyes as she detected what she had come for, tens and even hundreds of them, heaped in a large glass salad bowl, as if they were no more dangerous than demerara sugar and UHT milk.

There was no way she could just help herself and leave. She waited until Fred returned then, steeling herself, ordered a milky coffee and a slice of butterscotch pecan pie. Her sweet tooth got the better of her superstitions, even though she remembered uneasily childhood tales of the fairy mound and the dreadful consequences of partaking of food or drink while imprisoned within it. After all, this was the twentieth century. She was feeling a little faint. Her blood sugar count must be very low.

She polished every crumb off her plate and wiped her lips delicately with a paper napkin. It would be nice to get the recipe. These perverts certainly knew how to bake. She waited for what seemed an eternity until Fred was called back into the kitchen. Her moment had come. Quick as a flash, she weaved her way between the tables, opened her handbag and emptied the bowl full of condoms into it. On second thoughts, she took a small handful (she was wearing gloves, so as not to let the dreadful little packages touch her skin) and dropped them back into the bowl. She could hear Fred's voice. Any moment now he would emerge.

She fled, but not before Fred caught sight of her disappearing back and the bulging handbag crammed under one arm. He realized soon enough what she had filled it with. That night, as he snuggled up to his lover in bed, he went over the incident.

'What do you think she took them for? Is she a hoor or something?'

'Either that,' his lover replied, 'or she has a bloody marvellous sex life!'

'Well,' reflected Fred, who instinctively tended to look on the bright side of things, 'at least it shows safe sex has hit the hets!'

☆

Mother Genevieve was laid up in bed.

Her illness, she felt sure, was a consequence of these last weeks of stress. The three pregnant sisters in her charge were subject to the wildest changes of mood.

By turns they were wheedling and abject, convinced their condition was a punishment for their own or others' sins and desirous of approval or at least forgiveness from the head of the community; angry and rebellious, filled with a sense of injustice at what had happened to them and ready to criticize every move Genevieve proposed and contest every word she uttered; or else broody and sombrely beatific, vaunting a sense of superiority that was never made explicit, for they alone of all their order had been singled out to experience the twin joys of virginity and motherhood, like she who was a paragon for all their sex.

The archbishop had made no effort to conceal his irritation and alarm. He did not mince his words regarding Genevieve's evident failure in her duty to guide and protect those in her charge. The allegations he made, with a clear underlying implication of negligence on her part, subsided only after Dr Quinn had examined the three. She was well aware they might surface again at any moment and that her job was, to use no more delicate term, on the line. Demotion was the least she had to fear. If punishment was felt to be in order, she could well be shunted off to wash dishes and peel vegetables in a retreat house, or to clean and cook for a crotchety parish priest such as her own confessor Fr Ryan.

On top of that, she had been feeling strangely squeamish since that tea party with Mrs MacPhail and Miss (or was it Mrs?) MacFarrigle. Genevieve wondered if her problem was psychosomatic. Maybe her stomach was punishing her for having flaunted her Lenten ban so lightheartedly. The malaise expressed itself in twinges and aches which arrived without warning from parts of her body whose existence she had forgotten long ago, as if they were reacting with excitement to the introduction of a foreign element that flitted unpredictably from one area to another.

So she was delighted when Sister Esmeralda ushered Euphemia in to see her, promising to return with tea in a few minutes. Euphemia parked the familiar handbag on the table at the bottom of the bed and drew up a chair. When Genevieve asked about the ingredients of the cake Euphemia blushed, then baulked at this aspersion on her baking skills.

Not wishing to offend her guest, Genevieve suggested they recite a decade of the rosary together. They divided the Hail Marys in half. She stopped each time at 'fruit of thy womb, Jesus'. Euphemia took up 'Holy Mary, Mother of God' where she had left off. Although she tried to concentrate on what she was saying, Genevieve could not help noticing Euphemia's large, unfeminine hands, and the ponderous way she dealt with the beads. It reminded her more of a scout leader checking the knots in a rope than of a spinster at her devotions.

Tea arrived.

'So,' said Euphemia, sipping noisily from her cup, 'I hope you will be well enough to attend the ecumenical meeting next Thursday.'

Genevieve sat up in surprise and her voice had a touch of suspicion.

'How do you know about it? Will you be coming too?'

'Oh no, not at all. It's simply that we all have the greatest respect for the work you do with other denominations. You're going to set up a permanent committee, is that right?'

Mother Genevieve nodded.

'And who will be there for the Episcopalians? Cyril Braithwaite?'

This woman really is remarkably well informed, thought Genevieve, not without a touch of pique. Where can she be getting her information from? Euphemia went on without waiting for a reply.

'I had the good fortune to meet Mrs Braithwaite at a discussion group I attended a couple of times. Most sad about the separation.'

'He has separated from his wife?'

Genevieve felt obliged to show chagrin. In reality, she could not repress a touch of glee at the news. For all her openness to fellow Christians of different persuasions, she continued to believe in the material reality of transubstantiation and that for the clergy to marry was a great mistake. Scandals such as these were grist to her mill.

'And what led to such a dreadful decision?'

Euphemia leant over and whispered in her ear. Mother Genevieve sat bolt upright. It was more than ten years since she had heard that particular word pronounced, or even heard any confirmation of the continuing existence of a part of the male anatomy whose associations, in her case, went back thirty-five years to a stormy and passionate adolescence.

Hers was a tactical problem. Even to acknowledge that she had heard the word, that her visitor had pronounced it, might be sinful. On no account could she refer to the detail Euphemia had confided in her. At the same time, she could not deny the evidence of her senses. The church could hardly demand of her that she feign deafness. An unwonted and powerful emotion filled her breast. With alarm she recognized it as curiosity.

Better to leave the next move to Euphemia.

'How very sad!'

'Evidently he has yet to meet the right woman. That one was no match for him.'

This was a dangerous tack. Her guest must be diverted. Genevieve's strength sufficed to prevent her requesting further particulars, but only just.

'Are you married yourself, my dear?'

'My dear Albert! I buried him two years ago.'

'Where was he from? I have to confess that I had not encountered the surname MacFarrigle till I met you.'

Euphemia had paused with the china cup raised halfway to her lips. Genevieve noted that she was wearing new spectacles. The lenses were unusually large, exaggerating the dimensions of her eyes and the almost hypnotic intenseness of their gaze. The frames were of plastic, tinted gently pink, adorned at either side with what looked like gradually unfolding wings.

'From the West Highlands.'

I have caught her off guard, thought Genevieve. Now is the time to find out more.

'And which parish did you attend together?'

Euphemia relaxed. Her shoulders dropped, and she put down the cup.

'My dear, I left Glasgow twenty years ago and did not return until last autumn. I buried my dear Albert in London. You would not know the place. And now I really must be off.' She rose awkwardly and pushed her chair back. 'I have some urgent shopping to do.'

Genevieve was surprised but not displeased to receive a smacking kiss on her blue-veined cheek.

'Do take care of yourself. I shall be back before long. And I look forward to hearing absolutely everything about that meeting!'

As Euphemia left the convent and turned right towards Great Western Road, she failed to notice a fair-haired young man amidst the bushes directly opposite, wearing a suit that was just a little bit too large for him. He took a note of the time and jotted down a brief description of Mother Genevieve's visitor.

☆

Fraser Donaldson was sitting quietly at his desk in the open-plan office where he worked, checking the accounts of one of the archdiocesan charities, when he heard a voice just by his ear say, quietly but distinctly: 'I'm a poof.' The woman sitting opposite him looked up, her attention drawn more by the way Fraser suddenly froze than by the words, which she was too far away to have made out clearly.

Horrified, he gazed around him. There was no one near enough to have actually pronounced the phrase. Everything in the office was perfectly normal that afternoon. They were on the fifth floor of a new block just by the river. He could see the decorative pediment of the Victorian terrace on the other bank and, turning to his right, the postmodern flatlets that were selling with such disappointing slowness. Spring light filtered through the high glass panes of the windows. None of his colleagues had their desk lamps switched on.

Perhaps he had dozed off for a second. That often happened when you were falling asleep, that you took the beginning of a dream for reality. He reached the bottom of his third column before it happened again. 'I'm a poof.' Louder now, and more insistent. As luck would have it, his secretary was standing by him with a sheaf of letters requiring signature. She put her hand to her mouth and looked down at him with suppressed laughter.

He exchanged the few phrases he had to and dismissed her in irritation. She rushed off to the other end of the office and conferred excitedly with the man there who was her best friend. He looked in Fraser's direction with a broad grin, then shrugged his shoulders and got back to work.

Fraser had begun to sweat. What if it was his own voice? What if he had lost control of it and it was bent on outing him, here at his workplace, the hub of the Glasgow archdiocese, where the archbishop himself might step in at any moment? He decided it was best to keep his voice occupied, just in case it had taken on a life of its own, and made two or three phone calls, including one to Malcolm Mooney, who agreed to meet up with him for a drink after work.

Nothing untoward occurred before the coffee break. Fraser did not have an easy manner with his colleagues, finding it a struggle to join in the banter and chat at such times. Given his state of agitation that afternoon he managed extremely well. It lulled him into a false sense of security, and the shock was all the greater when the voice piped up again, loud enough for half the office to hear: 'Don't you see? I'm just a great big jessie!'

This time his secretary stuffed a handkerchief into her mouth, while several people at desks nearby laughed so much that tears came into their eyes. Just then the phone rang. It was the archbishop himself. Fraser's eyes nearly popped out of his head. How could his boss have heard from afar?

'Fraser, old fellow, it's about this new interchurch working party we're setting up. How would you like to be on it?'

Fraser nodded, speechless, then realized he had to say something and whimpered his assent into the receiver.

'Someone with a background like yours has a lot to offer. It's not every day the son of an Orange Lodge man comes over to Rome. And that's not all. There are even some clergymen in my archdiocese who could learn a thing or two about theology from you. So that's settled? Great. I'll send you a note with details of the first meeting. And remember, I'll be expecting a detailed report from you the day after.'

Takes one to know one, thought the archbishop as he put down the phone. You can count on a renegade to understand the enemy's moves. Good to have a man like that under your thumb. And he'll be able to keep tabs on the more radical ones from our side. They won't get away with much that doesn't get back to me.

Fraser, at the other end of the line, was still holding the receiver at some distance from his ear, looking at it in awe. He had no sooner replaced it than it rang again, and he jumped as if a wasp had stung him, then lifted it gingerly. The call was perfectly routine. As soon as he had a free moment, he made a beeline for the toilet and popped four valium tablets from the supply he kept at the bottom of his desk into his mouth.

☆

Mr Bleeper, the scholastic, swayed slightly as he faced his fifth-year religious knowledge class. Of all the trials he had so far encountered on his road to becoming a fully fledged member of the Society of Jesus this was the most formidable. The writings of St Thomas Aquinas and the spiritual exercises prescribed by

St Ignatius Loyola, the head of the order to which he aspired and after whom the school he was at present teaching in was named, held few terrors when compared with the scepticism and indifference of these lumpish Irish Catholic adolescents.

Mr Bleeper had known Cyril Braithwaite at Oxford, although he was as yet unaware of Cyril's translation to St Mary's Cathedral in the city of both their exiles. His own conversion to Rome had taken place amidst a haze of Tallis motets and pre-Raphaelite madonnas, with Cardinal Newman as a constant guide and inspiration. For one born in deepest Gloucestershire, in the heartland of England, Catholicism was a religion of choice, a state entered in adulthood which represented the apotheosis of everything the High Church of the Anglicans aspired to.

Waugh and Greene were Mr Bleeper's favourite authors. They stood out as beacon lights in the desert of modern English literature. Both had acknowledged the inevitable and taken the step back into Europe, a step that made them as one with Thomas More and the Elizabethan martyrs, with Byrd and Crashaw and Pope, undoing four hundred wrongheaded years of English history.

It was a rude awakening to see how these loutish youngsters, reared from the cradle in a mystery he had come to after years of searching, despised the riches that were theirs. He came near to recognizing himself a racist, to admitting that there was an inherent incompatibility between English and Irish blood of which his disciplinary problems were merely one expression. It made him long for the day when England as a whole would return to the fold and render fealty to the Pope. Then they would show these brutes what Catholicism could be. He imagined, as he often loved to, Prince Charles's coronation in the Catholic rite, at the point where the no-longer-young monarch bent to receive the crown from a pontiff specially flown in for the occasion. But it made him weak at the knees, and he had to stop.

He had known Amanda, too, at Oxford. Not that he had ever cast lustful eyes upon her. Sensual excitement came to him from a different quarter. Looking at the row of faces in front of him, their slouched shoulders, clumsily knotted ties and spotty foreheads, he reflected that he was safe from danger here. Nowhere in Glasgow would he find the choirboys who had moved him to such ecstasies in Oxford days. Only a handful of his present charges had that kind of purity and sweetness. Gerald Docherty was one.

Mr Bleeper was not looking forward to this lesson. If he had only consulted his colleagues first, he would never have embarked on a religious knowledge question time. To do so was to ask for trouble, and he had got it. The week before, searching desperately for an initiative that might arouse a flicker of interest in them, he had allowed each of the boys to write a question on a scrap of paper, without signing it, and had gathered them up at the end of the lesson. Only when going through them at the weekend, to make sure he could answer each query, had he understood the folly of what he had done.

Yet he was not a man lacking in moral fibre. He had resisted the initial impulse to burn the lot. He even decided not to censor them. He would face it out, shaming these shameless hoodlums by satisfying even the smuttiest of their curiosities with a straight face and a dignified intonation.

There came a knock at the door. It opened and the rector, Fr Flynn, entered. Mr Bleeper had taken this one precaution. He did not wish his courage to go unnoticed by the remainder of the staff, nor did he want the situation to get out of hand today, as it did with such sickening regularity. Immediately the boys sat up and a frisson went round by which not even the back rows were unaffected.

Fr Flynn muttered a gruff greeting and, sitting down, took what looked like a wad of raffle tickets from his pocket. He flourished it in full sight of the class before placing it on the table in front of him. A pen appeared from his breast pocket and clattered down noisily beside the wad. The whole thing was done theatrically and with considerable style, so that one of the long, dangling strips sewn on to his black habit at the shoulders fluttered expressively in the air, like a bird of ill omen momentarily set free.

That was the bill book. St Ignatius' Academy practised a form of corporal punishment which was renowned for its fairness and restraint. The teacher who assigned strokes was never the one to give them. All he would do was fill out one of the little sheets in the notepad, sign it and hand it to the culprit, who would then present himself outside a tall, thin door on the second floor at the end of classes that day. The strokes were administered with impassive accuracy by whichever teacher happened to be on duty, using a thin, bright Lochgelly strap with a built-in metal strengthener.

The scholastic distributed the questions among the boys. Each got one. Let them wallow in their own filth and take the measure of their putrescence. Mr Bleeper's only precaution was to ensure that Gerald and one or two other favourites did not receive questions which would sully their still boyish lips.

All went well, although he could sense the rector bristling behind him from time to time. It was not, in fact, as uniformly sordid as he had imagined. What was the sin against the Holy Ghost? Did St Paul speak Latin? Did St Catherine of Siena meet the Pope? What is a clitoris? What is the difference between Lent and Advent? Why do the Dominicans wear white and the Cistercians black? Or is it the other way round? How many prostitutes are there in Glasgow? Are you a virgin? When did Celtic win the European Cup? Is pubic hair different from the hair under your armpits?

He dealt with them one by one, manfully and with patient exasperation. What does Our Lady's obedience to God the Father tell us about the duty we owe to our parents? He had made sure Gerald Docherty got that one, which was first class. All at once the question he had been dreading arrived.

What is a homosexual?

Mr Bleeper hesitated an instant too long. He could feel the hairs going stiff on the back of his neck. Pointlessly, unnecessarily, he panicked. They were on to him. He would break down, right here in front of them. He got a grip of himself, and enunciated, in slow, surly tones, the answer he had prepared.

'A homosexual is a person with a warped personality.'

A loud raspberry came from the back of the class. Pandemonium ensued. Desktops rattled, pens flew, there were boos and catcalls and cheers and whistles. Mr Bleeper shrunk in his own eyes to the dimensions of a toadstool. Behind him, huge, formidable, he heard Fr Flynn's sombre blaring, a solitary foghorn in the horrid night of paganism. Gradually the din subsided and only the voice was left.

'Stand up the boy who did that.'

Daniel Kane stood up. Mr Bleeper was speechless. He had never found the boy so beautiful as in this movement of gentle, elegant and measured defiance.

'May I ask what you meant, Kane?'

'What Mr Bleeper said was a load of rubbish.'

Fr Flynn's fist hit the table with a deafening thud and with such force that it jumped from the floor.

'How dare you be so insolent? Come to the front of the class immediately.'

He was already writing out the bill with all the ceremony of a medieval scribe. He tore it from the book as a millionaire might do a cheque he had just signed for the foundation of a metropolis. One of Daniel's jet black curls slipped down on to his forehead. Beneath it the skin was white.

Mr Bleeper almost gasped. Out of the corner of his eye he saw that Gerald, too, was staring at the culprit with something close to adoration.

'Now get out of here. Wait for me at the door of my office.'

Daniel left and shut the door behind him. The silence was unbroken. Not a boy moved. Fr Flynn got up and patted Mr Bleeper with a feigned solidarity which did not deceive even its beneficiary. His already shaky reputation had taken a further plummet.

'Good work, Mr Bleeper. Just you carry on and I'll see to this upstart and his parents.'

☆

It was no easy matter for those who were not *habitués* to locate Knight's Bar on the regular, American-style grid of city centre streets that climbs up from the river bank to Blythswood Square. By eight o'clock the pub would be uncompromisingly gay. At six thirty in the evening it was still at a transitional stage. Over lunchtime it offered cheap but wholesome fare to businessmen and the odd businesswoman from the office blocks nearby. Some of the former nipped in again for a quick pint after work. Lingerers could plead tiredness as an explanation. Within half an hour such protestations would start to wear thin. There were good reasons for suspecting the motives of any man still in the bar an hour later, apparently forgetful of marital obligations, suit a little crumpled, tie fetchingly loosened as a deepening six o'clock shadow modelled his cheeks.

Fraser's strategy was always the same. He would slip out of the office after everybody else had left, walk in a direction opposite to his goal, make two wrong turnings and then scurry down the stairs into the basement bar, after a furtive glance over his shoulder to make absolutely sure nobody was following him. As he climbed the hill this evening, his heart beat wildly. He imagined for one awful moment that when the door into the lounge swung back he would find a reception committee consisting of the archbishop, Fr Feenan and Fr Flynn, all of whom he hobnobbed with regularly in the course of his job.

He had considered not turning up for his appointment with Malcolm. The dose of valium put paid to the voices. He tried to believe they were a hallucination, but if so, he was not the only victim. The amusement of his colleagues had been unmistakable. Malcolm had an antique and bric-à-brac shop near Kelvinbridge and had proposed meeting at the Orange Sun Café. Fraser refused. The café had windows on to the street and to be seen in it would have been too direct a statement for one in his professional position. Knight's Bar was safer and more discreet.

Malcolm was more patient with Fraser than most of their circle. A Catholic himself, he subscribed to enlightened teaching regarding his condition. It was acceptable to socialize with gay men and read gay books, to bitch and adopt a female nickname and even to cross-dress on special occasions, but not to seek any kind of physical or emotional satisfaction. Not conviction but a native inertia led Malcolm to adopt this position. It was the line of least resistance. Lavish dinner parties and extravagant sitting room curtains were an antidote to passion, whose ravagings he sincerely hoped never to feel again.

He and Fraser had known each other since university days, when both were deeply involved in union politics, though on different sides. At that time Fraser pursued Gaelic and Scottish Nationalist ends with a single-minded idealism he subsequently transferred to Latin and the Catholic church. A Conservative supporter, Malcolm took part regularly in student debates. Recent developments in British politics, however, caused him to switch his allegiance to the Liberal Democrats.

He was worried about Fraser. For a while he had hoped that religious devotion would veil his friend's sexual proclivities in a cloud of incense and lilies of the valley, and that when the cloud eventually lifted, he would have turned miraculously into a eunuch. No such luck. Fraser satisfied his physical needs in a more anonymous and dangerous manner than ever before. He was already living on the edge in his job, dependent on the goodwill or the blindness of his workmates to avoid detection. So why did he put himself at risk from the police by frequenting cruising spots along the river bank long past midnight? Did he need the stimulus of constant risk to keep himself going? Or was he trying to blot out some pain gnawing deep inside him which he refused to confront?

Concern was written all over Malcolm's good-natured, podgy face as he heard the tale of Fraser's incredible tribulations. Not for one minute did he believe the bit about the voices. The strain of these last years was evidently beginning to tell on his friend.

'Sounds to me like you need a break,' was all he answered. 'Can't you take off to Lanzarote or Rhodes or Tunisia for ten days or so and try to forget it all?'

But no, in spite of his conversion, Fraser's innate Calvinism was too strong to allow for such a hedonistic solution. And what if the terrible voices proved able to travel and continue to haunt him, even amidst the chaos of a crowded Mediterranean beach?

Malcolm was lucky enough to spot Colm on the other side of the bar. He beckoned him over and the conversation took a different turn. Fraser, who did not like Colm, looked glum.

'Tell us how you got on at Gavin's last night,' Malcolm asked.

'We had an absolutely outrageous time,' said Colm. 'There were seven or eight of us there and the atmosphere was fairly glum. Gavin's been turfed out of his job, and it looks as though he'll have to go down south to find another one. So we were all sitting moping over a couple of bottles of cheap wine. Then Gavin jumped up and announced a beauty competition.'

'That one really is a boy and a half,' commented Malcolm sympathetically.

'Well, off he goes and starts emptying out his bedroom wardrobe. You've no idea the tartish rags he has stuffed away there. Sequins, black tights, boas . . . you name it, he's got it. Jack got a stepladder and pushed it up against the kitchen table. Dave used a bottle as a microphone and we all had to do a catwalk up the steps, on to the table, then across the sink and down on to a chair. You got marks for approach, decorum, mascara, dress sense and banter with the public.'

Fraser was scowling. He hated this kind of playacting, indeed, anything that smacked of effeminacy.

'I don't understand how you can behave like that on a weekday night and then turn up at the choir on Sundays looking as if butter wouldn't melt in your mouth. Doesn't it mean anything at all to you?'

Colm rolled his eyes heavenwards and winked at Malcolm. Fraser picked up his glass and left to join another group. Shrugging his shoulders, Malcolm offered to buy them another drink.

☆

The kitchen of the archbishop's palace is a great, cavernous basement room to the rear of the building, sunk well beneath the level of the garden. There are heavy vertical iron bars on its windows. A little sunlight sneaks in during the afternoons, but on an early spring evening such as this only the faintest of glimmers tells of the declining day beyond.

Here Mrs Donnelly concocted the wonders which filled the archbishop's groaning tables: mulligatawny soup and rollmop herring, lamb chops, macaroni cheese, sausage rolls and salad, toad in the hole, bacon fritters, braised steak, and fish in breadcrumbs, always served with an abundance of potatoes and shiny, slithering greens. Rarely was the place free of the odour of cabbage, which only gradually yielded to the sweeter scents of lemon meringue pie, upside down tart, pavlova and rhubarb crumble. The archbishop might command the faithful; his housekeeper commanded his stomach, and felt only pity for those who misprized her status and influence.

Mrs Donnelly had switched on the big central light. The archbishop had been ferried off to the television studios for a live appearance. She had served him a sizeable lunch followed by a plate of sandwiches at four o'clock. Now she was her own mistress until tea and biscuits at ten. The nun who came in to help during the day had returned to her convent. The coast was clear for a meeting of the sodality of Blessed Maria Alfocorado, of which she was the proud foundress and chairwoman.

The members were assembled around the scrubbed deal table. Squeezed in at the corner, Cissie studied their faces. Many of them had been her companions at school. She knew the names of their children and who they had married, their professions and the size of their mortgages. Their husbands had played football on the same or opposing sides when at school, though they all supported one team now on Saturdays. The offspring of these unions sat in the same classrooms and worshipped in the same pews as their parents and grandparents had done.

There was something dreamlike, she reflected, about following this cohort of women though three decades, on a journey which added stones to their weight and increasing quantities of make-up to falling cheeks and double chins, without bringing them any illumination as to the actual purpose of their lives.

Cissie attempted to shake off her mood of depression and contemplated her peers: Dorothy Gallaher, Marie Therese McLaughlin, Deirdre White, Frances MacAweaney, Daphne McGlone, Sandra Luperini and Bridget Scott. They had come a long way from the halcyon tennis-club days of her late teens. Frances had been engaged to three different men in the space of a year, and Deirdre had been kicked out of the university for never doing any work and spending all her time in the women's union smoking cheroots and supervising a poker school. And to think it had all come to this.

Mrs Donnelly called the meeting to order by beating on the table with a wooden spoon. Cissie studied the housekeeper. She was the odd woman out. The archbishop had brought her with him from the stony wildernesses of western Ireland. No one knew a thing about Mr Donnelly. Some said he had been an alcoholic, others that he had been reported missing at sea. The fact that Mrs Donnelly was an unknown quantity gave her a power she relished. Her past could not be used to force her into line.

'Well,' she said, 'let me see what you have got.'

Wordlessly, almost noiselessly, the women produced handbags and string shoppers, purses, supermarket bags and boxes, and emptied their contents on to the table. The pile grew and grew until they had difficulty in seeing each other's faces.

Cissie was the victim of a strange hallucination. Every now and then she could have sworn she saw Euphemia sitting in the corner, a little withdrawn, observing what they were doing with wry amusement. But when she screwed up her eyes the shadows beyond the table were empty. Euphemia was not there.

'Praise be to the Lord,' said Mrs Donnelly. 'This is a fine harvest indeed.'

Deirdre White piped up immediately in her querulous, watery voice.

'I'm still not happy about this. What does it have to do with Blessed Maria Alfocorado? Is this really how she would want us to be spending our free afternoons?'

Mrs Donnelly's brow darkened.

'This is no time for quavering. You had your chance to pull out two weeks ago, Deirdre, before we all took the vow. I'll have none of your quisling talk in my kitchen.'

Her opponent was undaunted.

'I've been reading it up and it's different from what you told us. Maria refused to marry the man her father had chosen for her and ran away to the convent. The fact that her betrothed was struck down by lightning two days later could have been pure coincidence. Nobody is going to convince me it was a miracle. What had he done to deserve a death like that? And all she wanted was not to have sex herself. She wasn't bothered about stopping other people having it.'

Mrs Donnelly's voice grew thunderous and she half raised herself from her chair.

'Every single act of extramarital sex that takes place in this city of lust and depravity is an offence crying out for vengeance to God the Father! If we manage to prevent even one of them then our work will be blessed in His eyes!'

'Hear, hear,' cried Frances MacAweaney.

'Deirdre may be willing to turn her nose up at the prospect of a perpetual indulgence. The rest of us aren't going to pass it up so quickly,' said Sandra Luperini.

'But what does Blessed Maria Alfocorado have to do with collecting condoms?' asked Deirdre. 'If you ask me, it's a form of stealing.'

There was an awkward silence as the members of the sodality contemplated the heap of shimmering plastic packages on the table in front of them. A draught from beneath the back door lifted the uppermost ones and they settled back in a glistening wave.

Daphne McGlone came to Mrs Donnelly's rescue.

'The Holy Father has condemned these godless contraptions. That's good enough for me. People have to learn self-restraint. What sort of world do we want our children and grandchildren to live in? How can they possibly cope with so many temptations we never faced?'

'Nuns and priests can control themselves,' muttered Marie Therese McLaughlin. 'I learned to do so, not without difficulty, after I conceived my last child. Why shouldn't other people have to?'

'St Paul,' interjected Dorothy Gallaher, who fancied herself as a theologian, 'says that abstinence is the best thing of all. Marriage is a failsafe for those of us too weak to abstain entirely from the pleasures of the flesh. And let's face it, we could have saved ourselves the trouble. When you haven't had it for a while, you lose your taste for it, and a good thing too, if you ask me.'

Cissie had blushed at the mention of self-control, which was not her forte. Rob had wanted to use condoms after Simon was born, but she refused. They found other ways of getting round the problem, which actually made the whole thing rather nicer. And since she got over her menopause she had been having the time of her life. It made her feel such a hypocrite.

She looked fiercely at Bridget Scott, another hypocrite. She had made her husband have the snip after her second set of twins. No doubt they had both confessed afterwards and done their penance, once they had sorted things to their own satisfaction. After all, the priest could hardly force them to have him put back the way he was. That Joseph Scott had always been such a gentle, biddable man.

Bridget caught Cissie's scowl and guessed what she was thinking because the same idea had crossed her mind. Her friend's mute accusation stung her into speech.

'It's not just about stopping the babies the Good Lord wants to give us. These plastic things are used for practices I hardly dare speak about. But then, Cissie's the expert on that.'

'No one here is going to attack Cissie as long as I am chairwoman,' Mrs Donnelly interjected. 'She had the most perilous task of all and she carried it out with aplomb.'

There was a brief scatter of applause and everyone looked expectantly at Cissie.

'Well,' said Sandra Luperini, 'tell us about it. Did they set upon you?'

'Nothing of the sort,' answered Cissie. 'The young man was perfectly civil.'

'In that case you will have no qualms about going back next week,' said Mrs Donnelly.

'What? I have to do it again?'

'Of course, my dear. They'll have refilled that salad bowl the very instant you left. The devil's coffers are inexhaustible.'

'The lesbians,' squealed Frances MacAweaney. 'How do we stop the lesbians?'

There was a silence while the members of the sodality got their brains round that. None of them was conscious of having seen a lesbian, never mind imagining what one might do in bed.

'Forget the lesbians,' sneered Marie Therese. 'Where are we going to hide all this stuff?'

Mrs Donnelly's features took on a military rigidity.

'Do not forget that we are engaged in a war, a war against the decadent and degraded customs of the present day. We are soldiers fighting in the ranks of our Most Holy Father. The fact that he does not know what we are up to is neither here nor there. What matters is that we are operating in the spirit of his message. As your chairwoman it pleases me to think of you as a military formation, a phalanx of resolute souls moving into battle under my direction. Not all the secrets of a military organization can be shared with every one of its members.

42

Some are the concern of the commander alone. This is one. Bring me your condoms, ladies, and I will find a suitable home for them.'

☆

The archbishop tried to think exactly what Mrs Donnelly had given him for lunch. It was more than he could do to remember. The truth was, it had left him feeling exceedingly flatulent. Not that he had started farting yet. It was as if he had swallowed an air cushion instead of food, and it was gradually dilating in his colon.

His limousine had broken down on the way to the BBC studios, a most irritating occurrence. Mr Mannion, the chauffeur, was attempting to flag down a taxi. As he shifted in the back seat, behind the shaded windows, the archbishop reflected with satisfaction on what was in store. In his own estimation, he appeared on television far too rarely. He was an important moral leader in the community and it would be hard for the channel to dedicate too much air space to his views. His secretary Dominic Feenan had briefed him hurriedly that morning on the programme in which he was to take part. Unfortunately he had not the slightest recollection of the topic. He knew it was a religious discussion programme. Could it be Sunday opening? A further threat to the continued provision of separate schools for the children in his flock? This preposterous business about women priests? He would give them an earful about that if he had half a chance.

The taxi itself got caught in a traffic jam, so he only arrived in the nick of time. He was not even introduced to the producer. Someone took his coat and hat and plumped him down unceremoniously in a barber's chair. He was subjected to the ministrations of a gushing woman with untidy hair, a powder puff and a handful of coloured pencils which she applied liberally to his face. The bloated feeling had definitely not gone away.

Two minutes later he was in front of the cameras. With a touch of trepidation he saw the words 'Sex, Religion and the Family' in large letters on the hoardings at the back of the studio. Who else was taking part? Cyril Braithwaite, a milk and

43

water Episcopalian, nothing to fear there. He recognized the Presbyterian chap, but couldn't think of his name. If the truth were told, they disagreed about very little. He hardly stopped to look at the shabby, ill-dressed Quaker woman. After all, the purple waistcoat of a Catholic archbishop was hard to beat! And they were such a lacklustre lot, all heart searching, no answers and silent prayer!

But here was that horrible German woman, the theologian. They had crossed swords during a discussion at the university, where she taught. If he had his way, rebels such as that would be out of the church before they knew it. And she had brought a crony along with her, a not unattractive middle-aged woman, who was looking at him very sharply indeed.

The cameras swung into action. He had forgotten to ask if they were being broadcast live or not. The presenter was a dapper young man, deferential the way these people always ought to be. The channel was getting this show for free. They could hardly be grateful enough. Nothing would enter the coffers of the archdiocese as a result of his appearance. He scanned the audience and nodded to one or two friends.

Marital breakdown was the opening topic. The Protestants spoke first, mumbling the usual things about the importance of the individual, the search for happiness and the need for compromise. The woman he did not know said something he did not quite catch. His turn was next and he was preparing a barrage about the sacred nature of the nuptial bond when something peculiar happened. It was a harsh, ear-splitting sound like a strip of adhesive tape being torn violently off a plastic football. Suddenly his stomach felt more comfortable, and he grinned, looking round for the source of the noise. He was a little disconcerted to find the other members of the panel watching him. Everyone had fallen completely silent.

He said his piece against divorce, to his own satisfaction.

The presenter appeared to be rather nervous. He was staring at the archbishop very intently. The end of the cleric's speech caught him off guard, and he glanced in alarm at his clipboard and fired a question back about the importance of sexuality in marriage.

The archbishop got into his stride. He spoke about the man as head of the family, the preaching of St Paul on the role of women, and emphasized how procreation must be the principal aim of what he referred to as 'genital activity'. Chuckling to himself, he reflected that he was rather hogging things to the detriment of the other clergymen. Then the German woman broke in, and he remembered her name. Ute. Ute Schreier. She looked positively apoplectic.

'When will it end?' she cried. 'When will it end, this voyeuristic presence of the Catholic priest at the foot of the marriage bed? How am I expected to take seriously the advice of a man who has no experience of partnership or of physical love?'

He bent forward, eager to reply, when it happened again. This time it was like the sound of an old-fashioned motor car starting up; an intermittent deep burping, individual detonations getting louder and longer until they joined together and the engine triumphantly took off, all four pistons firing in turn. It was a most satisfying conclusion. As suddenly as the noise had started, it stopped. Again he felt an intense physical relief, and beamed.

The presenter had stopped in his tracks. There were ripples of laughter from the audience. The producer was addressing one of the cameramen in a stage whisper, who then swerved his machine, which had been focusing on the archbishop, to one side, while the microphone dangling just over his head like a ripe banana was lifted into the air. The sound engineer was holding his nose with a pained expression.

The Presbyterian had taken up where Ute Schreier left off. The archbishop was struck by Cyril Braithwaite's appearance. He was biting the side of his hand, tears of mirth streaming down his cheeks. Two emotions assailed the archbishop: horror, as an idea about the possible source of the strange noises flashed through his mind; and indignation that he was being squeezed out of the discussion. He glared at the cameraman, moved his chair nearer to the centre of the group, and prepared to speak.

'Take the Virgin Mary,' the German woman was saying. 'What kind of a model is that for me to follow? I am sorry, but I cannot compete with her, no matter how hard I try. She was a virgin and a mother at one and the same time. That is just beyond . . .'

Her voice trailed off. She was looking at the archbishop in

trepidation. It was not what he might say that she was afraid of. The third outbreak was absolutely deafening. Once, on a television programme, she had watched aborigines play on long wooden horns to produce a protracted, rather nasal whooping which apparently could be picked up fifty miles away and served them for long-distance communication from tribe to tribe. The anthropologist presenting the programme emphasized the miracles of breathing the players had to effect in order to sustain such volume and intensity of sound. A noise like this was now emerging from the archbishop's backside.

The studio lights went out. There was a babble of loud and alarmed cries. Two men picked the archbishop up by the armpits and hauled him through the swing doors, indifferent to his protests. He lost one of his soft leather moccasins as his feet dragged along the floor. They dumped him in a side room and promised to return.

In the distance he could hear a din of many voices, reproachful, unbelieving and hilarious. The full enormity of what had happened was borne in upon him. He bowed his head and began to weep.

TWO

In spite of his excitement, the sex in his hands was limp as he shook the last drops from it. This was the third time he had called in during the course of the afternoon. The very smell of the urinal evoked tension and danger and a wild exultation. Each time he returned, the blood at his temples throbbed more insistently. It couldn't be much longer before he made a contact.

He paused in front of the gleaming wall of water, for him as refreshing and energizing and rich in promise as a high cascade in mountain country. So much of the time, wherever his body might be, whatever his external occupation, his mind was here, alert and waiting, screwed to a pitch of intensity nothing else in his life could quite match.

Saturday afternoon wasn't the most promising spot in the week. Along with the old drunkards shuffling up and down the stairs there were fathers with their young sons, dropping the tiny trousers and directing the small jet with soothing or impatient words before they relieved themselves in a hurried, businesslike way, one eye constantly over their shoulders to make sure their offspring did not wander into a cubicle.

Such a pair had just left. The bespectacled man to his right stepped back and did up the buttons of his raincoat before making his way upstairs to the street, his bulk blotting out the daylight and casting an ever larger shadow on the wall. Only one other remained. He turned his head and their eyes met, ever so briefly, but long enough.

This instant of recognition was what he loved most. No words were ever spoken. So often, in the course of listless afternoons amidst the crowds of shoppers, he would shoot a glance into eyes that made nothing of it, for whom his interrogation had no meaning. Even when he felt quite sure of the man he had chosen, guided by a detail of dress or a way of walking or the set of a head, he could be proved pitifully wrong, left crestfallen, staggering beneath the weight of a proffered gift the other had not even perceived to be there. And then, when he was least expecting it, when he had given up hope and turned his mind to other things, he would happen on a pair of eyes like a deafening cry that set him reeling. And suddenly there was a tight knot in his stomach, constantly being tugged at, like the rope with which one dinghy curtly, insistently, pulls another after it, out of the harbour and into the open sea.

He followed the man on to the street. The other paused just long enough to check he was in tow, and, with a barely perceptible jerk of his head, set off purposefully in the direction of George Square. Puzzled and amused, he trailed him, careful not to reach the pedestrian crossing until the light had turned to green and the bleeping started, so that they would not have to acknowledge one another too early in the chase. The man had plunged his hands into the pockets of his padded jerkin. His shoulders were hunched, although it was not cold. His hair was a light chestnut colour. He looked to be in his early thirties.

They headed towards the merchant city, leaving the shopping crowds behind. All at once the man stopped, turned to face him, then disappeared up a tenement stair. So this was the place he had chosen! No one lived in this building and the offices would be deserted at the weekend. As he climbed, the footsteps above him paused. His heart leapt at the first and second landings. The third was dim, for the windows were placed halfway between one landing and the next. The man already had his sex in his hand and was pulling at it convulsively. He glanced at it, then at his face. The man clutched him and his eyes stared at the lettering on the office door beyond his shoulders. He smelt of plaster and lime. He must be a building worker.

'You're so young!' the man murmured, then pushed him away and came, spurting on to the wall just by the door. The next minute he was gone. The clatter of footsteps dwindled down the stair. He stood gazing at the shape the dampness had made on the crimson Victorian tiles, then unbuttoned his flies and masturbated, slowly, rhythmically, still dazed by the intense presence and sudden absence, filled with ideas and sensations at a level beyond words. If he had tried to articulate them he could only have moaned.

It was sunny outside. Dust motes danced in the half darkness of the close. There was come on his hand and he pulled out his handkerchief and cleaned himself musingly and methodically. What they had done gave him the impression of tremendous noise and he found it hard to credit the absolute silence that enveloped the whole place. Perhaps if he put a shell to his ear he would hear it, like the roaring of the sea. He leant back against the curved wall where the stairs looped round, and adjusted his trousers. There was not a drop on the pale beige fabric. He let out a deep exhalation, then chortled, incredulous, folded the handkerchief into a careful bundle with the moisture at its core and stuffed it back into his pocket. He would rinse it out in the bathroom back home so that his mother noticed nothing when she came to do the washing.

Ten minutes later he paused at the plate-glass window of a bookshop, scanning the picture books of Scottish landscapes ranged along the shelves to tempt tourists. A face was reflected in the pane just to his right. He looked round. It was Gerald Docherty.

'Hallo,' said Gerald.

'Hallo,' Daniel replied. 'What are you doing here?'

'I've been out to buy a sports jacket with my mother. Want to go for a coffee?'

☆

O mighty instigatress and high artificer!

Those of my mean standing are not gifted with the faculty of foresight. If we enjoyed such a privilege, I might never have undertaken this journey, which has proved to be of a most awful and terrifying nature. You, who in your position of even limited sublimity could nevertheless anticipate the dangers involved in such a course of action, might at least have shown compassion equal to your powers and warned us of what lay ahead.

Barely had our globule entered the territory destined for our activities than we were beset with perils beyond my capacities of description. I could say that we resembled a frail vessel on high seas amidst a storm of the utmost violence. The truth is that we were enclosed on every side. Sailors cannot be threatened with steep shores and cratered cliffs from both above and below. Yet this was our plight. And what is more, these cliffs moved to meet one another rhythmically, doing their utmost to crush us to fragments between them.

Nor were we able to dance on the surface of the sea. A corrosive and foul-smelling liquid enveloped us, sweeping with it the fragments and particles of your august and not inappropriately named fairy cake, which gradually dissolved into a uniform and colourless concoction where our globule was the only hard, resistant element.

Countless times we sent up thanks for the means of travel devised and supplied by those who govern you and us and of whose ministers we are the least in rank, yet not the least honoured in the magnitude of the services exacted. While the globule protects us on all sides, irradiating these interior darknesses with its red glow and affording us a view of the constantly renewed horrors we must penetrate, its outer perimeter is of sufficient flexibility for it not to shatter the already ragged and pitted edges of the pounding cliffs we were repeatedly propelled towards. Such an eventuality would inevitably have informed our hostess of our presence within her corporal precincts, with dreadful consequences for our mission.

Scarce a millimetre of this range of cliffs is truly white. Rather their colour ranges from dull cream to yellow, and a strange architect has dug deep into their recesses, then filled these cavities with silvery alloys that gleamed eerily as we moved past them.

This, the first of our torments, cannot have lasted much longer than five minutes, though to us it was an eternity of unremitting danger. Our globule was sucked onwards to the entrance of a cave over which hung a strange, movable banner of red flesh. Who knows, it may have been a sign which warned of the fastnesses we were to venture into. What followed was a tunnel of whose length I can give no reliable estimate. It thrust ever on and downwards, sometimes narrower, sometimes wider. Several of my minions cried out and flung themselves in grief to the floor of our vessel, filling the air with imprecations, convinced that we should never again emerge from the dread territory we had so foolishly violated.

Try to picture our situation. We are confined, not by barriers of stone or earth, but by walls of living flesh. These walls do not stand still but shift back and forth ceaselessly, while our ears are deafened by a relentless pounding which my researches tell me must be the effect of the circulation of our hostess's blood. Another rhythm sets her frame quivering, no less incessant in its variations as she draws in, then expels the air which gives her life.

Had the dimensions of our globule been even a little less restricted we would undoubtedly have become jammed at one of the narrower points in the tube we travelled down. I dare not think what would have happened to us then. Greater straits may lie ahead, but I trust none will be so great as to force us to abandon prematurely the vessel which has so far been the instrument of our salvation. Our forms are reputed to be indestructible and depend on neither blood nor air for their irrigation or sustenance. Could even they resist decomposition when exposed to the digestive juices of this huge organism?

As I pen this, my second missive to you, most august and high yet only intermittently merciful one, we lie becalmed in an organ whose size we can only guess at. Around us the process of erosion and assimilation proceeds in darkness. It is in part a process of putrefaction, for at intervals gas bubbles form within the liquid in which we are suspended and rise towards the tube through which we travelled. Not long after such bubbles depart upwards, a jolt shakes everything around us, as these products are liberated into the circumambient air. Other gases, for reasons I cannot fathom, take a different route and direct themselves towards those nether regions where our business remains to be done.

Thither shall we take our course when we have rested, partaken of the food of angels you entrusted to us, and deliberated as to our precise whereabouts. You may rest assured that a further and equally detailed report will reach your hands in due course.

☆

Alan turned over in Jackie's bed in yet another attempt to get comfortably settled. Although he had been sleeping there on and off for three months he had not managed to get used to it. She lived in a conversion on the first floor of one of those huge Victorian West End town houses. His side of the bed was next to the window, and the curtain she had did not reach far enough down to stop the orange radiance of the streetlamp from entering the room. What was more, it wasn't interlined and he could feel the chill of the spring night down his right side, unmitigated by the glass pane.

She did not move. He presumed she must be asleep and sat up in bed. He was dissatisfied. He objected to staying in on a Saturday night. If Alan did come round at eight o'clock he expected a meal to be laid on, followed by leisurely sex. This was not Jackie's style. She had a major presentation to do on Monday morning and had spent the entire evening crouched over her drawing board, intent on a design project. Being ignored in this way dented Alan's self-esteem and he had sunk into a sullen silence she deliberately refused to take any notice of.

Jackie was certainly a catch, a distinct improvement on the secretaries he had gone out with until then. The problem was he still hadn't moulded her to the kind of relationship he wanted. He had certain basic needs she just didn't pick up on, or managed to ignore. It was good she had a proper career because she could talk intelligently and she impressed his friends. The fact that her earnings were quite a lot higher than his disturbed him. Maybe that was what limited his influence in their relationship. Normally if you had sex with a woman regularly enough she would start doing the usual things for you, like washing clothes, ironing and cooking. With Jackie it didn't work like that, and this puzzled him.

He had gone to bed before her, selecting the least forbiddingly intellectual of the contemporary French novels from her bookshelf to flick through. He had turned out the light, then awakened to find her beside him. Now Jackie sat up too.

'Can't sleep?'

'No. You neither?'

'It's my own fault for working late. My mind won't settle. I keep seeing graph paper and lines that never meet. Tell me a fairy tale.'

I could think of better ways to unwind, Alan reflected, and said nothing.

'Or tell me about the farting attack again. That's a great story.'

Alan sniggered at the thought of it.

'You find it a hoot, I find it a hoot, but my boss doesn't see it that way. There was hell to pay, with him and higher up the line. How long am I going to be stuck in religious broadcasting? I'm fed up with the holy-holies.'

'Darling, you make such a good presenter on those programmes. With your dapper suit and neat little tie you look as if butter wouldn't melt in your mouth. Why don't you stick with it? It's a cushie little number that makes minimal demands on you. And your parents are proud of their boy for making it so far.'

'Maybe I could write something sensational for the tabloids.'

'"Archbishop's Backside Steals Show"'? There's enough to make a story in that little fiasco, especially if it went out live.'

'And it's not the only odd occurrence on the Glasgow churches scene. There are rumours about a convent in the West End. You'd have to know Catholic doctrine to appreciate the ridiculousness of it all. But you know what they say. No smoke without a fire.'

Jackie yawned. Feeling more wide awake than ever, Alan struggled to keep the conversation going.

'What about music journalism? An interview with the lead singer in Ceòl, for instance?'

'Have you tried?'

'Oftener than I care to remember. No go. Since they got on to the London and New York circuits they don't have time for small-beer Glasgow journalists like yours truly.'

'Why not try Chariots?'

'Who're they?'

'An all-woman group. They're doing a gig in the Exhibition Centre next weekend I want to take you to. The lead singer is supposed to be lesbian, but I see no reason that should put you off. And they're all Glaswegians.'

Alan paused for thought.

'What are your plans for tomorrow? Although I have to work at this presentation, I could squeeze in a pub lunch somewhere nice. Drymen maybe? Or Balmaha?'

'Sorry. I've got to put in an appearance in Govan. Family duties. I haven't seen my mother for three weeks and she'll take it really badly if I don't go for the Sunday meal.'

Jackie was not pleased. She snorted and turned over, pulling the downie roughly in her direction. A cold draught hit Alan's side. He wondered what his chances were of developing frostbite in an unheated Glasgow bedroom.

☆

Earlier that same day, at the Halt Bar in Woodside Road, Mick McFall had heard his adjutant's second report on the case of the pregnant virgins.

Craig wasn't looking too good. Long hours spent amidst the undergrowth opposite the Oratory of St Bridget, dimly concealed by the evergreen bushes, in both fair weather and foul, had left him with a heavy cold. He snorted and snivelled as he spoke. Something more serious was bothering him which he couldn't bring himself to mention straight away. He would work his way up to that one.

'As I told you last week,' he began, 'Mother Genevieve has been laid up with a stomach complaint and has not stepped outside the convent for more than ten days.'

Mick sipped at his drink and put it down, impatient to hear what progress had been made.

'She has received only four visitors during that period, two men and two women. I checked them out as you asked me to.

'Cyril Braithwaite, the Episcopalian prebendary from the cathedral, called by. Mother Genevieve was unable to attend the meeting of the new ecumenical committee. He's on it too, so presumably he came to fill her in on what had happened. She had three visits from Father Joseph Ryan of St Pius XXVII's parish in Springburn. He's her . . . ' Craig glanced at his notes and wrinkled his nose in distaste. 'Her spiritual advisor. That's something a Mother Superior has to have so they can make sure she is running the convent properly. The first of the women was Cissie MacPhail. She and Mother Genevieve were at school together. Her husband, Rob MacPhail, works in the transport department of the city council. All of that is reasonably straightforward. It's the other woman that's giving me problems.'

Craig's voice faded off into silence. Mick leant closer, all of a sudden reminded of the lad's inexperience. He felt a twinge of guilt at the thought that his assistant might find the details of adult private lives hard to stomach. But that was not what troubled Craig.

'What kind of problems?' he asked gently.

'It's just that it doesn't all fit together.'

The younger man's voice rose in pitch. Mick realized he was close to tears, tears of frustration and puzzlement. Craig got a grip on himself.

'Her name is Euphemia MacFarrigle. She came twice and stayed for about forty minutes each time. The first time I followed her down Great Western Road she went into a betting shop, then led me right into the centre of town. I had a funny feeling she knew I was on her heels and wanted to play around with me.'

He was warming to his subject.

'As far as I can gather she is a regular client at three bookmakers' in the West End. They are a bit terrified of her because she has yet to back a horse that didn't win. What saves them is that she never bids high stakes. Otherwise she might clean them out utterly. All the same, she makes enough from her betting to live more than decently herself and support someone else besides.

'Anyway, she went into Dino's Café and ordered a coffee. I positioned myself in a corner seat by the window, where I could be inconspicuous but see everything that was going on. Then a funny thing happened. This guy was sitting on his own reading the paper. He looked really strange. He must have been in his late sixties but his hair was black and shiny. I could swear he dyes it and wears make-up. He uses powder and lays on the mascara with a trowel. It really turned my stomach.

'He put down his paper and caught sight of Euphemia. I've never seen anyone look so astonished. Then he got up, went over to her and greeted her as if she was a long lost friend. Everybody in the café looked round.'

'And what did Euphemia do?' Mick asked.

'She was horrified. She couldn't get away from him fast enough. I had the impression he remembered her from some time in the past and wanted to renew the acquaintance. She pretended not to know him, grabbed her handbag, paid at the till and went out, leaving him standing there like a nincompoop.'

'And then?'

'I went over to him and tried to get him to talk. He told me his name was Alfred Coutts, and gave me a sheepish kind of smile.'

'And what did you get out of him?'

'Hardly anything. He wanted to talk about me, Mick.' Craig rolled his eyes and looked at his employer appealingly, as if he could offer him retrospective help in this difficult situation. 'If you ask me, he was one of them. You know, a . . . a . . .'

He couldn't quite bring himself to say the word. Mick nodded knowingly, relieving him of the need to articulate his fears.

'It made me feel squeamish. I went hot and cold all over. I've never been near one before. So I just scarpered. Maybe I could have got more out of him, but I'd had enough for one day.'

Mick gestured towards Craig's drink, and the younger man gulped the liquid down. The litany of his tribulations was not yet complete. For all his distaste, Craig could handle the story so far. It was unsavoury but it cast him in a good, not to say a heroic, light. What came next was different. He looked at Mick pleadingly. A large droplet of catarrh wobbled at the end of his nose and he rubbed it off with his index finger.

'The second time, I followed her home. It may be she is living with someone. The flat she stays in has a different name on the door plate. It doesn't say Euphemia MacFarrigle, but Edwin MacFarlane. I hung around, and a man came down a little while after she'd arrived.'

'Is she a transvestite? Did they look alike?'

'Not at all. What really bothers me is that . . .' He took another swig from his beer. 'You're not going to believe this. When I went back the next day, the house had gone.'

Mick gave a low whistle, just out of sympathy. He didn't believe a word of it.

'What do you mean?'

'Ninety-eight Otago Street wasn't there. It's a gap site. The building has been demolished.'

Mick patted Craig on the shoulder. He was clearly running a temperature and must have been doing so for some days now without realizing it.

'You go home to your Mammy, my lad. You've done very well but I think you've been overworking and you need a rest. I'll look after this case for the next couple of weeks till we get you back into shape.'

☆

The church and academy of St Ignatius are situated on the summit of a hill only a few minutes' walk from the city centre. A football pitch, interestingly and perhaps significantly, occupies the ground between the church and the school buildings and rounds out the complex. At the time of the school's opening towards the end of the last century, when a notable Jesuit poet was briefly one of its masters, the tenements and town houses nearby were homes to prosperous business-men, bankers and the better class of clerks. These people have long since deserted the area for the leafy avenues of the West End or less cramped quarters in Shawlands, Pollok and Mount Florida on the south bank of the river. Garnethill is now given over to shabby lodging houses and cheap hotels with peeling paintwork. The stench from the neighbouring brewery wafts down deserted streets, spreading an aura of decomposition and dissolution which the crumbling stonework can only intensify. The tuck shop where the boys stock up on sweets during their morning break has been taken over by an Indian family. The fluttering saris and gaudy headscarves of the mother and grandmother and their women friends provide a forlorn and incongruous note of colour amidst the general, unremitting greyness.

The church façade proclaims its dedication to the order's founder in proud gold capitals: *Divo Ignatio Sacrum*. The interior is a peculiar mixture of Italianate extravagance and Presbyterian restraint. Columns of green marble with cream and black veining mark off the sequence of side chapels from the central nave. A particularly gory wooden statue of the crucifix-ion is tucked into a dark corner by the main door. Its bleeding, swollen feet, pierced by an outsize metal nail, emerge from the shadows just above eye level and have given more than one unwary visitor a nasty shock. The dome surmounting the crossing is not an illusionary painting, like that of St Ignatius' church in Rome, but a genuine construction of masonry and plasterwork. The pale green copper clothing its exterior makes it a city landmark, identifiable from a considerable distance. Mosaics of indifferent craftsmanship and questionable taste adorn the apse above the high altar. One of the largest images is of a pelican feeding its offspring with its own blood, and is reproduced in silhouette on the crimson uniforms of the academy, with an appropriate Latin motto recommending altruism. High up in the left transept a choirloft clings uneasily to the wall, suspended above the void like a perilous eyrie with its cargo of fledgling voices and souls. Mr McElhinny, music master and director of the choir, had a predilection for Renaissance church music and was constantly in search of good treble singers. No sooner had he trained one set of protégés to his satisfaction than puberty took its inevitable toll on their voices, wreaking havoc on their mental and musical purity at one and the same time.

The boys were, strictly speaking, supposed to gather here each morning and preface their day's work with attendance at mass. Sadly for their mentors, ever smaller numbers felt inclined to fulfil this obligation with the passing of the years. It was the feast day of the school's patron saint, and an unusually large crowd filled the church. Proud parents joined the customary levy of parishioners to watch the archbishop and a bevy of lesser clerics in a concelebration of solemn high mass. The front rows were crammed with a seething throng of crimson blazers, the small fry nearer the altar, the taller boys to the rear. Prefects patrolled the aisles and called mischief makers to order in penetrating stage whispers which succeeded in their aim of drawing the attention of doting parents. These filled the rows behind, the mothers in clothes which they would only otherwise have risked at a family wedding and were delighted to have the opportunity of dusting down and donning on this one day of the year. It was curious that hats they knew would provoke hilarity under normal circumstances should inspire respect on such an occasion. Envious, cowed sisters wearied their parents with endless questions, or peered forward, trying to catch a glimpse of more privileged siblings over the shoulders of the families in front. The middle-aged stalwarts who formed the committee of the Old Ignatians Society had abandoned their wives and taken their station in the right transept, proudly sporting school ties and the distinctive crimson handkerchiefs, tucked into their breast pockets.

Mr McElhinny nodded to Gerald, who had a mirror poised to one side of the organ manuals so that he could see the choirmaster's head and shoulders. He began the voluntary. Once it was over, he would take his place beside Colm in the tenor section. He loved dotting back and forth during divine service in this way. In the sacristy some forty feet beneath them, Fr Feenan was adjusting the archbishop's vestments when a boy rushed in carrying a telegram from the Vatican. The archbishop glanced at it in alarm, then let it fall to the ground, for they were late already, and there was no time to discuss its contents with his secretary. The sacristy bell clanged and the procession of seven priests and twelve acolytes with thuribles swept out into the body of the church. The congregation rose to its feet and the organ intoned the opening verse of the school's Latin hymn. Left alone, the messenger dutifully picked up the discarded telegram. He could not help glancing briefly at its contents before placing it on a dresser next to an uncorked bottle of altar wine, from which he took a sip. All he had made out was the one word 'earplugs'.

Everything went smoothly during the first part of the ceremony. St Ignatius' was renowned for its excellent acoustics, and the austere harmonies of Palestrina penetrated to the most distant recesses of the interior, elevating the spirits of all present, along with clouds of incense, towards the high windows. As the archbishop sat listening, he noticed how powerfully his heart was beating. He did not wish to articulate his fear, yet dread possessed him at the thought of the sermon that lay before him and its concomitant dangers. Since his televised humiliation he had kept public appearances to a minimum and taken regular doses of the tablets Dr Quinn had supplied. He was determined to believe in, indeed to prove their efficacy, in spite of the doctor's deprecation. Nevertheless it was clear to him that if, as

59

Quinn insisted, his malady was the result of stress, today's performance was more than likely to cause a further outbreak.

The gospel ended, he rose and made his way down from the altar. A subdued organ accompaniment filled him with foreboding. As he climbed the twisting stairs into the pulpit he checked the state of his abdomen and decided it was normal. The sermon he had prepared was based on a military metaphor. Ignatius had started out in life as a soldier and had been wounded fighting against the French at the siege of Pamplona. It was while recovering from the injuries sustained there that he made the decision to give his life entirely to God and become a soldier of Christ. The archbishop expanded on the thrills and perils of warfare and on the qualities required of every soldier worth his salt, thus cunningly preparing for the second half of his sermon, in which he would translate these sterling qualities into spiritual terms.

It was at this point that a shrill whistling, only just perceptible at the limits of hearing, became audible. Betty McGuigan, sitting in the nave close to the seventh station of the cross, reflected that it sounded like a pressure cooker working up to the moment when you have to turn the gas down, and looked around to see where it was coming from. A number of women in the congregation were doing the same.

The archbishop was describing the spiritual travails of St Ignatius that had led to the writing of his famous exercises. In order to bring home their importance to the boys, he compared them to various activities they might engage in on the sports field. As far as he could judge, he was getting the message across, for the attention of the front rows was riveted upon him.

He was leaning close to the microphone so that the sound of his own voice deafened him to the other noises he was producing. Intermittent as these were, they were perfectly clear to the first-, second- and third-year pupils. It was like someone opening an ancient, unimaginably heavy wooden door on unoiled hinges, with a painful slowness which made the laborious and fascinatingly varied creaking that resulted more rather than less distracting.

Eddie McGlone had been chewing gum thoughtfully in time to the rise and fall of the archbishop's intonation. He took the sticky ball from his mouth and carefully attached it to the back flap of the blazer of the boy in front of him, then looked quizzically at Frank Cullen, who was sitting next to him.

'The old geezer's farting,' said Frank in his usual matter-of-fact way.

A medieval chronicler describing the scene would have said that the demon trapped in the poor cleric's backside, unable to disrupt proceedings with the effects he had so far employed, now began to take his job seriously. From the noises that emerged, anyone would have thought that an irate trumpet, imprisoned in the windings of the archbishop's colon, was desperately signalling its presence in the hope of being rescued.

Guffaws of laughter swept the rows of boys. Their parents held out only a little longer. Hats bobbed up and down, fascinator veils were swept back so that the streaming eyes behind them could be dabbed, and several old Ignatians used their ceremonial handkerchiefs to mop their tears of mirth. After a brief pause, which allowed the sacrilegious trumpeting to be heard all the more distinctly, the archbishop beat an ignominious retreat into the sacristy. As he turned, he brought his rear end into the proximity of the microphone in time for a particularly loud blast. Even the other priests on the high altar were convulsed with uncontrollable hilarity.

Up in the choirloft, Mr McElhinny gestured wildly to Gerald.

'Play something,' he hissed. 'Anything! The loudest piece you can find!'

☆

It was quiet enough when there was just herself and Bill to feed. When they had guests Mrs Donaldson rarely had time to sit at the table. She would hurry back and forth from the kitchen, often gulping her food from a standing position, which Alan found intensely irritating. The moment one course was on the table she got busy with the next one. Even at the end of the meal there was coffee to be taken through to the sitting room where they all adjourned.

Today was a special occasion. Only once or twice a year did she succeed in bringing her 'four men' together for Sunday lunch. Fraser had piled up the plates and helped her clear away the remains of the main course. She placed the tinned fruit salad in her favourite cut glass bowl at the centre of the table, arranged whipped cream and orange jelly on either side, popped a Swiss roll in its polythene wrapping down next to them, in case anyone still felt peckish, and sat down. The coffee was percolating contentedly in the kitchen and the dishes could wait until later in the day.

'So why are you in your dressing gown?' Alan asked Craig. 'Don't you feel well or were you just too lazy to get your clothes on?'

'Craig's staying with us for a bit. He's been feeling poorly,' Mrs Donaldson butted in. She had an infuriating habit of answering questions put to any member of the family, which made it practically impossible to have a conversation even when she was in the kitchen.

'But have you got a job? What have you been doing with yourself?' Alan insisted.

'Whatever it is, he's not going to tell us about it,' interposed Mr Donaldson, who had as usual refused to take his cap off when he came to table.

'You keep quiet,' his wife told him.

The meal had been delayed for a full half hour while they waited for him to get back from the pub. Weekday nights were not enough these days, he had to go on Sunday as well. Soon he would start burping as he always did between the main course and dessert. Mrs Donaldson wished she could stuff the napkin she had so carefully ironed and starched right into her husband's big mouth.

Craig grinned sheepishly. 'The job's top secret for the present. But it's exciting enough and the pay is good.'

'If you ask me, he's working as a plain-clothes officer for the police,' said Mrs Donaldson, surprisingly close to the mark, 'and he's been left out on duty all night. He's got a really dreadful chest cold. I can tell you' – she smiled at her eldest son with the benignity of those who do not doubt their own absolute power – 'they won't be getting him back this week.'

'As long as it's not a job with the Catholic church,' Mr Donaldson declared. 'It's enough of a disgrace to have one son turn a Pape without the others following suit.'

He scowled at Fraser, who promptly dropped the wobbly piece of jelly he was balancing on his spoon. With his mouth gaping open he looked like a fish.

'You leave that boy alone!' snarled his wife. 'There's just one God and, even if we don't understand Fraser's way of serving him, it all comes down to the same thing in the end.'

Dad objects to having a son who's a Pape, thought Alan. What would he say if he knew he was a poof as well? He smirked but said nothing.

'Have you been taking the tablets for your blood pressure?' Fraser asked his father, with a determination to be charitable, which furthered enraged the retired welder.

'I wouldn't have problems with my blood pressure if you had two sensible ideas in your head to rub together!' he bellowed.

'Leave him alone, Dad,' murmured Alan.

'And as for you, when are you getting married? Nearly thirty and no sign of a woman! What with those religious pro-grammes, you're turning out the next best thing to a monk! Why couldn't this woman bear me a son with some spunk in him?'

Alan pushed his chair back and rose to his feet but his mother bustled round and persuaded him to resume his seat.

'See?' she turned to her husband. 'See what you've done? You're at it again. I go to endless trouble to get them here on the same day and you offend them all, one after another. No wonder we see so little of them.'

She felt tears coming, and dabbed at the corner of her eye with her napkin.

'Oh, Mum,' cried Fraser, and got up and put his arm round her shoulder.

Mr Donaldson went on unperturbed. He was determined to give his firstborn the benefit of his experience.

'I know a man has to try a few women out when he's young, just to learn what it's like.' He leered at Alan meaningfully. 'But there comes a time when you need to settle down. What's a man without a family, eh? What's a man without sons?'

Alan coloured and gazed moodily at his fruit salad. It was not the first time he had been subjected to a sermon of this kind.

'Tell us the latest about the farting archbishop,' suggested Craig, to divert the conversation and because he was interested.

As the youngest he was still considered exempt from the procreative imperative.

'He won't be back on the programme for a while, I can tell you,' Alan answered. 'Actually, I felt quite sorry for the old fellow.'

'Served him right, damned Pape!' said Mr Donaldson.

'Did you see the programme?' asked Alan, a little nervously.

'We certainly did,' beamed his mother. 'Every time you're on, my dear, there we are, glued to the set. Oh! there's the phone!'

A minute later she put her head round the door.

'Alan, it's for you.'

It was his producer.

'The archbishop's been at it again. Drop whatever you're doing and get round to St Ignatius' as fast as you can. I want to know what this is all about.'

☆

This was either the fourth or the fifth time Cissie had visited the Orange Sun. She had lost count. And she had not been able to bring herself to steal any condoms on this or her previous visit. Her failure had not gone down well with Mrs Donnelly, who had curled her lip and hummed and hawed, then threatened to send another volunteer in her place. No offers were forthcoming, however, and Cissie lacked the conviction to refuse to return.

She had seen them twice before. On both occasions they were alone. She had taken to sitting over her coffee in a leisurely fashion before approaching the counter with her handbag, and this gave her an opportunity to survey whoever else happened to be in the café. Their names were Kevin and Clive. She had picked them up when a friend came over to speak to the healthy one and was introduced to the one who was sick. She had never seen anyone look so unwell before and she knew it must be that illness.

There was not a pick on him and his hair was coming away in patches. Leathery and tanned, his skin was drawn taut around his cheekbones, giving his eyes an unnatural brightness, as if he had to look at everything with a special intensity because he knew he would leave it before long. At the same time his gaze would gloss over without warning, and she was not sure whether he was rapt in thought or merely so debilitated that he had lost any capacity for reflection, reduced to staying alive and nothing more. The first time she saw him she could not take her eyes off him. Even when she forced herself to look away, his image haunted her. Two sentences went through her head. He's going to die. He's had sex with that other man.

She liked the other one instinctively. He was younger, chubby-cheeked, with gel in his hair. He talked constantly to his friend, reading him bits from the paper and gently urging him to finish the soup he fed him with a spoon, or guiding his hand to the coffee cup he could still just grasp. She imagined he must not naturally be a serious person. He would like dancing and staying up late at night. She had had friends like that when she was his age. She had never got to stay out late as often as she wanted to. But she had enjoyed herself all the same. She decided Kevin was like her in a way. He was the wrong kind of person to be faced with a tragedy of this sort, and yet he handled it so well.

Clive had blotch marks down one side of his face and on the backs of his hands. Sometimes he would respond to the things Kevin said but mostly he just sat there and survived. He wore ugly iron rings with strange designs. From his name he must be English. Kevin was from Glasgow; she could tell by the way he spoke.

Suddenly Cissie thought of Simon. He had been down in London for three years. There was no word of a girl or of him getting married. When she tried to ask him about romance he deflected the question so deftly she had never been able to get any indication as to whether he had been in love or not, or who with, if he had. What if he was sitting in a café like this? What if he was sitting next to an ill man, like Kevin? Somehow the idea did not frighten her. She wondered if Simon would cope as well as this boy did.

They were with a group of friends this time. She really ought to be going but she could not bring herself to leave before them. There were three friends. They all looked perfectly healthy. One had a leather jacket like Kevin's. The other two wore neat suits and bright ties. They must work in offices. Maybe one of them taught at the university. They were all careful to include Clive in the conversation, although he only stared at them, startled, then relapsed into his habitual torpor.

Now he was asleep. She felt glad for him. At least he would not be suffering at such times. One of the boys in suits, the one with red hair, had a good line in patter and kept the others laughing. The chap next to him went for more coffees. Clive had slumped a little. His right forearm slid off the side of the chair but his other hand was poised just next to Kevin's. All at once he juddered back into consciousness, with a moan and a look of panic in his eyes.

In that split second Kevin grasped his hand. His vigilance had not faltered for a moment. Cissie found herself thinking, absurdly, that Clive was very lucky. She snapped her handbag shut with a decided air, got up and strode out of the café.

Harry, who was at the till, called to Fred in the kitchen.

'That woman's just waltzed off without paying!'

Fred craned his neck round the door and Harry pointed to where Cissie had been sitting.

'Oh, don't worry about her,' said Fred. 'She'll be back. She's a regular.'

☆

On Monday morning the anteroom in the archbishop's palace was unusually crowded. Alan Donaldson was not the only journalist who, having gained access to the building, failed to penetrate beyond the doors of the archbishop's study. When he arrived he found a man he vaguely knew from the *Herald* sitting next to a scandalmonger from a national tabloid. They glared at him then returned to their feverish and reciprocally mistrustful whisperings. The same nun in a soiled apron who had opened to Dr Quinn several weeks before brought an additional wooden chair for Alan to sit on, next to the two remaining visitors.

One, a Mother Superior of indeterminate age with small, lively grey eyes, couldn't sit still and kept shifting position, clutching her abdomen and smiling vacantly to either side. Beyond her sat the investigator Mick McFall, who knew Alan's name from his television appearances. Alan recognized the former schoolteacher's features, as they often drank in the same pubs in the West End or near Charing Cross, and wondered what his connection with the Glasgow Catholic hierarchy was.

One of the double doors to the archbishop's study swung back and everybody jumped. Dr Quinn emerged, looking harassed and squeezing his consultant's briefcase convulsively. His expression was distinctly peeved. He had allowed himself to be convinced against his better judgement, and had arranged for a room to be made available for the archbishop that very evening in a private hospital on the city's outskirts. The archbishop had insisted that tests should be carried out without specifying what these should be or what it was they were intended to reveal. Quinn was thinking hard about the instructions he could give his colleagues there. In spite of the size of his fee, he regretted more and more being associated with this case. It could bring him nothing but discredit.

As for the pregnancies, he was doing his best to banish them from his mind. They struck him as being of the same order as the farting attacks and potentially even more damaging. He was unable to decide between two possible courses of action: to publicize the medical anomaly and so vindicate the sisters' virtue, or to lie and initiate a witch-hunt for putative fathers. His eyes met Mother Genevieve's. He frowned at the unwelcome reminder and tossed his head. She dropped her gaze as if she were guilty and he flounced out of the room and down the main staircase.

Fr Feenan popped his head round the door and nodded ominously to the Mother Superior, who got up, straightened herself and disappeared through the double doors. Alan could not have said exactly what was strange about the way she walked. She neither hobbled nor limped. Nothing in her gait suggested that she was disabled or in pain. Rather she gave the impression of someone who had lost touch with the middle and lower parts of her body and was struggling to make their acquaintance once more, as if she could not predict the exact nature or the effect of any movements initiated beneath the level of her chest. If he had had to choose a single word to sum up her state, he would have described it as one of rejuvenation. The idea startled him but his impression would not be contradicted. He suddenly felt he would like to discuss doctrine with her.

Theology had been one of his Ordinary subjects at university and his interest in it revived at the most unpredictable times.

You could have heard a pin drop in the anteroom. All ears were strained to catch the slightest hint of what was going on inside. At first no words could be distinguished. Now Mother Genevieve's tones became audible, mournful to begin with, then horrified and protesting. The scandalmonger rose slightly from his chair and McFall put away the comic he had been reading. Then the hall door opened and Cyril Braithwaite was ushered in. His appearance was slovenly in the extreme. His suit looked as if he had bundled it up and sat on it for hours at a time. His dog collar was stained and his shoes were unpolished and scuffed at the toes.

He was looking round politely, greeting the strangers present with a thoroughly Anglican benevolence, when the double doors opened wide and Mother Genevieve shot out, as if propelled, so that she almost fell into his arms. Her embarrassment, thought Alan, was utterly disproportionate to the incident. He wondered what special significance the prebendary had for her if he could provoke confusion of such magnitude. Cyril was affectionate and reassuring. He touched her forearm and she started as if his fingers carried an electric charge. Yet she showed no inclination to leave and hovered on tiptoe, gazing up at the considerably taller Protestant clergyman with the kind of hero worship a secondary schoolgirl might nurture for an art teacher she has heard deliciously smutty rumours about.

Cyril broached the subject of the ecumenical working party and left with Mother Genevieve for a neighbourhood teashop. He had merely come to offer the archbishop his condolences, not expecting to find such a crowd of visitors, and willingly abandoned this plan at the prospect of a lively theological discussion. As they were leaving, Fr Feenan summoned McFall into the archbishop's presence.

The anteroom was empty when McFall emerged, so no one noted his downcast expression. The journalists had given up hope and gone to lunch. Smells drifting up the stairwell of the palace indicated that Mrs Donnelly's preparations for the same meal were almost complete. McFall stuffed a cheque, which threatened to be the last he would receive on this case, into his pocket and let himself out, once he had inspected with longing interest the closed doors on the ground-floor landing.

✢

'Death, thou shalt die!'

Colm's mother timed her arrival beautifully. The CD of Britten's *Holy Sonnets of John Donne* had just reached its triumphantly uplifting conclusion when she opened the door and edged in carrying the supper tray.

Gerald did not know her well. His mother and Colm's were good friends and had been at school together, but he had rarely dealt with the woman directly. He stood up to greet her and helped pull out the middle one of a nest of tables and spread a lace cloth over it. She set down two china cups of smoking coffee, milk and sugar and generous helpings of shortbread and fruit cake, both home made.

'Well, boys,' she beamed, 'I'll leave you to get on with your chat.'

Colm was the only one of six children not to have got married. He had stayed on as the rambling family flat emptied progressively, a respected professional with a promising career in health administration and one of the pillars of the choir at St Ignatius'. He was a good if distant uncle to his five nephews and three nieces, and he and his mother lived more than comfortably on her widow's pension and his salary.

This was only the second time Gerald had been honoured with an invitation. On his first visit he surveyed the bookshelves while Colm opened the piano and dusted down the keys. Music and spirituality were Colm's twin passions. Lives of composers, books about singing technique and the art of accompaniment stood next to a large section on meditation, finding one's path to God, liberation theology and the new face of the church since Vatican II.

Colm lived his life in compartments, passing quite consciously from one to the other. His mother and immediate family were kept separate from his fellow choir members and from the musical friends he attended concerts and operas or organized 'at homes' with. Visits to Knight's Bar and the more outrageous queens of the West End and Maryhill formed yet another sector.

When he took his mother for a night out at the theatre and encountered someone from a different part of his life, he would nod frostily to them and comment: 'Just a bloke I bump into from time to time.' The choir included several former schoolmates, married men with thinning hair and three or four children, who sniffed an exciting aroma of exotic, illicit freedoms around Colm. Their curiosity was whetted by his more outlandish friends but the questions they put to him remained unanswered. After a Jesuit education and university years under the strict supervision of their parents, these schoolmates had begun solid, unsensational careers and married from home. They brought their wives, more worldly and often impatient convent girls, the gift of a tremulous virginity, which had to be jump started even in the hot days of youth.

'So tell me about Daniel,' Colm began.

Gerald thought of Daniel as unique, a creature without paragon. He and Daniel belonged to different species, disparate phoenixes who could not possibly be placed beneath a single heading. Though they were only sixteen, Daniel was in every way more worldly wise. He claimed so many people in showbusiness, in the arts, and even in parliament, were gay that Gerald grew dizzy and ceased to listen. When Colm was included in the list, Gerald reacted with disbelief. Now he began to suspect Daniel was right. The idea that there might be a whole race of phoenixes, whose mothers could meet his when shopping, or on the way home from mass, was simply too huge for his mind to grasp.

'What do you want to know?' he asked.

Colm paused and sipped his coffee. Gerald was sweeping crumbs of fruit cake from the palm of his hand into his mouth. The older Ignatian was in a difficult position, unable to articulate, even to himself, his desires or motivation. He was on the point of doing something he had never before risked, of fishing a person from one of the ponds in his life and transferring him to another without endangering the barriers between them. He was shrewd enough to know that many of those who sang in the choir must, beneath a veneer of piety and conformism, share his tastes, and he watched new recruits from the lower forms mature with a mixture of tenderness and exasperation. He believed he could identify, before they identified themselves, those who would never marry, entering the priesthood or living out long decades as frail virgins at the behest of ageing parents. The latter eventually passed on, leaving them sole survivors on the abandoned raft of what had once been a family. Those who did marry chose the most androgynously boyish, the least voluptuous or curvaceous of mates.

For years now Colm had resisted the temptation to intervene, to speak. Unwary forthrightness would have made his own position untenable. He was determined to adhere to the principles of his church, which permitted, indeed encouraged, the greatest excesses of camp in public and private life while vetoing any erotic or emotional satisfaction. He cast himself as a potential educator who would show others the path to a chastity he had achieved, and maintained, at considerable cost. What held him back was the difficulty of convincing himself that his concern for Gerald was utterly devoid of erotic colouring.

'Daniel's not the kind of boy I would have expected you to choose for a friend,' he began. 'You're such a gentle, studious type, and he's a real rebel.'

'I like him. He's exciting.' Gerald was defiant and uncertain.

'You know how the school authorities look on him. It's bound to get back to your parents that you have been associating with him.'

'Why should they care? He does well enough academically.'

'Getting through exams is not all that matters. I'm concerned about his moral nature. What has he done to you, Gerald?' asked Colm, changing tack. 'What is he trying to draw you into?'

Gerald coloured.

'Have you done anything unnatural?'

'He says you're just the same as we are,' Gerald blurted out. 'Why are you pretending you're not?'

'Gerald, I'm only concerned for your good. And what do you mean, ' "the same as we are"?'

Gerald's head was in his hands. He was about to break down. Scenting victory, Colm softened.

'Look, the kind of cross you have to bear is one that is familiar to me and to more people than you might think. The road before us is a harsh and stony one but we can learn to walk it if we are forthright and take hold of ourselves. I just can't stand by and see you debauched needlessly before you get a chance to find out what you are!'

'"Debauched"?' wailed Gerald. 'But I love him!'

'"Love"?' Colm echoed the word incredulously, in a sort of shouted whisper. He could not afford to raise his voice in case his mother heard. Indeed, he was worried that she might notice Gerald's sobbing and interrupt them at the crucial moment when he was just beginning to get his message over.

'Love is something that comes from God, Gerald. How can anything you and Daniel do together resemble that? What is that boy turning you into?'

Settling into a sullen silence, Gerald pulled out a handkerchief and blew his nose.

'What's more,' Colm went on, 'there's a legal question. I don't know exactly how far you two have gone, but I have a very good idea. Do you know you could be hauled into court for it? What would your mother say? Can you imagine what that would do to her?'

He had gone too far. Gerald leapt to his feet.

'Are you threatening me? Don't you understand we all live in glass houses?'

'Gerald, Gerald,' murmured Colm. 'This is not what I intended at all. Sit down again and let's talk about this like sensible people.'

'I don't want to be a sensible person. I want to go. I'm not going to listen to you any longer. Get me my coat.'

Gerald spoke through gritted teeth. Colm gazed at him, then shrugged and saw him out.

☆

Cissie was pleased but surprised to get Mother Genevieve's summons. She had a frugal lunch and did her shopping, then called round to find her old friend in the process of packing up. The familiar sitting room was even barer than usual. The holy pictures had been taken down and the few nick-nacks scattered along the mantelpiece and on the coffee table had been gathered into plastic bags and dumped in an armchair. The door which

72

led into Mother Genevieve's bedroom was propped open with a middle-sized black suitcase whose strap had already been firmly tied.

Tea would, however, be brought, Cissie was informed. It was late spring. Her hostess did not switch on the electric fire but dragged the suitcase in so that they could shut both doors and run no risk of being overheard.

Cissie sipped her tea and looked at Mother Genevieve expectantly. The nun's expression was wooden, as if stunned. She clearly did not know where to begin. Her visitor took advantage of the silence to munch one more Jaffa cake.

'Well, Brenda,' she prodded, struck by her own boldness. She had not used that Christian name with her friend for more than twenty years. 'Spill the beans. What's afoot?'

Mother Genevieve still refrained from looking at her directly. She smoothed the dark skirt primly over her knees and took a deep breath.

'Cissie,' she said. 'You and I go back a long way.'

Cissie nodded impatient assent.

'There are many things we have never spoken about. You are a married woman and I am a bride of Christ, though recently I have come to doubt the precise meaning of that expression. My dear' – she swung round and faced Cissie head on – 'I have observed you with interest and affection all through your years of marriage. At times I have envied you. More often I have thanked my stars for the path I had chosen. It was a path of peace and dedication. I dealt firmly and fairly with those entrusted to my charge. What little ambition I had was satisfied in the station I had reached. And I was untroubled by the lusts of the flesh.'

Cissie bridled, and Mother Genevieve hastened to lessen any offence that might have been taken.

'The expression is not of my choosing. I am forced to use it until I can find one that is more appropriate. Anyway, all that has been called into question now.'

She coloured and became more agitated.

'We have drunk tea and consumed cakes on innumerable occasions. But not since we were girls have we truly opened our hearts to one another. Something prompts me today to share my troubles and perplexities with you, perhaps against my better judgement. I demand no corresponding confidences. All I ask is that you should hear me out and divulge the contents of our conversation to nobody.'

There was a silence. Cissie had the impression of a huge weight of water gradually building up behind a dam which was about to crack.

Mother Genevieve stared intently at the unlit electric bar, hands joined in her lap. She sniggered ironically.

'Perhaps we ought to say a decade of the rosary together. But my heart would not be in it. I have a horror of insincere worship.'

'Come on, Brenda,' said Cissie, who was losing patience. 'Get to the point. They've given you the boot.'

Mother Genevieve nodded, speechless. A large, brilliant tear trembled on either cheek.

'It's because of the pregnant sisters,' Cissie insisted.

The nun's eyes were big with astonishment.

'How do you know?'

'How could I have failed to notice? And I'm not the only one. Euphemia MacFarrigle and one or two others have cottoned on. Word is getting around.'

'That's not all . . . ' The dam burst and Mother Genevieve wept unrestrainedly, but without entirely relaxing her vigilance. There was a subject even closer to her heart which she could not contemplate broaching, one she must struggle with alone. Her unburdening would be only partial.

'It's so unfair!' she wailed. 'I was called in to see the archbishop yesterday. Why should I get blamed for the whole thing? Even if those girls have misbehaved, it isn't the end of the world. It won't be the first time babies have been born in a convent. The trouble is, it looks like a miracle! I'd much rather they were just plain pregnant, if you really want to know. The truth is they're still virgins.'

Is the woman going out of her mind? Cissie asked herself. She kept silent. Mother Genevieve's emotion had touched her and she was conscious of an urge to share her own peculiar burden whenever the opportunity should arise.

'When it all came out, do you know what solution those fools

74

in the hierarchy came up with? Earplugs! Men! They're nothing but incompetent men!'

Cissie could not stop herself giggling. 'What on earth were the earplugs supposed to do?'

'The idiots decided they had been fecundated via the ear, like the Virgin Mary! You can imagine how stupid I felt when I had to tell the community. Nothing could have been more calculated to undermine my authority. Well, the archbishop has problems of his own.' She winked knowingly at her friend. 'It's in the public domain by now. Loyalty no longer binds me to silence. And just before that disastrous sermon he got a telegram from Rome. Can you guess what it said?'

Suddenly Mother Genevieve could not speak for laughter. She would never have believed that she could weep tears of sorrow and hilarity within minutes of one another. She laughed so much that Cissie became alarmed and got up and patted her back.

'It said "Remove earplugs immediately. All forms of contraception against canonical law"!!'

Mother Genevieve's voice rose in a hoot as she came to the end of the message. Cissie's high peals rang out and the two old schoolfriends sat and roared with laughter until the sister whose responsibility it was to refill the teapot put her head round the door and they had to sober up.

'So what's going to happen to you now?' Cissie asked when they had mopped their cheeks and poured more tea.

'It's not me I'm worried about, it's the community. He's sending in Philomena O'Sharkey.'

Cissie's face was blank.

'Mother Rodelinda of the Seven Sorrows,' added Mother Genevieve, as if that would clarify things. 'She has a special devotion to the Suffering Virgin and she's determined to make any other virgins she can get her hands on suffer too. When we were both in the novitiate she was famous for mortification and long fasts on cold tea and dry bread. She's a vindictive, sanctimonious little minx, if you want my view of it.' She was taken aback at her own frankness. But there was no point in stopping now. 'She had her own convent in Ireland, stuck out in the backwoods. She's very competitive and she could not forgive me for getting a post in Glasgow. Two years ago there was a mini rebellion. I think she had been excessively severe and the other nuns refused to take any more of her nonsense. So her bishop packed her off to the Vatican to study theology, and appointed a moderate in her place. And now our archbishop has decided to give her my job. She'll be crowing with delight. What really worries me—'

She broke off and looked at Cissie, who noted a tenderness she had never seen before in the nun's expression.

'—is what this means for those poor girls. You must know what having a baby's like, Cissie. They need all the love and spoiling I can give them. Now it's going to be one long, uninterrupted round of punishment. The strange thing is,' she continued, resolving that a half truth must suffice for the time, 'seeing them has . . . has awakened the woman in me. It has . . . awakened my sensuality.'

There was an awkward silence. Cissie did not encourage Mother Genevieve to expand on this topic. She had heard quite enough to cope with for one day.

'And are you leaving Glasgow?'

'No, I am to be allowed to continue my work on the ecumenical commission. For the time being I will lodge with Father Ryan in the parish house at St Pius XXVII's. It's not ideal but it's better than banishment. I'll be able to keep an eye on my girls from afar.'

They're not the only people I don't want to be separated from, she thought, and reproached herself for her duplicity.

Cissie sat digesting the news. 'There are interesting times ahead,' she concluded. 'And I am delighted we shall be facing them together, Brenda.'

☆

It took Mick three afternoons to find Alfred Coutts. The proprietor of Dino's Café grew positively fulsome and offered him a free marshmallow with every cup of coffee he drank after his sixth. He began suffering from insomnia because his intake of stimulants had increased so much.

On the first afternoon two teenage boys called in for a half-hour's chat about their approaching exams. They sat in their crimson uniforms at the table next to Mick's, then took their leave: one to the train station, the other to a bus stop for Hyndland.

Mick paid no attention to them. On the second day he started losing heart and toured the cafés and tea shops of the town centre without glimpsing anyone remotely fitting Craig's description of Coutts. This made his excitement all the greater when, at half past three on the third afternoon, a man who could only be the one he sought sauntered in and ordered a cappuccino. Mick conjectured, accurately enough, that he was a retired drag queen, aged somewhere between sixty-five and seventy. He was carefully made up and his skin had an unnaturally youthful sheen. It looked flaky, as if it might disintegrate when touched. His hair was white at the roots and he had been rather too generous with the lipstick.

Mick watched him wolf down a sausage in batter, a roll stuffed with chips, and a plateful of beans. Presumably he lived on his own and came here now and again for meals. His appetite would explain the sagging jowls and the indeterminate waistline hidden beneath a stained and baggy raincoat.

'Mr Coutts, I take it?' said Mick, sitting down next to him.

'Are you one of my admirers? Do you remember me from a show?' asked Alfred, fluttering eyelashes Mick had not noticed until they were set in motion.

'I believe I do,' he answered. 'How long is it since you left the stage?'

'Five years, three months and seven days since my last performance.' Alfred had a pronounced, mincing Home Counties accent. 'Never thought I'd end up this side of the border. But with property the price it is down south, it struck me as a sensible place to retire to. Bit dull, mind you.' He rolled his eyes heavenwards. 'I was famous in the sixties as Widow Twankey at the Alhambra. You'd be in your teens then, wouldn't you? What a little sweetie you must have been! Don't think you could have seen many of my later shows, though! You look far too innocent for that!'

Mick let the former actor take his hand. He was man enough not to be flummoxed by this sort of thing, although it did make him feel uneasy.

'Actually,' he hesitated, 'I was hoping you could put me in

touch with a common acquaintance. Apparently she spent a lot of time down south too. Does the name Euphemia MacFarrigle mean anything to you?'

Alfred dropped his hand at once.

'What do you know about Euphemia? How strange! I bumped into her here a couple of weeks ago. It was the first time I'd set eyes on her in nearly twenty years. And, can you credit it, she hadn't aged a bit! It was quite uncanny! You'd have sworn she'd discovered the elixir of long life!'

All at once suspicious, he lunged close to Mick and peered short-sightedly into his eyes.

'So what's your interest in her? What's in this for you?'

'A mutual friend asked me to check her out. She's been giving him a bit of trouble.'

'Trouble of what kind?'

'Difficult to put your finger on, actually. It's more that she looks as if she could give him trouble, if you see what I mean.'

'Hmm . . . ' Alfred tilted his head to one side and considered. 'Well, why don't we leave this dump and go somewhere nicer? You can buy me a drink, or two, or three' – he clapped his hands together – 'and I'll tell you all about me and Euphemia. Not that there's much to tell. We just met once, after all. Gave me a real start to see her here again. And she tried to cut me stone dead, the standoffish old besom.'

They got up and Alfred allowed Mick to give him his arm and help him round the corner into the Highlandman's Retreat, though his gait was sprightly enough and he had no obvious need of assistance. Mick selected a quiet corner in the pub, behind a wooden partition where a stained-glass window gave on to an inner courtyard. He set a pint and a chaser down in front of Alfred and contented himself with a gin and soda. Alfred drank with gusto, then wiped the froth from his lips and cleared his throat.

'It was nineteen sixty-seven,' he began. 'Sixty-seven or sixty-eight. I was doing a panto up here. Near to the end of the run the lady I was in digs with had a heart attack and they had to find somewhere else for me to stay at short notice. That's how I came to ninety-eight Otago Street. They've knocked the building down now. I know, I went round to check when I came back to live in Glasgow. Euphemia was the only other person in the flat. Not that she owned it; it belonged to a bloke named Edwin. I never saw him. The rent went straight to his lawyers. His surname was MacPherson or MacPhee, one of those Scottish names with an F in the middle. It was the top flat, and Euphemia had two rooms; a bedroom and the big, front sitting room with the triple windows. When you were in there all you could see was sky, just like you were in the cockpit of an aeroplane.

'Me and some of the lads in the panto used to get up to tricks. I didn't always take my togs off after the performance, and we would go for an Indian round the corner from the theatre, pretending I was a girl and they were my two blokes. It was innocent fun, though I don't know what the police would have said if they had caught us. I suppose the danger added a touch of excitement to it. We'd stayed particularly late that night and it was nearly two when I got back to the flat. I'd had one too many, I can tell you. I kept tripping on the pavement with my high heels. Getting to the top of that last flight of stairs was sheer purgatory. It's one thing crossing a stage in a tight skirt; the close in a Glasgow tenement is something else.

'There was a light under Euphemia's door. While she was always pleasant, she kept herself very much to herself. I don't know when she had her meals, but she never used the kitchen at the same time as me. Anyway, I was on too much of a high to think of sleeping. I felt like a bit of company so I knocked on Euphemia's door and went in. Not just like that, you understand. I would never intrude. I knocked and she said: "Oh, come in," in a funny, surprised little voice, and so I did.

'What a room it was! Euphemia was sitting right up at the windows in front of a big desk. On it she had spread charts and tables, and I could see she had been doing calculations in a notebook at her elbow. There were two columns of sums down either side of the page. A cabinet on the wall was filled with stuff you'd expect to find in a chemistry lab: bottles and tubes and retorts, green and yellow and purple powders, metal pincers, suction tubes and pumps. It could have been the set for the magician's cave in *Aladdin*!

'Normally I don't think she'd have had much to do with me, but that night she was really beside herself with glee. She said nothing about the way I was decked out and I was so curious to find out what she was up to that I forgot about it myself. She sat me down and made me a cup of tea. While she was getting it I took the chance to have a good look round. The decor was dingy to say the least. There hadn't been a painter in that room for nearly a century! She had a couple of framed portraits of women in old-fashioned dresses. A long, thin roll of paper was hanging from just below the picture rail, with a tree on it and all sorts of branches sprouting out. It was covered with old-fashioned writing in different colours of ink and there were little creatures perched on the ends of the branches with bodies like monkeys, but human heads.

'Anyway, she sat down and told me she had been working on a horoscope.

' "He's been conceived!" she shouted, with a big smile.

' "Who do you mean?" I asked.

' "Him," she says. "The one I have to help. Or one of the ones. He'll be born this autumn."

'And then she took me to the window and pointed out all the stars. It was a clear, cold night, the kind you hardly ever get in Glasgow, and the constellations were spread out like a map, or like points of gleaming spindrift on a great, dark sea. To her it was an alphabet, and she could read what it meant. She took me from one point of the compass to the other like we were in a ship, calling in at each of the points of light. She was familiar with the places and the distances between them. Then she told me how it would all have changed by the time he was born. I found that bit difficult to follow, but it clearly said a lot to her.

'By this time we had run out of tea so she reached in behind the funny glass things and produced a bottle of malt whisky. We drank it neat. I didn't know whether she was mad or not. It was like being back on stage and, because that's always been where I've felt happiest, I just went along with the script, trying to humour her and feed her the lines she needed.

' "What's so important about this bloke?" I asked.

' "He's going to be a poet," beams she. "He's going to write great poetry. And maybe plays and novels as well."

' "And why does he need your help?"

'At that she clouds over and looks kind of sad.

' "Because he'll only just make it. There's a lot pitted against him, a lot we need him to fight. He has to go through that first. The problem is it might get too much for him."

' "Why can't you help him right now? Pretend you're his auntie or something? Get them to make you his godmother?"

'She looked at me as if I were really stupid.

' "I don't have unlimited powers, you know. There are rules that limit even my freedom of action. Quite soon I'm going to have to go and I won't get back for a long time. It could be as much as twenty years."

'She looked really upset when she said that, and I leaned over and patted her arm, gently, just to let her know I cared.

' "Well," she shouts, and jumps up, "let's go for a walk."

' "A walk? At this time of night? Are you crazy?"

' "I'm not going to get any sleep and neither are you. We can be two respectable middle-aged ladies out for a perfectly innocent stroll, though the police are going to be a bit curious as to the time of night we've chosen!"

'I didn't want to risk my glad rags any longer so I insisted on slipping into something a bit more comfortable. She came through into my room and I showed her all the stuff in my wardrobe: dresses, nightgowns, spangled bras and so on. I must have liked her a lot because I wouldn't normally share my fantasy life with someone I'd just met. Euphemia entered into the spirit of the thing and said she wanted me to look convincingly dowdy. She brought out one of those pastel-coloured coats you can still see on Glasgow wifies, along with two hats and a rainmate for each of us. She said it was going to rain later on and we had to be prepared.

'That walk is as clear in my mind as if it had been yesterday, even though all those years have passed. Because, do you know what she did?'

Alfred turned round and put one hand on Mick's shoulder to emphasize his point. The other was holding his third pint. He was about to down what was left of it.

'She prophesied. She foresaw it all. She told me everything that was going to happen in this city and a thing or two that hasn't happened yet. That's why I'm inclined to believe the whole business about the boy and her coming back to help him and whatnot. First of all we went over the river and down Woodside Road to Charing Cross. She told me it would all be knocked down and they'd dig a tunnel underneath and make a double bridge. The upper part of the bridge would be a building instead of a road, a building like a road that never quite materialized. Then she pointed towards St George's Cross and said it would all come down, there'd just be a wasteland with a few relicts standing here and there. The city would look as if it had been devastated by bombing raids.

'All this, she said, was nothing to what it would be like over the river. The Gorbals would disappear without a stone left standing and they'd put huge towers in place of the tenements, towers like stacks at sea with tempestuous winds blowing constantly around the bottom of them. And inside they'd be like caves, damp and dark with slime and greenness dripping down the walls. And nearby they'd worship Allah. Of course I took her for completely nutty there and then, but you go and look, my sweetie, just you go and look around and you'll see that everything Euphemia said has turned out to be true.

'We walked right down to the Broomielaw and she moved her hands overhead like they were aeroplanes. She said she could see a new bridge, ten lanes or more of traffic sweeping above the Clyde downstream from where the railway crosses. And to the right, on the south bank, a great, ephemeral garden would arise. There'd be plants growing that had never been seen in Scotland and would never be seen here again. They'd flower for a summer and then it would all be swept away just like it had never happened.

'The last bit was specially for me, she said, because I worked in the theatre and would care about that sort of thing. There would be one year when actors and dancers and performers came to Glasgow from all over the world, and there would be more plays put on in twelve months than in the twelve years that had gone before. The streets would be filled with music and dancing and a babble of languages from Europe and America and the rest of the world.'

It was nine o'clock by the time Mick saw Alfred Coutts on to his bus and made his way back to Kelvinbridge on foot. His head was spinning and he knew only one thing for certain. The temptation to investigate 98 Otago Street had hardened to a resolution in his mind. He could put off penetrating Euphemia's mysteries no longer.

THREE

The London train was delayed for more than forty minutes. Fr Feenan took Dr Quinn into the station cafeteria for a cup of tea while they waited. The consultant was distinctly uncomfortable. It did not suit his image of himself to be seen in such lowly surroundings. Nevertheless, if the personage who was about to arrive was as important as everyone assured him, his trouble would prove worth it in the end.

Fr Feenan had done his utmost to persuade Dr Quinn to be part of the welcoming committee. With the archbishop in hospital the responsibility of meeting the Vatican's special investigator fell to him. He was not looking forward to giving an account of what had happened. Recent events would be particularly hard to explain. Wielding the authority of the medical profession, he hoped that the consultant could substantiate the more incredible details.

At last an announcement over the intercom brought them to their feet and they made their way to the platform. As the crowds of descending passengers thinned out, a man dressed entirely in black was left standing on his own. He was shaped like a snowman. Fr Feenan was struck by the resemblance in spite of the opposite colour. He had a pointed nose. His head was perfectly round, bald except for a scattering of white hair just above the ears and along his neckline. He doffed his hat and bowed in an endearingly old-fashioned manner.

'Father Felipe Gutierrez?' asked Feenan.

'Pliced to mate you,' came the reply. 'The weaver is very bud. What a putty.'

☆

Heroic wonder worker! Most devious binder and sunderer of spells!

You will be overjoyed to read that we have emerged unscathed from an extremely hazardous phase of our journey. It appeared we must be smothered or pulverized and all traces of our heroic enterprise lost to the world. Resourcefulness and determination secured our freedom only to leave us utterly adrift in a void for which we had neither plan nor chart.

But let me not hurry my tale. When last you heard from us, we were becalmed in the upper part of our hostess's stomach, like a tiny vegetable bobbing on the surface of a grey, unwholesome broth. Such was the acidity of our environment that our globule was bleached to a uniform white and we feared the outer plating had grown perilously thin. Those minions whose responsibility it is to maintain our vessel have, however, tested its resistance by beating repeatedly at vulnerable points on the casing and assure me there is no danger of a puncture in the foreseeable future.

We slept and watched by turns. At the end of my third period of rest I looked out and found our situation radically changed. The separation of the different elements was almost complete. We had sunk to the bottom of that vast dungeon and become embedded in a repulsive, slimy sediment. Before my very eyes this substance was sucked forcefully towards the exit point, carrying us with it, helpless and fascinated.

Now began a second tunnel journey, slower than our first, yet no less terrifying. The sickening stench which surrounded us penetrated our capsule. I issued every crew member with a supply of pills which deaden the olfactory nerves while leaving the intellect unclouded. If the mechanism is in perfect trim, I understand this second journey can take as little as five or six hours. In cases like our own, where the vital functions have had time to grow sluggish and decay, matter can be trapped in these nether regions for as much as a week.

How strange this organism is! That which it least needs, the rubbish from which no further advantage can be drawn and which in due time will be ejected back into the world, is stored closest to its most precious parts, where our journey is to reach its climax, the sites of ecstasy and generation!

No praise can be too high for the exertions of our navigator in the course of our remarkable odyssey. As the tube down which we were travelling gradually silted up, all motion ceased. The mass of densely impacted matter where we were confined impeded the operation of his instruments. Nonetheless, by calculating the distance we had travelled and estimating the direction in which we were moving, he was able to give an approximation of our whereabouts.

In the course of a hurried and fraught council of war we resolved that our only hope lay in boring our way out. It was no easy task to gouge a road amidst the almost solid circumambient slime, but our globule was able to penetrate the tunnel's outer membrane without effort. A perforating tool emerged from the front part of the module and began to whirr round like a slow propeller, simultaneously diffusing a sedative liquid to prevent her whose guests and prisoners we are from feeling even minimal pain. The rear of the module emitted unceasing healing rays so that the tissues merged seamlessly behind us. Our explorations must procure no lasting damage. We are, after all, artificers of pleasure and not pain! The exhilaration we felt may well have been due to the consciousness that we were no longer helpless pawns of fate but had taken the direction of our journey into our own hands. What a joy to leave that seething mass of shit and strike out on a different path!

The labyrinths of this creature's anatomy are unfathomable. Our navigator worked on the basis of hypotheses. Twice he insisted that we should alter our direction, and even then he had only the vaguest inkling of where our mining operations might lead us. To our alarm we entered a huge, empty chamber. Shrunken as we are, even the smaller organs of our hostess resemble enormous caverns. But at least those have functions to fulfil and their inner shaping makes them easily identifiable. The organ where we now wandered was a nothingness. It took a considerable time for us to travel its furthest extent and we feared that we had merely exchanged one prison for another.

At this point one of the minions sighted what looked like the top of a carnivorous plant hovering above us, its fronds searching through the darkness like a predatory creature anxious to fill its maw. Before we could take stock of the situation, we were wafted upwards and launched on a very different path.

You taught me that when a predicament reaches its most desperate point, help is not far to seek. As ever, your advice has proved well-founded. Our navigator let out a shout of joy and relief when he realized that, while believing ourselves astray in the inner darkness, we had in fact happened upon the quickest and most natural pathway to those areas we wish to reach.

On my last mission but one I had occasion to visit a covered market in a human metropolis. Beneath a huge glass dome, floor after floor of shops offered merchandise of every imaginable sort to satisfy the needs, real and fancied, of humankind. The architect, with an ingeniousness I could only admire, had arranged for lifts to transport the denizens of this trading centre from one level to another. The lift shafts were transparent and curved upwards towards the sky like the stalks of outsize flowers. At the top a bouquet of electric droplets mimicked the blossoms one would find in nature. I was entranced, and paused to watch the lifts as they rose and fell with their living cargo, like fireflies liberated into day, or drops of moisture defying every pull of gravity.

Such is the sensation as we now travel a road innumerable eggs have travelled before us – a sensation of lightness, soaring and fulfilment. The days when our hostess could conceive and nurture new life are gone. It would be in our power to flout even this law of nature had you so commanded, but you have not. Nevertheless we are uplifted by the certainty that it cannot be long before we reach the place of fertilization, a threshold untrod for long decades where our preparatory labours are sorely needed. If our hostess's days of procreation are long past, her days of pleasure have yet to begin.

O prodigious one, flagrant, antique and consummate! It will not have escaped your notice how greatly the tone of this missive differs from those preceding. How could I ever have doubted that you watched over us, that your merciful gaze accompanied us through each peril, and that you smiled indulgently on our faintheartedness and lack of faith? How could I do other than acknowledge, needlessly and inevitably, that events have vindicated your foresight and perspicacity, proving yet again, if proof were not superfluous, your suitability for the exalted functions allotted you?

☆

Daniel's mother did not like him having friends round to the house. It was a nuisance to her to have extra mouths to feed and she was not interested in small chat with her son's schoolmates. He had been allowed to invite Gerald on the pretext of looking over history notes together with a view to the examination looming in ten days' time.

George Kane had a small but prosperous business based in the city centre, which sold office equipment to companies mainly in the central belt. He travelled in his dark blue BMW between Glasgow and Dundee, Edinburgh, East Kilbride and Ayr, and rarely arrived home before nine in the evening, when he would heat up whatever his wife had left for him in the microwave and have it in front of the television with a can of lager. It was customary for him to spend Saturdays in his Glasgow office, sorting out accounts and preparing for the week to come. On Sundays he accompanied the rest of the family to morning mass, then either washed and polished his car with loving attention or drifted off to the golf course.

His wife brought up the four children more or less single-handedly. She was a schoolteacher who had recently been promoted to subject principal, and took large quantities of administrative work and corrections home in the evenings. The house ran with clockwork efficiency. The evening meal was on the table at some time between two minutes to and two minutes past six. If it got as late as five past the children began to feel disoriented.

Mr Kane's commercial success meant that early on in their marriage they were able to move from a flat in Partick to a semi-detached with four bedrooms in Bishopbriggs. His wife had her own car and the couple were thoroughly independent of one another. Now that the firstborn, also named George, had left home, each of the other three children had a room to him or herself.

In the run-up to exams, fifth-year pupils were allowed to absent themselves from St Ignatius' in the afternoons for study purposes. It was five o'clock and Daniel was growing rather tired of the beheading of Charles I, the Interregnum and Oliver Cromwell. He had been sitting with both elbows on the desk, hands over his ears, murmuring important dates and details under his breath and trying to fix them firmly in his memory. Now he turned round and saw that Gerald, sprawled on the bed, had fallen asleep.

89

His crimson blazer lay on the carpet where he had tossed it when they came upstairs. He had kicked his shoes off. One of his socks had a hole in it and the big toe of his right foot stuck out. The nail was slightly twisted. Gerald's head rested on the pillow on his clasped hands, elbows spread wide so that Daniel could see where the sweat in his armpits had darkened the pale blue fabric of his shirt. His lips were parted.

Daniel knelt down by the bed, leant over and kissed him. Gerald's eyes popped open but he did not move or say a word. Gently, deliberately, Daniel grasped the knot of Gerald's tie and eased it back and forth, loosening it until he could slip it off over his head. Then he undid the top buttons of the shirt and slid his hand underneath, caressing Gerald's chest and navel and stroking his side. He could see that Gerald had an erection and Gerald's own hand moved to his crotch as he bent over him.

Their attitudes to sex were very different. They had not done it many times together, always out of doors, in places where they had to be furtive and expeditious, given the constant danger of a park warden coming upon them in the bushes, or of someone entering the close they had laboriously climbed to the top of. Gerald was intensely romantic. He would often close his eyes as if the anatomical practicalities of sex were too base for him to see as well as feel. He refused to talk more than was absolutely necessary about the things they did or might do.

He cast Daniel as expert and initiator. Daniel's very limited experience did not really equip him for this role but a sense of adventure and a love of exploration meant that he adapted comfortably enough. He had a matter of fact, down to earth approach. He could still not quite get over his surprise that a refined and virtuous creature such as Gerald should concede him these intimacies. He had no illusions as to how any adult person, and Gerald if he told him, would judge the kind of encounters he had so far survived on. It struck him as only a matter of weeks before Gerald discovered how depraved the one who had the privilege of being his boyfriend actually was. Time was at a premium. Never before had Daniel had sex twice with the same person. So he wanted to make the best of this opportunity to learn as much about lovemaking as he could.

He loved Gerald. There was no doubt about that. He felt

fiercely protective of his friend, even to the extent of wanting to protect him from himself, or what he saw as the unpalatable aspects of his own personality. He would have laid his hand in fire for Gerald. But this was no reason not to experiment as imaginatively as possible with the potential for pleasure their two bodies offered.

They were naked except for one sock, their clothes scattered across the floor between the bed and the desk.

'Have you ever done penetration?' he asked, pretty pointlessly, for he knew Gerald had not.

'What's that?' asked Gerald, trying not to sound too interested.

'It's like a man does with a woman, only you put it up the backside. I've read about it. Want to try?'

Daniel rolled over on to his back, knees in the air, and looked at Gerald expectantly. His friend flushed and his eyes widened in alarm.

'But I don't know how. I'm sure I can't do it. Doesn't it hurt?'

'When they describe it in the books it sounds great. You have to use spittle or Vaseline or something to make it go in smoothly.'

Daniel, who had been planning this session for some time, jumped up and produced a tin of Vaseline from his desk drawer, the seal unbroken. He held it out encouragingly to Gerald, who shook his head.

'Shall I do it to you, then?' Daniel proposed, ever ready to compromise.

Daniel was too precious to Gerald, and they had been intimate for too short a time, for him to contemplate refusing anything he asked. He nodded and spread his knees wide, with a mixture of trepidation and excitement.

'I'll do it with my finger first. That should make it easier.'

The business was rather problematic. Gerald was tense and tight, and Daniel only had the vaguest image in his head of what penetration might turn out to be like. Nevertheless he was young and his erection was resilient. After a great deal of huffing and puffing and the application of generous quantities of Vaseline they got it in. They both came almost immediately. Daniel withdrew, collapsed on top of Gerald and dozed off, his face thrust into the pillow and his neck in the crook of his friend's shoulder. Gerald stared contentedly at the ceiling. Daniel's body was deliciously sticky and fragrant on his. His backside was smarting a bit.

There was an irritated knock at the door.

'Come on boys,' came Daniel's mother's voice. 'Tea's on the table.'

'Oops,' said Daniel, opening his eyes, not daring to move.

She rattled at the doorhandle but did not put her head in. They heard her footsteps going downstairs again.

☆

Mick McFall caught a glimpse of his reflection in the windowpane. The woollen balaclava he was wearing gave his head a disturbingly stumpy outline. He was glad he had not pulled a stocking over his face. He looked frightening enough as it was.

There was no great expanse of sky to be seen beyond the triple windows. The building opposite blocked any view. Perhaps the retired panto dame had simply spent three hours letting his imagination run riot on free drink, taking the mickey out of him in a thoroughly enjoyable way.

He had had to repress a movement of surprise when he found that No. 98 really existed. It annoyed him that he had even allowed himself to think there might be a tenement stair just off Gibson Street which appeared and disappeared at will. He must have walked past this building at least a hundred times when a student. Good friends of his had a flat round the corner in Westbank Quadrant and the quickest way to get there for coffee after classes led along this isolated branch of Otago Street.

It was June and the weather was rainy. He sheltered for nearly an hour in the mouth of a close opposite, until the only lighted window in the top storey had gone out and he could presume all the occupants were in bed. If his theory was right, and this Euphemia MacFarrigle was nothing more than a pious old dame besotted with priests and nuns of a kind he had often come across in his youth, then he had no wish to cause her an unnecessary shock. Since starting his new career he had entered private dwellings unlawfully on at least six occasions, always with the most satisfying results for his investigations. It was marvellous what a letter or a receipt could achieve, either in convincing the occupant to accede to his client's requests or in proving to his client that the suspicions he or she entertained were totally unfounded. Such minor infractions of the law helped you cut the Gordian knot and put in a bill a lot more quickly than more respectable methods would have allowed.

He planned to slip in and out as quickly as possible, giving the place a summary once-over that would show how perfectly ordinary everything was. He was inclined to go back and give that Coutts a piece of his mind. As for Craig, the poor lad evidently wasn't cut out for detective work. His imagination was liable to get the better of him at the slightest opportunity. Mick felt decidedly on top of things as he entered the close at No. 98, slipped the balaclava over his head and got out his torch.

There appeared to be no one living on the lower floors. The brass doorplate outside the top right flat read Edwin MacFarlane, as he'd expected. The storm doors on to the stair were not closed. Picking the Yale lock took a matter of minutes. It was once he got into the unlit hall that a funny sensation started to come over him. Maybe it was only the curtain hanging over the doorway, which had brushed his shoulder when he least expected it. But it didn't feel like an ordinary hall. He became obsessed with the idea of another heartbeat whose rhythm kept chiming with his own, a heartbeat that emanated from the walls and was larger than life, more than human.

Mick told himself that the silence made the pumping of the blood unusually loud in his ears, and that the two beats were nothing more than different aspects of a single pulse. Then he realized how overwhelming the silence was. The low whish of rain, the restlessness of the trees in the park at the end of the street and the gurgling of the river behind them had kept him company during his long wait outside. Now it was as if he were hermetically sealed off from the rest of the world.

There! The first sound that made plain, straightforward sense came from behind a door on his left. The old dearie was fast asleep. The rise and fall of her breath was not quite a snore but regular enough to reassure him there was little likelihood of being disturbed. He got his bearings again and turned the handle of the sitting-room door while pressing it inwards so as to minimize the noise. Now he could use his torch safely; if anyone had been awake, they might have noticed its ray in the hall along the bottom of a bedroom door and given the alarm.

His face in the window was like another person's. He had to calm himself. The mantelpiece had a mirror above it in which his torchbeam flared up as if catching fire, dazzling his eyes. He swung it to the left and noted that the upper part of a door leading into a shallow cupboard was smothered in postcards. He did not look at them closely but continued his circuit and encountered, with a shock of recognition, the glass cabinet with retorts and test tubes Coutts had mentioned.

The desk by the window had been carefully tidied. One stray letter lay in the cleared space at the centre. The handwriting was most peculiar, an exaggerated, flowery copperplate of the kind people used in the last century. The paper was crisp, fresh and white. Who would be bothered to write like that nowadays?

He lifted it and read the words 'O mighty instigatress and great artificer!' All at once the door opened and the light went on. When he saw who had entered his jaw dropped in horror, and both torch and letter slid from his hands.

☆

The interior of St Pius XXVII's church in Springburn was totally dark, with the exception of a small row of candles Mother Genevieve had lit in front of the statue of the madonna. Every now and then she rose from her vigil and did a circuit of the church, pausing by the doors at the far end and looking up into the great inverted hull of the nave, as if she could breathe in strength and tranquillity from the blackness that filled it.

She was at some distance from the candles now. A draught from beneath the sacristy door set the flames trembling and their fragile yet persistent light played on the garments of the statue, its white robe and enveloping blue mantle. Occasionally a glimmer reached its face and the mournful features emerged from the darkness. It was like a rivulet of lava seen at dusk from the valley below, running along a mountainside then cooling into invisibility.

Her first four days at the parish house had been exceedingly difficult. Although she confessed her woes to Fr Ryan, and not vice versa, in their years of frequenting each other she had come to an accurate enough assessment of his character. He was a not unintelligent man, an ambitious creature who had failed to make progress in his ecclesiastical career because of a single misdemeanour from the time of his training in Rome. Her efforts to ascertain exactly what had taken place had so far been fruitless. The consequences of this crime still dogged him and there was little probability of his rising beyond the care of a few souls in this particularly grim and poverty-stricken corner of Glasgow.

As a result his soul was consumed with bitterness, a bitterness to which she had exposed herself unwarily in earlier days, before experience taught her to restrict their converse to absolutely official channels. Never again would she share with him the trials and aspirations of her spiritual self. Itemization of the week's petty foibles, a word or two about administrative difficulties in the convent, followed by absolution and a cup of tea, this was all that was required.

To be thrown into an intimacy neither of them desired, when rigid boundaries had been so clearly established, was harsh indeed. Fr Ryan could not refuse the archbishop's request that he provide her with a temporary refuge. His resentment at her presence came out in a thousand tiny ways, from helping himself to all the butter at table before she had a chance to take any, to pointedly filling only one of two cups when the housekeeper brought them supper in the parlour at ten o'clock. On her first full day there, lost for anything to do and sunk in evermore morose reflections as the morning wore on, she had picked up his daily newspaper and read it from cover to cover, not without enjoyment. He must have realized, and from then on took it to his study immediately after breakfast to prevent her getting her hands on it.

Mother Genevieve felt all the more helpless because it was not she who had inflicted her presence on the furious priest and, to her knowledge, it was totally beyond her power to decide when the disturbance would be removed. Under normal circumstances she might have mustered up sufficient fortitude or benevolence simply to bear with him or to confront him and reach some kind of truce. As it was, the battle going on inside her occupied all her energies.

From waking to sleeping she was obsessed with the thought of Cyril Braithwaite, or rather of the magnificent member with which she sincerely believed him to be endowed. This was what she had felt unable to tell Cissie during their last interview. Her inner eye envisioned it from all angles: the front, the rear, above, below, from one side and another, in every possible gradation of tumescence and detumescence. At times she could almost feel it in her grasp, anxious, trembling and live, like a question to which she alone was capable of supplying the answer.

She had tried every tactic known to her to banish it from her thoughts, yet the more she struggled the more insistently it haunted her, the more tenderly and temptingly her mind flitted towards it at every moment of the day, whatever the occupation she was engaged in. When she did forget about it for a while it was not the respite that stayed in her mind but the shock and intensity of her realization that it had abandoned her, and the power with which the image returned.

Her feelings towards him were a mixture of admiration, indulgence and impatience. When he had wandered into the archbishop's waiting room in his soiled dog collar and his crumpled suit, she was swept with a wave of maternal solicitude. She could have desired nothing more than to have the opportunity to minister to this man, to wash his clothes and scrub his shoes, make sure that he shaved in the morning and brush the dandruff briskly from his shoulders before he left the house. The idea of his clothes made her think of removing them from him, and then she saw him naked, and then . . . She did not put the feelings that followed into words.

He was perhaps the most creative presence on the ecumenical commission. Although something about the way he spoke betokened a great inner sadness, which she hoped was only passing, his fund of tolerance, wit and good humour was inexhaustible. Confronted by the meanmindedness and narrowness of other Christian denominations, he neither condemned nor challenged. Rather he would play with the ideas they put forward, picking them up, tossing them into the air, then catching them and reassembling them in a different formation that opened up possibilities no one present had suspected before he started talking. In spite of the breathlessness with which she hung on his every word, she knew that she had been able to come to his assistance in the course of some extremely problematic discussions, for she had an agile enough mind herself, which the daily affairs of the convent gave her little opportunity to exercise. He did not respond with approval but with a twinkle in his eyes, as if they had shared a joke, or as if they were playing on the same side in a ball game and had excogitated, then executed a particularly graceful and nimble manoeuvre.

While she knew it was not fair, she managed to gain some inner peace by blaming the drift of her thoughts on Euphemia MacFarrigle. If Euphemia had not told her, she would never have known, and her enthusiasm for Cyril would never have been anything more than Platonic. The funny thing was, she could not for the life of her remember exactly how Euphemia had put it. She even caught herself doubting that Euphemia had said anything whatsoever. She tried to imagine what the words might have been. 'He has a huge dick.' 'He's too big for her.' 'She can't take it all.' None of them had the right ring. None of them quite fitted, or made sense when repeated in Euphemia's characteristically husky tones.

Another way of distancing herself from her predicament was to look for psychological explanations. Her obsession with the prebendary's member was a consequence of experiments in a shack on the banks of the Kelvin when she was just plain Brenda MacCafferty. Being discovered there by a search party of nuns and teachers in a compromising situation had not only led to her becoming a bride of Christ. It had provoked a neurosis of which her obsession with Cyril's dick was merely the most recent expression.

The thought of the shack filled her with nostalgia, and she sighed. She was one of several girls who went there, and it was a piece of bad luck that nobody else had been with her on that crucial afternoon. If the boys they met up with had been Catholics she was convinced her mentors would not have reacted quite so hysterically. But they came from the Protestant direct-grant school in Kelvinbridge. The experiments were a prelude to mixed marriages, so punishment had to be absolutely exemplary.

It was generally the girls who took the initiative. She had waited more than half an hour that afternoon before hearing a timid knock on the door. They fumbled and petted in the dark interior with its smell of resin and leaf mould. He was tall and at first she had buried her nose in the luxurious blue fabric of his blazer until he bent over her and they started to kiss. He refused to lie down and she had had to undo his buttons herself and take it out and feel it half-swollen in her hand. She was just wondering what to do next when the door was wrenched open and Mrs MacBride, the French teacher, shone her torch full on the criminal conjunction.

A night-service bus roared by on the main road just outside the church, its tyres sending up a sibilance of rainwater. A crowd of revellers returning home set up a raucous chanting which faded into the distance. Mother Genevieve took her place once more on her knees in front of the madonna. She had had nothing but black tea for ten hours and she felt very light-headed. Her idea was to fast the lust out of her. If her body lacked nourishment, there would be no energy left for lascivious musings.

The madonna must surely come to her aid. She looked up. The face was in shadow. She remembered seeing a halo of electric bulbs just above its head when she had visited the church in daylight. Made bold by desperation, she stood up, fumbled at the back of the statue and found the hanging cord and switch. The lights flicked on and she had to shield her eyes. The madonna looked somehow different.

But it was no use. The same image filled her thoughts. She buried her head in her hands and heard an unexpected sound. She looked up again. The madonna was laughing. It started with the lips twitching, then the mouth opened and she glimpsed the beautifully symmetrical, pearl-like teeth. From a snigger it became a hearty guffaw. The shoulders were heaving. While one hand still held the plaster bouquet, the other was lifted to wipe the statue's cheeks. The movements were unreal, rigid, like a film from which the intervening frames have been removed, and which proceeds by fits and starts.

With a wail of fear, Mother Genevieve leapt to her feet and scampered towards the door. She had locked it behind her to forestall unwarranted intrusions, and now she dropped the key and had to run her hand to and fro along the floor before she recovered it. She looked over her shoulder and the madonna was still laughing, the halo of bulbs rocking backwards and forwards above her head so that crazy shadows flitted over the whole church.

A moment later she was outside, the door slammed shut behind her. She ran straight for the parish house and upstairs to Fr Ryan's room. When she shook him awake he was more astonished than annoyed. He pieced together from her fragmented cries that something unbelievable had happened to the madonna in the church. It was not hard for her to persuade him to pull some clothes on over his pyjamas and follow her.

When they got back, all was quiet. The candles had gone out but the halo was still switched on.

'It moved, it moved, I swear it moved!' moaned Mother Genevieve.

Fr Ryan's lips were setting hard in a smirk of contempt and irritation.

'Wait!' she cried, patting him on the arm, and knelt once more in the position she had risen from. She bowed her head and closed her eyes. There was a long silence. Nothing happened. What was she to do? For desperate predicaments, desperate remedies. She visualized Cyril's penis.

'Good God!' cried Fr Ryan. 'It's a miracle!'

The laughter was deafening this time.

☆

Craig found two messages on the answering machine when he went to the office the next morning. The first was very hard to understand. It was in a foreign voice. The speaker had a strange habit of changing the vowel in the middle of a word, so that a different word came out, one which had no real connection with what he was trying to say. The gist of the message was a request to call back on a direct line to the archdiocesan offices. The man underlined the importance of absolute secrecy.

The second message was from the Western Infirmary. McFall

had not told Craig of his plan to violate Euphemia's sanctuary. The younger man was nonplussed to learn that his employer had been found in a state of shock at dawn, huddled in the damp grass on a gap site in Otago Street. McFall lived on his own. No one answered from his home number, so the nurse in charge had contacted his office.

It took Craig some forty minutes to reach the hospital. He was concerned. His employer liked a drink or two but, in all the time they had known each other, he had never gone on a bender of such magnitude. At the same time the mention of Otago Street rang like a warning bell in Craig's ears. He tried not to think of what it might imply.

They had put McFall in a private room. Apparently there was nothing wrong with him. He was sitting up in bed still wearing his bedraggled clothes, clutching the sheet to his midriff. The male nurse informed Craig that his boss could not stay the night and had to be taken away, then left the two of them alone together.

Craig sat down beside the invalid. McFall got up, tiptoed to the door, opened it, checked no one was eavesdropping, then closed it again securely and came and sat on the edge of the bed.

'It was terrible,' he whispered, as if confiding an enormous secret to his second-in-command.

'What was terrible?' Craig was trying to keep his cool. McFall ran a hand through his matted hair.

'She caught me.'

Craig looked puzzled.

'That MacFarrigle woman. She caught me.'

Craig persuaded Mick to get back into bed, and tucked the sheet up around his shoulders.

'Why don't you tell me what happened from beginning to end?' he said. It felt rather good to be the strong one for a change. Mick's face creased up with fear. He got a hold of himself and took a deep breath.

'I went to the house to suss things out. You know, illegal entry and so on. Long as you don't get caught it does no harm. The house was there,' he assured Craig, wide-eyed like a child retelling a fairytale. 'Number ninety-eight was there and I got in, no trouble. I'd just found this funny old-fashioned letter on the table when the light went on and she . . .'

His voice died away on a high note as if he himself could not believe what had happened, and he began to blubber silently. It was distressing to watch. Craig took out a neatly ironed handkerchief. His mother was an indefatigable ironer. After spending more than a week at home, he had returned to his bedsit laden with ample supplies of every kind of linen. She starched both vests and handkerchiefs. He shook it out, dabbed at Mick's eyes and blew his nose for him.

'She was absolutely terrifying. Not old at all. I'd have put her in her mid-thirties at most. A hefty woman. Huge boobs. She was wearing a big robe that trailed on the ground behind her, turquoise and green and grey with designs on it that looked like characters and equations. Then again, it was like a picture of the sky, one of those star maps you get in encyclopaedias. She was livid. She stood there glaring at me, and as she glared, I shrank. I just got smaller and smaller until she bent down, picked me up and put me in a bottle . . .'

Again his voice faded away to nothingness. Craig let him cry for a bit longer, then took his hand and squeezed it, hoping to draw him back to his tale.

'It was horrible. She lifted me up on to the table and set me there just like a specimen she was going to use in an experiment. She kept marching up and down, hollering at me in absolute fury.

'You've no idea how scary it was being that small. The table was like a city square. A bluebottle went buzzing past, as big as an aeroplane. A pencil was like a fallen tree you had to scramble over. The glass of the bottle was smoky so I couldn't see through it properly. All I could make out was this huge, bluish form of an enormous, enraged woman venting her anger on me. Then when she had let off a bit of steam she got some stuff out of the cabinet, you know, the chemistry cabinet' – Craig nodded, although this was the first time he had heard it mentioned – 'and started telling me all the things she'd like to do to me.

'She placed substances round me in containers shaped like wine carafes. One was full of glowing embers, another had a kind of living smoke that didn't rise up out of the funnel, but circled round and round as if it were a whirlpool made of gases. There was a blue liquid in another one – shot through with stars that gleamed and went out in a constant dance. It made my eyes hurt to look at it. Then one container had a big face in it, pressed up against the side, watching me. I was terrified she was going to let it loose. It was like seeing someone in the hall of mirrors in the fairground. The face would pull away, circle round, then come back and stare, like a fish in an aquarium.

'She threatened to dissolve me, so I'd just be a consciousness without a body, or to make me so sensitive to sounds and colours that I wouldn't be able to stand being alive. She claimed she could turn me into a toad or make me impotent and stop me having sex with a woman ever again. She said she could make me feel so guilty I'd just run off and commit suicide the minute she released me. She even talked about taking me downstairs the size I was and leaving me in the street for the cats to play with or the rats to gobble up.'

'And what did you do?' Craig interrupted. Mick looked him straight in the eye, as ingenuous and direct as a child.

'I wept,' he answered. 'I just stood there and wept my heart out with fear. The odd thing was, in spite of the tears, I could tell she was calming down. She kind of enjoyed making this long list of terrible punishments she would inflict on me for daring to snoop into her private affairs. Last of all she picked up a retort with a boiling, amber-coloured liquid in it and poured it into the bottle I was trapped in. I thought she was going to burn me to death. In fact it knocked me right out. Next thing I knew I was cowering in the weeds and dank grass with a policeman tapping me on the shoulder like I was a down and out, wanting to know when I would move on.

'She's behind it all,' he declared solemnly, waving a squat finger in Craig's face. 'The virgin births, the farting archbishop, it's all her doing. And either I quit this city or we put a stop to her. Otherwise I'll never feel safe here again.'

This guy is really bonkers, thought Craig. I have to start looking for a new job.

'Yes, yes,' he murmured consolingly. 'Now let's get you home and into some dry clothes. Otherwise you'll die of pneumonia before Euphemia has a chance to get her hands on you again.'

The renewed terror in McFall's features warned him that this was dangerous material for jokes.

☆

Alan straightened his tie. His producer had assured him that a clip would be in the national news that evening, and he was determined to look his best. Even so, he had not had time to write his lines and would have to improvise. A red light winked from the camera in front of him.

'Behind me is the church of St Pius XXVII in Springburn, Glasgow, where a miracle is believed to have taken place in the early hours of this morning. The event has galvanized the local Catholic community, and large crowds have been visiting the church all day. Mother Genevieve from the Oratory of St Bridget in the city's West End was keeping an all-night vigil when the miracle happened. There are differing accounts as to what actually occurred. Some say the statue moved, others that it spoke to her, others that it laughed. The archbishop is not available for comment, and Mother Genevieve herself is at present resting in the parish house. But here with me I have Father Patrick Ryan, whose parish this is and who has been Mother Genevieve's confessor for many years. Father Ryan, do you believe that we are dealing with a miracle here?'

'Oh, absolutely. I saw it with my own eyes.'

'What exactly did you see?'

'She laughed. The madonna laughed. It's a message of hope and joy to the faithful of my parish and throughout the West of Scotland.'

'Was there anything special about this particular statue?'

'It was here when I came to the parish. I understand they brought it over from Ireland in the early years of this century. It's a funny thing, you know, but I had remarked how the little girls tended to have a special devotion to that statue. Children can often sense things we older and wiser folk fail to pick up on.'

'And why do you think your parish has been chosen out of all the parishes in this city?'

'God has an especial care for the poor and the deprived and I believe he wants to draw the attention of the world to the plight of my parishioners here in Springburn. People have to turn back to God and the Virgin Mary, otherwise there's no way we can find a solution to the horrors of this godless modern world.'

The producer was waving his arms in a signal to stop.

'Father Ryan, thank you.' Alan turned to face the cameras straight on. 'Alan Donaldson, *Reporting Scotland* from the parish church of St Pius XXVII, Glasgow.'

The camera panned away from the two men and down in the direction of the crowd. The crew had taken up position on the grassless, treeless sloping ground between the parish house and the church. Along the ridge of the hill above them stretched unbroken, joyless phalanxes of council tenements. Many of them had shattered or boarded windows. Fragmentary obscenities were sprayed on the lower walls.

Two constables stood sentinel on either side of Fr Ryan's front door, protecting Mother Genevieve's repose, while a group of three directed traffic on the main road below. It was utterly clogged with sightseers in search of a parking space. Some had rolled down their windows to let blue, white and gold streamers trail out. Horns were tooting and there was a general air of festivity. A private operator had laid on a special bus service christened the Holy Hotline. It ran from the city centre and was in the process of setting down its third load of passengers. In spite of the drizzling rain, the open-top deck was crammed and the pilgrims gave out a great shout as they drew to a halt in front of the site.

The shrill tones of a hymn to Mary could be heard coming from inside the church. The doors were jammed with people trying to get in and out. Two booths had been set up, selling holy postcards, rosaries and plastic models of the Sacred Heart and the Infant of Prague. With unbelievable alacrity, someone had devised miniature statues of the madonna which laughed when you turned them upside down. They were selling like hot cakes.

Families were milling around, eating candy floss and toffee apples, picking up and putting down squawling babies, jostling prams and exchanging news excitedly. A group of women had formed a small circle and were chanting the rosary in singsong, raucous voices. They were on their knees, and at the end of each decade they would shuffle around in awkward imitation of a dance. It was a satisfying mortification to feel the gravel and ash graze their skin. Alan only hoped they would look out for discarded syringes.

His producer was exasperated, but there was nothing to be done.

'I can't get either the nun or the archbishop,' Alan insisted. 'You just have to be patient. Why don't we try interviewing some of the crowd?'

That did little to improve things. Alan found it easy enough to adjust to the way these people spoke. His producer, who was English, could not understand a word.

'How can we possibly broadcast the stuff?' he asked. 'We'll have to use bloody subtitles!'

☆

Sister Juliet stamped her foot, then kicked over the metal bucket. The clang as it hit the flagstones was satisfyingly loud. A tidal wave of filthy grey water washed over Mother Rodelinda's sandals. The hem of her habit was drenched and the dampness soaked upwards towards her knees.

'I've had enough! I'm not scrubbing any more floors!'

Her two companions did not dare to move. They were still bent double, habits hitched up around their waists, wire brushes gripped in red, swollen hands. Waiting for a response, they watched the water form rivulets and drain off towards the stank in the middle of the floor.

A tantrum or an explosion would have been more bearable. The cool, calculated venom of Mother Rodelinda's voice as she spoke through gritted teeth chilled them to the bone.

'You have upset the bucket. You have dirtied the floor.'

'I don't care! It didn't need washing in the first place.'

'You have wet my sandals. You have soiled my habit.'

'I'm pregnant! I should be resting! I shouldn't be set to do tasks like this!'

'You have raised your voice in the presence of your Mother Superior. You have forgotten, yet again, your vow of obedience.'

Sister Juliet was wilting. She could feel her courage wane with her anger and give place to the familiar, leaden helplessness of these last terrible weeks.

'That's not the vow you have most trouble with, of course. How dare you name your shame to me, you hussy! It amazes me you have the insolence to open your eyes in the morning after the disgrace you have brought on us all! "Should"? "Should"? Can a fallen women like yourself ever use that word again?'

Mother Rodelinda's voice rose in a slow crescendo of spite. The three younger nuns were by now frozen. The clatter of the brush as it slipped from Sister Juliet's fingers to the floor was deafening.

'What do you know of "should" and "ought"? The swelling on your tummy is an obscenity in the eyes of God and man, do you hear? The little thing kicking away inside you is the devil's work, nothing more and nothing less! And the milk you will suckle it on, if the poor creature is unlucky enough to survive, will be the milk of depravity and lust! What kind of nourishment is that for a mother to give her child?'

Sister Fatima gasped. Sister Viviana was weeping soundlessly. Sister Juliet stood motionless, her cheeks hot and burning, her fingers spread wide, locked in the gesture that had let the brush fall.

'Can you imagine a punishment that would be commensurate with what you three have done? And you complain about scrubbing floors? Think of this floor as your soul, my girl! Were you to scrub it ten times a day for ten years you could not take away the blackness that disfigures it! Even I, Mother Rodelinda of the Seven Sorrows – and my name is apt, for I am an expert in the trial and mortification of this dull flesh of ours – even I am at a loss where your crimes are concerned. If I set you to lick these flagstones clean with your tongue, it would not diminish your guilt by so much as a hair!'

The saving thing was that Mother Rodelinda took so much pleasure in her own eloquence it inevitably set her in a good mood. The three nuns sensed the lightening of the atmosphere and stood transfixed. The least unwary move might set her raging again.

'You are a wily, devious character, Sister Juliet. That

fact cannot escape one who has had to struggle so long and mercilessly with her own inborn sinfulness. Who knows if this latest outrage of yours is merely a trick? Perhaps your real aim is to get three days' solitary confinement with spiritual reading so that you can put your feet up, relax and let that little whippersnapper grow even fatter on your laziness, while you gorge yourself on thoughts of the brute that fathered it on you?

'Oh no, Sister Juliet, oh no. I am no woman's fool, and no man's either. You will work twice as hard after this piece of cheek, and I shall make sure you get only stale bread and cold tea to keep you going! What is more, you will stand to your meals while the rest of the community sit. That way no one will be able to forget your disgrace, not for a moment. And you will quiver with longing to taste even the watery broths the others feed on!'

☆

Dr Quinn's private consulting rooms were in a maindoor flat in one of the balmy recesses of Hyndland. He was rarely in time for the first appointment at 2 p.m. and the nurse was used to seeing him hurry in in the blackest of tempers, having given some foolish intern or incompetent nurse a thorough dressing down before lunch. Today would be worse than usual because the first patient on the list was a newcomer and she'd had to put a call through to the doctor before he'd even had the chance to remove his greatcoat.

'Good afternoon, Mother Rodelinda,' he said, gripping the receiver between chin and shoulder while he smoothed out a copy of that morning's *Herald* on the desk. He wanted to have another look at Alan Donaldson's article about the Springburn miracle.

'No, I cannot agree to sedate any of your sisters. All three are in surprisingly good health and I have not the slightest intention of interfering with them.'

He listened for a moment.

'Whatever disciplinary problems you encounter must be resolved using your own resources. I understood that was what our archbishop called you in for.'

Had the woman no notion of medical ethics? He listened again.

'Punitive measures are your concern, not mine. I take absolutely no responsibility for the consequences of any measures you may adopt, let this be clear. And allow me to add, Mother Rodelinda, that there is a special charge for telephoning me during private consulting hours. I do not think the archbishop will be pleased when he sees the bill you have been running up for the archdiocese.'

He slammed the phone down, hung his coat up, and checked to see who this afternoon's patients were. The name Felipe Gutierrez, at the head of the list, filled him with unease. He had begun to see the Glasgow archdiocese as a ship which he would do well to abandon before it foundered irrevocably. But the harder he tried to extricate himself the more obstinately its members involved him in the minutiae of their increasingly demented lives.

The idea of gaining closer intimacy with the Vatican investigator's body inspired him with distaste. He glanced at the small sink to his left and resolved to wash his hands particularly thoroughly after any examination. The thought struck him as uncharitable when the cleric entered the room beaming, dressed as usual entirely in black and carrying a bunch of gorgeous flowers before him like a lance.

Felipe looked around, took a glass from the shelf above the washhand basin, placed the flowers in it and set them significantly on the desk between himself and the consultant. They must have cost him a bomb. No two were alike. There was a lily of the valley, a gladiolus, an iris, a crisp orange tulip and a strikingly turgid, pale purple lupin, as well as other blooms whose names he did not know.

'It's charming of you to bring me these flowers,' the doctor said, peering over them at the priest. 'Very few of my private patients are so thoughtful.'

Felipe joined his hands in his lap and looked at Quinn appealingly.

'I half problem,' he began. 'Problem with my bauxite.'

Quinn did not understand.

'My ess,' grinned the priest, proud of his English and of the broadmindedness which allowed him to use such a modern word.

'Oh dear,' responded Quinn, beginning to feel out of his depth.

'Etching. I half constant etching. And then . . . ' he gestured towards the flowers.

Quinn waited, breathless. A single tear trailed down the Jesuit's sallow jowls.

'I did not boy them, oh no,' shaking his head mournfully from side to side. 'Not boy. I get them fry. Tuttily fry.'

The consultant had to master a mad urge to run for it. His heart was beating so loud he could hardly catch the cleric's words. There was a pause.

'So you didn't pay for the flowers. Who gave you them? Did you bring them from Italy?'

'Oh, no. First an etching, then the flowers. Bless hims. Bless hims growing from my bauxite.'

Quinn wondered if madness could be contagious and, if it was, what risks he ran of catching it from these people. As he did so, Felipe stood up, turned his back and dropped his trousers in a neat, swift movement. His buttocks were enveloped in great, billowing underpants which he edged downwards with a timid grace. They settled around his ankles like a seagull coming to rest and folding its wings.

He bent right over. Fascinated in spite of himself, Quinn rose from his chair, circled round the desk and peered into the cleric's cleft. It was unbelievable but true. Amidst the fawn-coloured hairs a bright green shoot protruded. He gave it a sharp tug and Felipe yelped with pain.

'No!' he pleaded. 'Not before tame! Impassable!'

Quinn sat down again without saying a word. Felipe pulled his pants up and fastened his trousers round his ample paunch.

A welter of feelings assailed the consultant as his patient eyed him expectantly: wonder, compassion, the temptation to laugh, fear . . . He was sure he could get a colleague to sign him off for six weeks because of stress. But it would look bad and there were important political manoeuvres going on in the hospital he could ill afford to miss. Psychotherapy was another possibility. He could keep up a front and go to see a psychotherapist about it all. He certainly needed to talk.

'Did this problem start when you came to Glasgow? Or had it already been bothering you when you were in Rome?'

'Oh, no,' Felipe murmured. 'Just sprung and simmer. No bless hims when the weaver is culled.'

'But did you get anything last year?' he persisted.

The cleric shook his head, serene and melancholy. Quinn suspected he did not understand and gave up the attempt to find out more. He reached for his prescription book and scribbled.

'Put on this cream twice a day and come back in a week's time. I'll read up about it and see what can be done. Maybe surgery would help.'

☆

The intensity of waiting meant that Mr Bleeper nearly jumped when Gerald knocked on the door. He had a study in the parish house next to the main school building. It was a Victorian edifice in mock-Renaissance style with an imposing staircase in the central hall and wooden panelling throughout the first-floor rooms. Mr Bleeper's was no less sombre than the rest. The early summer sunlight entering the window with its generous triple bays did little to dispel the gloom; a combined effect of heavy green curtains, bookshelves lined with works of abstruse theology, and two ponderous armchairs. Their ageing leather upholstery was still mysteriously redolent of tobacco, although he knew for a fact that the two previous occupants had been non-smokers.

Gerald paused inside the door, half in and half out of a sunbeam thick with motes. For Mr Bleeper he had the air of a dancer awaiting a change in the music.

'Do sit down, Gerald.' He gestured towards the empty fireplace. 'Now, what is it that has been troubling you?'

The castors squeaked as the chair shifted under Gerald's weight. His hands did not release the ends of the arms, as if he was prepared to take flight at any moment. Mr Bleeper sat down opposite him, settling his black habit carefully around his knees.

Gerald said nothing. Mr Bleeper coughed nervously, then became absorbed in contemplating the pale ruddiness of the schoolboy's skin. He felt an urge to get up and caress the back of his neck, for him the most wonderful and vulnerable exposed place on his pupils' bodies.

'Are you having difficulty with your work?' he prompted. 'Your Highers are over now, and I really can't imagine a student of your calibre having anything to fear from the results . . .'

There was another silence. Mr Bleeper hastened to fill it, if for no other reason than to stop the flow of his own thoughts.

'You're coming back to us next year, am I right? I do think it's most sensible of you. Those who rush on to university at the absurdly early stage that is the norm in Scotland are far too immature to benefit from it.'

'It's about Daniel,' Gerald blurted out, afraid that if he did not stop this chatter the courage to speak would utterly desert him. 'I went to confession on Saturday and the priest wouldn't give me absolution.'

'Yes?' said Mr Bleeper. 'Go on. I don't quite see the connection.' He could feel his face flushing. If he had been a little more honest he would have admitted that his sex had tensed, ever so slightly, at the mention of Daniel's name.

'I haven't been to confession for three months. I haven't been able to go to communion or anything. My mother has noticed, though she hasn't asked me about it. She's too tactful. You see' – for the first time in the course of the interview his eyes met Mr Bleeper's straight on – 'I'm in a state of mortal sin.'

To relieve his growing agitation Mr Bleeper got up and went over to the window. On the street outside, the junior boys were thronging the door to the tuck shop in a huddle of crimson. Out of the corner of his eye he glimpsed two sixth years disappearing into a lane, presumably to have a smoke. He tried to remember their names but could not.

'And what is the mortal sin?' he asked.

'Things I have done with Daniel. Things I can't talk about. They are things against nature, things the church says are wicked.'

'They *are* wicked, Gerald. It is not merely a question of what the church says. Such things can corrupt your young soul horribly, with a corruption it may take you years to shake off.'

The words came mechanically, as if another person was speaking, but they sounded right. Mr Bleeper had lifted his gaze and was staring at the sky, scanning the contours of a small cloud hovering above the Normal School at Cowcaddens.

'I know,' agreed Gerald, 'I know. I suppose I have always known. But when we do them they don't feel wrong. They feel wonderful. Like sort of dissolving. Like another person taking over and moving and acting. I find it so beautiful.'

He was crying as he spoke. Mr Bleeper did not dare look round. He could no longer shut his excitement out from his consciousness. He was afraid that if he turned towards the fireplace Gerald might note the telltale swelling beneath his black habit.

'Exactly what did you do together? Did you let him penetrate you?'

Gerald nodded, sniffling at the same time.

'Do you realize the gravity of that sin? Do you know that you are defiled? That he has used you as a man uses a woman?'

'The devil makes it feel beautiful so as to tempt me. You don't need to say it. It's just that I was defiled even before I met Daniel. This thing has been growing inside me for as long as I can remember. Do you know what it is like?' He looked at Mr Bleeper, begging for confirmation. 'It's like a plant growing inside a building. Gradually it sends its creepers up along the walls and through them. And the building starts falling apart. The plant is strong and dark and indestructible, and its roots go far beneath the foundations of the building. And the only thing to do is to demolish the whole structure.'

Mr Bleeper rushed across the room, the black wings of his habit fluttering behind him. He knelt in front of Gerald and grasped the boy's hands.

'No, Gerald, no. You must be strong. Together we can defeat this. God's forgiveness is infinite. It can encompass even your sin.'

Gerald's tears had stopped flowing and he spoke with a strange firmness and resolution.

'No, a crumbling wall has no strength. It can only be torn down.'

He freed his hands from Mr Bleeper's and went on with increasing conviction.

'I came to see you because the priest said I had to warn the school authorities. To tell them about Daniel, in case he corrupted other boys. I said Daniel was leaving, but that didn't seem to make any difference. Now I have told you I will go back and get my absolution. I came to you because I believed you could be trusted. You are not to say anything. I am not a traitor. I do not want to betray Daniel. If you say anything I shall deny every word of it.'

'If I agree to keep silent, Gerald, it will not be because you threaten me. And my silence will have a price.'

Gerald looked at him in puzzlement.

'You must have nothing more to do with Daniel. No doubt your confessor has told you that. Not a word, not a phone call, not a single glance is to pass between you. He could use any of these to draw you back into his net. Promise me you will do this and your secret will be safe with me.'

'But where am I to find the strength?' Gerald broke out, close to tears again.

'Pray to St Ignatius. He can sustain you. I suppose it is in the nature of our order, where men are always with men, and all their needs and thoughts are turned in upon their own community, that the sin that has defiled you should be a constant torment. St Ignatius has come to the assistance of countless youths in the past. We are soldiers under his command, and a good leader never abandons his men. He will not fail you.'

Gerald rose wordlessly and went to the door. Mr Bleeper suddenly had an idea.

'Why not keep a journal? Write down the tribulations that assail you as you labour towards purity. Speak to God in its pages. Perhaps that will help you to resist.'

Gerald said nothing. The door closed noiselessly behind him.

☆

Rob and Cissie had a ritual about going to bed. It was so time-hallowed that they only became aware of it when, for some reason or another, either of them broke the usual pattern. Rob went first because he liked to read for half an hour. He preferred heavyweight novels from the last century, which he could lose himself in, and there was always one on his bedside table next to the lamp and the radio alarm. Cissie would linger to watch the late-night news on television and then switch everything off and put the fireguard up in front of the fire. Their flat was on the ground floor, and she liked to pause in the darkness and see the streetlamp cast its orange light across the sofa and the carpet while she breathed in the familiar smells, especially when there were freshly cut flowers in the vase on the sideboard. With Rob already tucked away she could take her time in the bathroom. She undid her hair and put on a little perfume, just to renew the day's fragrance. It was a touch of coquetry she would have found it hard to renounce. After all, you never knew your luck.

Tonight there was no sign of her. Rob read a further chapter, then yet another, then finally turned out the light and burrowed down beneath the duvet. Generally Cissie would arrive before it was time to sleep. She was being inconsiderate and his irritation prevented him nodding off. He craned over to see the luminous figures on the alarm. Half past midnight. He got up, put on his dressing gown and slippers and padded down the short hall. All the lights were still on.

Maybe she had fallen asleep in front of the fire. He opened the door gingerly, and she looked up from the sofa in surprise. She had been playing with something, moving it backwards and forwards over her middle finger. It was a condom. There were shadows under her eyes, her smudged cheeks suggested she had been crying.

Without saying anything, he took the poker, stirred the fire and tossed on a few more coals. The additional burst of heat was welcome. Instead of taking his place on the sofa beside her, he sat opposite. She was still playing agitatedly with that rubber thing, moving the circle up and down as if it were a wedding ring.

'Why haven't you come to bed?' he asked.

Tears brimmed in her eyes and her shoulders quivered. He went over and put his arm round her.

'The Pope doesn't approve of those contraptions,' he observed. 'And anyway, we hardly need them now.'

'Don't joke about it!'

She snuggled in closer to him. He had come to mass with them just to keep up appearances as long as Simon was at home. That was one of the conditions on which she had been able to marry him. Now he refused to have anything to do with the church. Religion was a taboo subject between them, although he could not resist the occasional jibe about her pious doings.

'So tell me,' he said.

Only then did he look down and realize that Cissie's open handbag was at her feet, crammed with the things.

'Are you planning to set up business in contraceptives, or what?'

'I'm just realizing that I got it all wrong, horribly, horribly wrong.'

'Don't tell me you've lost your faith? Not you, of all people?'

'No, it's more important than that. Think of all the damage we have done. Of all the lives that could have been saved.' She waggled her middle finger in its glinting plastic sheath at him.

'I thought the idea was to stop babies being born.'

'It's AIDS I'm talking about, Rob. I've been going to the Orange Sun Café, the place the gays and lesbians go.'

Rob's mouth dropped open. Was she going to leave him for another woman? He had picked up one of her magazines the other afternoon. He often read them when her back was turned, secretly finding them just as interesting as the *Economist* or *Transport Weekly*. A woman had confessed how, once her children left home, she discovered that her husband had never interested her sexually and had gone on to find happiness with a friend from the Mother's Union. The mysterious sodality where Cissie spent so much time took on a different colouring. She read the alarm in his face and smiled sadly, nudging his arm.

'Don't worry, darling, I'm not thinking of joining them. Mrs Donnelly sent me there to steal condoms as part of her purity campaign to clean up the diocese. She said they encouraged people to be promiscuous, and it was our duty to confiscate as many as we could. Now I think about it it strikes me as absolutely preposterous.'

'It's amazing the things that can make sense after a few decades of the rosary,' observed Rob, wondering what was coming next. 'So what made you see the light?'

'There's a man with AIDS who comes into the café regularly with his friends. Today his lover was in on his own. I couldn't help asking. He died last week. The man started crying and I felt so guilty! Imagine if that had been Simon! And I've been helping people to catch the disease!'

Rob shook her gently.

'I wouldn't put it quite like that. Isn't it like the child trying to empty the sea with his pail? However many you took away, I'm sure they had plenty to put in their place. And it's hardly your fault if people don't use them.'

'But I got it all so wrong, so totally, totally wrong. Why am I such a conformist, Rob? I follow the rest like a sheep, merely because I want to be part of them, to be like them. To be liked by them.'

She had clenched both her fists and was beating them gently on her knee.

'I must say, I was never very keen on Mrs Donnelly,' said Rob. 'I found something sinister about her when we met at the Easter social. Are all your friends involved in this business? Can nobody be salvaged?'

Cissie straightened up, more hopeful all of a sudden.

'Euphemia. She never had anything to do with it.'

'My old friend Famie. She sounds like a real odd bod. But interesting. You keep promising to bring her round to the house and then never do.'

'She's unconventional. I don't know how to deal with her a lot of the time. But you're right. I think I'll tell her the whole story and see what she suggests. I'd like to make reparation in some way . . .'

Rob turned her face to him.

'Are you serious about all this? Or have you fallen asleep in front of the fire and dreamed it all up? It's hard to believe, you know. From baking fairy cakes to stealing condoms is quite a leap.'

Cissie laughed and kissed him. Her lips were surprisingly eloquent and he returned the kiss more passionately. She looked down into his lap in that direct fashion of hers he had always found so exciting and so disarming.

'It won't fill that thing you've got on your finger,' he said, 'but it'll do. Coming to bed now?'

☆

Fraser lifted his head and gazed at the grimy sandstone frontage of the tenement on the other side of the street. His desk was positioned by the window in the spare bedroom. From this vantage point on the second floor he could spy most of what was going on in the flats opposite. Behind one first-floor window an old couple were snugly settled in front of the television. It was nearly ten o'clock. In a few moments Mrs MacPherson would lurch to her feet, waddle unsteadily to the door and return after the briefest of intervals with tea and biscuits on a tray. The pair never went out, not even on a Saturday. Fraser would often play a game with himself, addressing questions to them and inventing their answers in his mind, as if they could keep him company unwittingly across this distance.

The pretence was useless tonight. Every other window was dark. The students had made their way noisily downstairs twenty minutes earlier, armed with carrier bags filled with drink, no doubt bound for a party that would keep them occupied until the small hours. Fraser wondered if he was the only person under sixty left at home. He had been poring over a project for restructuring the finances of the archdiocese for more than an hour. He did not really need to bring work back from the office. It offered a tenuous connection with the church which filled out lonely weekends and kept temptation at bay. The dangerous time was coming. He already knew that this evening resistance would be in vain.

He perched his pencil behind his ear, pushed the chair back and got up to make a cup of cocoa. As he paused at the door and looked back, the circle of light cast by the lamp, and its reflection in the windowpane, were emblems of his sense of utter abandonment. It was as if he had lost touch, had let a thread slip from his fingers years ago, and was now totally adrift. Another voice spoke for him when he was in company. He had forgotten his own language, and the possibility of ever communicating with other human beings again was beyond his grasp.

Experience told him the only salve for this pain was sex. The river was just five minutes' walk away. On the evenings when he held out, stayed at his desk till long after midnight and then collapsed into bed, the walkway by the water under the dank trees was so present to him that he almost believed he had been there, even though there was no mud on his shoes and his hands did not have the familiar, lush yet acrid smell of rhododendron leaves.

He had not been to the disco for three months. If friends dragged him along, and he had had enough to drink beforehand, he could confront the brash lights and intensely smoky air. To go alone would be impossible. At least by the river bank there were no witnesses to his self-abasement.

Lost in thought, he allowed the milk to boil over, colouring the flames of the gas cooker a brilliant green. While he stirred his cocoa, the crucifix nailed to the wall next to the units caught his eye. He looked with tender reproach at the emaciated brass figure stretched across it. Why did it not come to his assistance at times like this? Why was its love not enough to fill his loneliness, as the great mystics promised?

Five minutes later he was out in the street. He zipped up his jerkin against the cold. He should have put on a jumper. It was too late now. In order to get started on the expedition he always had to shut out half of his conscious mind. More than once he had left home without his keys. He glanced up and saw that he had forgotten to switch the desk lamp off. The lighted window comforted him, as if there were someone at home waiting for him, ready to welcome him back unquestioningly once he had done what he had to do.

The streets had the peculiar mobility that possessed them on Friday and Saturday nights. You could tell from the noise where there was a party on. There were few solitary walkers. Groups and couples strode purposefully towards an invitation or a pub. The pavements resembled a busy strait filled with hooting ships, none stopping nearby, each following a carefully plotted course, trained on its destination, oblivious to its neighbours and to those who have nowhere to go.

Fraser swerved sharply and trotted down the steps where the bridge began. The river valley was a different world. It should have been a silvan paradise disrupting the monotonous symmetries of the prosperous West End. The flotsam and jetsam riding the grimy waters and the sour effluents that swirled in livid eddies belied the illusion. The factories and warehouses on the city's outskirts, and the bitter estates on windswept hillsides to which its poorer classes had been banished, threaded the park in liquid guise, spectral but insistent.

There were stretches of the gorge sunlight never reached.

Sycamore and ash on the upper slopes gave way to hawthorn shrubs and rhododendron on the lower. The ground was too waterlogged and steep for grass to grow. The paths were a mess of slippery mud that rarely dried out even in summer. Winter frosts hardened them to cutting edges that were treacherous to the feet.

Fraser's heartbeat quickened, filling out the silence as he left the other world behind. He strained his eyes against the blackness to detect shapes moving in the shadows or poised beneath the high arch of the bridge. When he got to the usual spot by the locked toilet he thought he was the only person there, until his sight adjusted and he could tell which dark-nesses were human, which inanimate. A cigarette glowed to his right.

As so often before, fear swept through him and he backed away, moving off the path into the protection of some bushes. He nearly yelped when a hand was laid on his arm. It did not release its hold. The touch was reassuring and he offered no resistance as he was drawn deeper into the undergrowth. They embraced at length and the closeness made Fraser gasp for air. He was like a diver working on the seabed who must take this opportunity to fill his lungs because he does not know how long it will be until he can come up again.

The man who held him was burly, even fat. Fraser noted with surprise and fatalism that he smelt of incense. He could have sworn his garments were ecclesiastical and his flesh had the bookish odour of a religious order. Methodically, almost wearily, Fraser did what was required of him.

As he thrust, his feet sank into a carpet of crushed bark and sodden leaves and his mind broke up into different parts. Each had its own voice. One was keenly aware of his physical excitement as he approached climax. Another was surprised and disoriented, as if one of his aunts had come upon him in that position and could only murmur her distress and alarm. Another asked why he was not using a condom and accused him of a further sin in endangering his own life and that of a man whose face he had never seen. Yet another observed wrily that to bring a condom would admit premeditation. He was the classic puritan for whom each sin had to be an inexplicable, involuntary occurrence other selves could immediately disown. And far above, the most distant part of his mind watched him and his accomplice from a star, amazed to see what strange creatures these human beings were, and how hard to distinguish from the shadows where they hid.

Afterwards they stood, hands still touching, leaning against the same broad tree trunk. They had been close for too long. Fraser resolved to make his getaway. The other man turned and peered into the darkness.

'Till me your gnome!' he hissed. 'Your gnome!'

The man grasped his elbow and Fraser whimpered with fear as he shook himself free. Stricken with panic he sprinted along the path towards the thundering weir, that strange foreign accent still echoing in his ears.

☆

'Juliet, can't you stop marching up and down?'

'It's time we turned the lights off. What if Mother Rodelinda discovers we are still awake?'

Sister Juliet had squeezed a rolled towel against the bottom of the door. There was no way someone patrolling the corridor outside could tell they were breaking the rules. And if they tried a sudden entry, the towel would hold them up long enough for Sister Juliet to lie down on the lower of the bunk beds and pull the coarse blanket up about her ears.

'I want to sleep!' complained Sister Viviana. 'What chance have I got of resting with this child doing gymnastics in my belly and you pacing back and forth like a caged beast?'

'I'm thinking,' Juliet answered demurely, taking her hand away from her mouth to do so. She had been biting her nails in her effort to concentrate.

'About what?'

'About a way out. How we can escape.'

'How can you talk like that?' gasped Sister Fatima. 'You speak as if we were in a prison.'

'And aren't we?' Juliet snapped back. She was losing her patience. 'Can't you see the bars on the window? Do you think it is just an accident that we have all been moved to the same room, that the door is locked behind us every night, and that it is a ground-floor room with a rather crude form of burglar protection which actually serves to keep us in?'

'The Mother Superior has done it for our own good, and for the good of the order. She is concerned for our reputation,' said Fatima.

'Reputation, my foot! We are prisoners and she is keeping us here against our will. I want to get out, not just to save myself but to save my baby!'

Fatima began to weep.

'Why are we suffering in this way? What are we being punished for? I believe this is the devil's work, and something awful is going to happen when this thing inside me sees the light of day!' She placed her hands fearfully and reproachfully on her swollen belly.

Juliet bent over her, eyes blazing.

'How dare you speak that way? How dare you swallow the twaddle they stuff us with? It's a child, a human child, however it came to be there, and you have to start looking after it. As of now!'

Viviana's cooler tones intervened.

'I've spent night after sleepless night racking my brains, trying to find an explanation. You know, I read a story once about a woman who became pregnant without ever sleeping with a man. It turned out that an officer who saved her life during the siege of a fortress had raped her while she was asleep. And she didn't even notice.'

'Fat lot of use that is!' scoffed Juliet. 'Do you really think one man could have raped each of us on the same night, in three separate rooms, without anybody realizing?'

The idea intrigued Viviana.

'We'll have to wait and see if the babies resemble one another,' she observed.

'How did the story end?' asked Fatima.

'The woman put an advert in the paper, he answered it, and they got married.'

There was a silence.

'I suppose we could put an advert in the paper,' hazarded Viviana.

Juliet's response was a snort.

'How could we when we can't even post a letter or make a phone call? Do you think Mother Rodelinda is going to invite a journalist in to speak to us and give him tea and cake?'

'Maybe the archbishop was right. I think I can remember having earache a week or two before all this started,' murmured Fatima.

'And each of us is about to give birth to the Saviour,' said Juliet.

Viviana stuck an exploratory finger into her ear, then shook her head.

'It's just too hard to believe.' She laughed. 'And what if it's a girl?'

'Anyway,' said Juliet, 'the Vatican's put a stop to that one. Fat lot of use shutting the cage door when the bird has flown!'

Fatima looked puzzled.

'But nothing went out. Something came in.'

Juliet was no longer listening. She had sat down on the edge of her bed and was palpating her breasts delicately and proudly.

'It can't be long now,' she said.

'Stop that!' cried Fatima. 'You know we're not allowed to let each other see our nakedness!'

Juliet ignored her.

'What'll it be like to have a baby sucking at them?' she mused, then giggled excitedly. 'They might be twins. Just imagine if we had six!'

Viviana peered over from the upper bunk, appraising Juliet's breasts with interest.

'What worries me is whether we get to keep them. Won't they just whisk them away?'

'That's why we have to escape,' said Juliet with triumphant logic.

Fatima rolled over in her bunk and covered her head with the pillow so as to blot out this seditious talk.

'And have you got an idea yet?' asked Viviana.

'Yes,' answered Juliet. She smiled and carefully pulled her habit up around her neck, then got up and started patrolling as before. 'We could use Mrs Kerr the cleaning woman.'

Viviana nodded. It was an astute suggestion.

'Do you think she would carry a letter to Mother Genevieve?'

Fatima had lifted the pillow and was listening intently.

'Worth a try,' said Viviana.

Juliet stopped so that her face was right up against Fatima's in the upper bunk and prodded the younger nun's chest with a menacing finger.

'If one word of this gets out, my dear, Viviana and I will know who the traitor was. You will have us to reckon with. Do not imagine that we will be more merciful with you than our superiors have been with us.'

FOUR

I take the pillar as my symbol of despair. It is a pillar of polished mahogany that rises from the banister at the point where the school stair reaches the final landing. That is the floor we have classes on. It is my despair materialized, a concentrate of molecules of pain that have taken on the hardness and the compactness of wood. Sometimes I find it strange that I alone should know what it means. The other boys pass by indifferently. Now and again one will place a hand on it and swing himself round from the landing on to the first steps. I am the only one who returns at lunchtime each day to pay homage to it, the only one to whom it speaks. I could swear that it is growing bigger although I know this cannot be true.

Pain is a peculiar thing. It is a new country I have stumbled upon, where reality has dimensions I cannot fathom, where the rules of gravity are contravened. Sometimes I wonder if the pain is inside me or outside me, and whether I am feeling it or just looking at it, looking at an alien object I can walk around, distinct and tangible as the pillar.

How much of the pain is mine? How much of it is pain I have inflicted on Daniel? When I watch the pain go out of me and into him like a lance, and he winces because I have ignored him, or will not look at him, or move away from a group of boys the moment he comes close, does that lessen the quantity that stays with me? Can I infect him? Is his pain like a pillar too?

My feet tread the earth of the country of pain. When I awaken in the mornings I am afraid to swing out of the bed and set my feet on the floor for the first time. This morning I lay on top of the quilt and peered at the pattern of the carpet. I thought if I managed to put my foot in just the right spot, I could be out of the country of pain and back in the place where I used to live. But for all my poring and conjecturing I found no frontier. I stretched my foot as far out from the bed as I could and lurched out on to the right spot, but it made no difference.

Sinful imaginings throng my nights. I know this is because of what Daniel and I did together and no longer do. Why does my body have to play such cruel tricks upon me? Why do these messengers come to me in the darkness, when I cannot protect myself, and why are their urgings so sweetly persuasive, so irresistible?

I have tried to pray but even the crucifix has lost its purity. It strikes me as a bad joke that I should have to fortify myself by staring at the image of a naked man. Have they done that deliberately, just to mock me? Am I really to become like him? What would it be like to hang there, nails cutting a widening wound in the soft flesh of my palms, my arms aching, my feet slipping on the bevelled ledge that is their only support?

☆

Cissie wondered if Euphemia was into creative writing. The results were unimpressive. As far as she could make out it was a science fiction story about explorers on a dangerous journey. Even then, there were details which didn't tally. What was the point of all the anatomical references? And the language was so antiquated. Maybe it tied in with the odd handwriting. Was Euphemia doing exercises in calligraphy?

She put the sheet down on the table and looked out of the window. It was a typical Glasgow July day. Rain had been falling heavily since the morning, so heavily you would imagine the storage tanks of heaven were exhausted, but still it kept falling, drenching the façades to an even darker shade of black. Puffy grey skies shut the city in like the padded interior of a trunk. Although the light was muted, the view from this top-floor sitting room was splendid. Strange that the tenements on the other side of the street didn't get in the way. Cissie had always thought of Otago Street as a sunken place, cradled in the valley of the Kelvin.

Euphemia was taking ages to make tea. Cissie had been delighted and a little unnerved to receive the unprecedented compliment of being invited back home. What made her even more nervous was the fact that she had bared her soul to Euphemia without so far eliciting any obvious reaction. Most likely her host was dithering in the kitchen so as to get time to absorb the story she had heard. You had to be fair. It was not an easy tale to believe.

The chemistry cabinet held little of interest for Cissie. Unable to settle on the sofa, she studied the portraits for a moment then transferred her attention to the cupboard door with its rows of postcards.

They were all of angels, drawn from galleries and churches in Greece and Serbia, Italy, Austria and Catalonia, Andalusia and the Balearic Islands, Crete and Rhodes and the Dalmatian coast. There were devotional paintings and detached frescoes, diptychs, triptychs and huge storied chancels, icons, candlebearers and carved wooden statues, angels on fountains, heads of cherubs on baptismal fonts, stained-glass windows and embroidered copes and chasubles.

Six podgy, decapitated cherubs snuggled luxuriously in a nest of wings, like a flower head in its glory of petals. Another angel, with extraordinarily languorous eyes, was reduced to a face seen sideways on, framed in a halo amidst cascades of feathers. St Michael had a sullen expression and a beauty spot on one cheek. Frizzy golden curls swirled around the perfect oval of his face, and he wore a jewel in the form of a fleur-de-lis at the crown of his forehead. Did he spend long hours on his coiffure? Or did he find it like that when he woke up every morning? One hand held a sword whose cold tip grazed his nose, while the other balanced scales with tiny people in them, poised with joined hands like divers about to jump. A gorgeously elegant Raphael led Tobias down a country path. The boy was carrying a fish. They had just come over the breast of a hill and were deep in conversation. Cissie wondered what they were talking about and if the angel's wings were ever entirely still or jogged up and down as it walked. What would they smell of?

She found it hard to get the whole array of postcards into focus. When she concentrated on one it invariably grew bigger and occupied her entire field of vision, so that she lost any notion of its place with respect to the others.

Euphemia had a soft spot for Annunciations. A madonna in deep blue with narrow, Oriental eyes hunched her shoulders as she drew her robe angrily around her neck. A glorious lily, tufted and shaggy like the curved backbone of an animal, marked the centre of the picture. The vase holding it was concave, regularly ribbed yet organic. Cissie felt sure it had at one time housed a living creature, like a conch. Beyond it knelt the most golden angel she had ever seen. Normally she would have thought of gold as one colour, but here it ran to twenty or thirty different shades, on cuffs and hems, in the varying intensity of the wings, in the tartan cloak of blue and gold that billowed at the angel's back, and in the eternally youthful brilliance of its hair.

She loved the musicians. Some played lutes like halved water melons. Others drew bows across upside down violins, flat slabs of wood cut in the shape of lyres. Two knelt face to face on either side of a miniature organ, one touching the keys while the other opened and closed a delicate bellows with just four fingers of its right hand. Called in to celebrate the Nativity, a choir of angels strummed guitars, their rounds mouths gaping as if they were fish stranded in an alien element.

From what Cissie could make out, angels could be as big or as small as they wanted. A search party in sumptuous gaberdines checking on the activities of the three kings were only about half the size of the coarse shepherds peering through the gaping rafters above their heads. A madonna disappeared upwards into a sky that consisted exclusively of angels, a seething mass of orange bodies with the pliability of plasticine, and if Cissie squinted a bit they turned into rank after rank of sulphur-tinted cloud. The madonna's tensed, downward-pointing feet had the grace and strength of a ballet dancer's, yet they quivered like the wings of a butterfly.

On another card four angels linked arms to form a circle around a descending dove. Cissie had seen people do that on television after jumping out of an aeroplane before separating to activate their parachutes. It occurred to her that the only way the painter could have studied bodies in that position was to get them to swim along the surface of a pool while he lay on the bottom and watched from beneath. Certain angels had braking problems. Clutching an outsize palm or a halo, they arrived at breakneck speed and, as gory martyrdoms reached their culminating orgasm of cruelty, narrowly avoided crashing into the pillars of a ruined Roman temple, or getting tangled in the ragged thatching of an outhouse.

There was a tinkle of cups and teaspoons and Euphemia at last entered with the tea tray.

'Do you like the postcards?' she asked. 'I call them my family photo album.'

Cissie moved to help her and they settled the things on a small table in front of the fire.

'Well,' said Euphemia as she got comfortable in her chair, 'I think I had better introduce you to my friend Derek.'

☆

During the morning break yesterday I was standing in the upper playground chatting to Michael Seenan and Dominic McConochie when who should I glimpse through the wire netting but Daniel. It gave me a real shock to see him there. He looked odd in that context, not wearing his school uniform.

Of course he's going to the art school now. If I'm honest I have to admit that it had been at the back of my mind that he was studying just round the corner. I never thought he would be so bold as to come and look for me. He doesn't know that I have made my decision and am past all that now.

My heart started thumping like mad. Our eyes met for an instant but I turned away. And then I heard him calling me. 'Gerald . . . !' he called, 'Gerald!' There didn't seem to be any point to his call. He didn't expect a reply. He was putting his pain into words but it came over like a natural thing, an animal cry. It made me think of a lone wolf in the steppes whooping eerily even though it knows there is nobody to hear for miles around.

I pretended not to notice and carried on chatting, although I could see from both Michael and Dominic's eyes that they grasped the drama of the situation. The cries stopped after a while and all you could hear was the usual background of shouting boys and footballs bouncing on the tarmac. When I thought it was safe I turned round again, just so as to fix the spot in the wire netting where he had been standing. It was going to be my last sight of him and I wanted to get it right in my mind.

But he was still there! He raised his hand and waved and sort of smiled.

'These poofs are certainly persistent,' said Michael Seenan with a smirk.

I looked straight at him and punched him hard in the face, mechanically, as if my mind were on other things. He groaned and backed away and when I looked again Daniel had gone.

I must have hit Michael very hard. There was a lot of blood and we were both hauled up before the rector. When Michael blurted out that Daniel had been outside the playground Fr Flynn blanched and stopped asking questions. Evidently he knows about the whole thing and finds it deeply embarrassing. But he gave me no punishment and even patted me on the shoulder as I went out. He has never touched me before.

After I got home tonight I decided on the how. Mum and I had washed up after tea and I went into my bedroom to start translating Virgil. That's the order I do my homework in: Latin, then French, then English last of all, because it's what I like best. I'd pulled my tie off the moment I got in and dropped it on the bed the way I always do. Something about the shape it had fallen into reminded me of the time Daniel and I made love and his mother nearly caught us. He loosened my tie gradually, gently so that he could slip it over my head and put his hand under my shirt to touch my nipples. I remember seeing it there, lying on the floor like a garland cast aside in the course of a feast. But when I saw it again on my bed it was like a noose. And I thought yes, the school tie, yes. And the thought made me laugh. It's such an appropriate choice.

☆

Little lances of falling rain hit the sides of the phone booth Alan was standing in as he popped his coins into the slot and tried Jackie's home number. She was not at the office today. Waiting for the connection, he peered up the muddy hillside at the church of St Pius XXVII with its habitual crowd of devotees and sightseers at the door. The crew had packed away lights and cameras, and their van roared past him down the road towards the city centre just as Jackie picked up the receiver.

'It's incredible!' he blurted out. 'We've got it on celluloid!'

'Got what?' asked Jackie frostily, although she knew exactly what he meant.

'The miracle! The moving statue! Mother Genevieve did it again!'

'How does she make it happen?' She was curious in spite of herself.

'I can't explain it. She kneels down in front of the madonna and bows her head. Presumably she's praying or making an invocation or something. And then the statue begins to laugh. It makes me feel quite peculiar.'

'But do you believe in it?'

'How can I not believe? I saw it with my own eyes. I feel superstitious about using the film. As if I would be desecrating something, or betraying a secret.'

'And have you managed to interview her?'

'No way. The archbishop has placed an absolute ban. Nobody has got in to see her these last few days except the odd Basque Jesuit, the one who can't speak properly and walks in that funny way as if he was struggling to hold his buttocks together.'

There was a pause.

'Alan,' said Jackie warily, 'we can't go on like this.'

'What do you mean?' asked Alan. He could tell what was coming.

'I never see you. Before you used to complain about me having too much work. Now I find myself wondering whether I'm in a relationship or not.'

'But Jackie,' protested Alan, 'this is the biggest break I've ever had. I've been on national television, had front page articles in the *Herald*, the lot. I can't afford not to milk it for all it's worth. It won't last for ever. It's my chance to get out of religious journalism. I know it sounds contradictory, but what I'm really doing is building a springboard to get me over into music. I've been on to Ceòl again about that profile.'

There was a silence at the other end of the phone.

'We start editing at eight o'clock. I'm sure it won't take that long. Can I come round after eleven?'

'Oh, just do whatever you want. But if I'm in bed don't disturb me. You can use the spare room. I need my sleep.'

The mansion has been tidied and is ready to receive its visitor.

Imagine, O lofty one!, a house of many chambers that has been neglected for a decade. Damp has seeped in through the cornices, swelling the wallpaper until it breaks off with its own weight and hangs in great, heavy curls. The walls are marbled with a pattern of fungi and blotches. The once splendid paintwork is dowdy and discoloured. Pictures hang awry, tapestries have slipped from their fastenings and droop like furled flags.

A stench of mould and corruption meets the nostrils on all sides. The carpets are hidden beneath bouncing whorls of dust like giant thistledown. Rats scuttle from one side of the room to the other and spiders of every colour and size have stretched ponderous webs across the windowpanes. The shutters beyond are securely fastened so that neither light nor air has penetrated the place for many summers. The folds of the curtains are the haunt of dead moths and forgotten chrysalids.

What a weight of melancholy assails the spirits as one wanders from room to room! Here was a place made ready for life, its celebration and begetting, a place that even when new creation was no longer a possibility could yet witness innumerable joyous encounters, tussles and congregations. And at the very point when its life should have begun, it was abandoned, turned to a thing of disgrace, a faculty that simply should not have been there.

Yet life had not abandoned it completely. We were not long in finding the succulent, responsive pillar at its core, and I would stake my indestructible spirit that it shivered at our arrival, as if to say, there is lust in me yet, but give me the opportunity and I can preside at the festivity of joy as was intended!

We are exhausted. I will make no attempt to conceal this fact. The image of the mansion is a decorous and appropriate one and allows me to evoke the enormous labours to which we have dedicated ourselves in these past hours. But you must remember that we were dealing not with dead but with organic matter, with living membranes and tissues which were not dumb and indifferent but initially opposed our efforts to reawaken them.

The return of sensitivity to places long since numbed is

invariably experienced as a return of pain. We imagined we could hear the passageways and thresholds, the vaults and corridors and arches crying out in protest that they had become accustomed to neglect and hopelessness. Why were we stirring them back to life? What prospect could there be that they would ever witness the encounters they had been framed to welcome?

The morale of my minions has been alarmingly unstable. When we reached the end of our second tunnel journey, and the navigator assured us we were at our destination, contradictory feelings fought for the upper hand with them. Relief at having completed their journey and a justified pride that so many dangers had been successfully braved were countered by disbelief and exhaustion. Had the scene of their activity truly been reduced to such an appalling state? And was the most considerable part of their mission still to be accomplished? Had they in fact done so little?

I taught them, O sublime one, a new song. I myself could not tell you the source of my inspiration. It is an error to say that the song was new. Rather, I discovered it, revived it with all its magic of rejuvenation where it had been lying in wait for me, in a forgotten and unsuspected byway of my consciousness. I knew well that our task was not only a hygienic one, that cleanliness was not our only objective. We needed to find a note that would set these chambers resonating, make them quiver with anticipation of the joyful, destined throbbing they will soon experience.

So my song achieved a double purpose. Its rhythms heartened my minions as they laboured, giving them the comfort of shared effort and achievement, while at the same time nurturing each tissue in these precincts. It was a pampering, fondling, caressing yet challenging song, a song that had fragrance and colour as well as music. Our task was a hard one, but in the end its fragrance dispelled the awful stench with which we had first been welcomed.

Now we have replenished ourselves with magical food and are preparing to rest. The navigator is debating the easiest way for us to leave this organism. I understand that there is no hurry and we can take time to recuperate before embarking on the final stage of our expedition. And so I bid you farewell with the fond hope that you will once more visit me, as you have so often done, in my dreams.

✫

Mother Genevieve was startled when the door burst open and Cyril strode in followed by an incensed Fr Ryan and a burly policeman. She had been staring moodily out of the window at the council tenements on the ridge of the hill. A piece of sewing lay untouched on her lap. Sitting in this trance had become her principal occupation.

'Officer,' Fr Ryan was saying, 'why did you let this man in? Are your orders not perfectly clear?'

'First of all, father, my orders do not come from you. And secondly, he says the lady here is wanting to see him.'

The policeman folded his arms and stood by the door. He would leave the others to sort out this particular mess. Cyril looked at Mother Genevieve as if astonished to find she still existed.

'Of course I want to see him, officer,' she said calmly. 'Please be so good as to leave us alone together.'

'There will be trouble for this, make no mistake,' threatened Fr Ryan, waving a knobbly finger at the unwanted guest who had catapulted him into the national headlines. 'Do you realize you are going against the express orders of our archbishop?'

Mother Genevieve waved a weary hand in his direction, as if he were a bluebottle she couldn't take the trouble to squash.

'Go,' she said curtly. 'Enough. Go. Begone.'

Her whole body had begun to quiver with excitement and she wanted Fr Ryan out of her sight as quickly as possible so that she could discover whether she was right, whether her moment had in fact come.

'Let's leave them to it,' said the policeman with gentle reasonableness. 'You can phone your archbishop from downstairs and I'm sure he'll take whatever action he feels is appropriate.'

The door closed. Mother Genevieve could not bear to look at Cyril. It was as much as she could do to grasp that the focus of her visions, the source of her miracle, was here in the room with her. The fantastical member was, so to speak, within her reach.

134

She stared out of the window again. The council tenements, amazingly, were unchanged, though rain was now beating against the glass, blurring the view. Cyril had pulled up a hard wooden chair in front of her and was clearing his throat, preparing to speak. She savoured deliciously the last few moments of her resistance before the ultimate barriers fell.

'Mother Genevieve,' he began, taking her hand.

She turned to him, her eyes ablaze.

'Call me Brenda,' she murmured.

'Brenda' – and the words came in a great rush – 'I've come to get you out of this. I don't know what's going on. I don't even want to ask myself if this is a miracle or a trick, and what your role is in it. All I know is that it is a disgrace and it has to stop. Whatever brought you or me into this church business had nothing to do with laughing virgins or rigged-up statues. I don't know how you do it, or if you do it, but it is destroying you and destroying all the respect and affection I feel for you.'

Respect, affection . . . Another word hovered on Brenda's lips but she said nothing. She squeezed his fine hand with the big, strong fingers in hers, encouraging him to go on.

'They're using you, my dear. Stuck here in this miserable parish house, which looks like a prison even if it hasn't always been one, you can't have realized. But everybody is making capital out of this affair: the hierarchy, the newspapers, the souvenir sellers. Do you know that they have built an arcade all the way from the bus stop to the entrance of the church? You are at the centre of this horrible sideshow, and if we don't do something quick it will swallow you up for ever.'

Calmer now, he spoke gently and deliberately. Both his hands were in hers.

'The ecumenical committee has met twice since I last saw you. I cannot tell you how deeply your absence affected me, Brenda. Since Amanda left, my whole world has started to come apart and I have found myself doubting even my vocation. Not that I've stopped believing in God or in love. I just can't relate them any longer to these piddling arguments about celibacy and the pill, or abortion and good works and women priests. You were the only one who made it meaningful, Brenda. And you've not only abandoned the committee, you've got involved in something that betrays the very image I had constructed of you. You are my last hope, for religion and for womanhood. Please don't let me down.'

He had expected her to offer resistance. Instead she asked him dreamily where he planned to take her.

'Tomorrow, at precisely one o'clock, a taxi will come for you. Pack a small suitcase with the things you need for three or four nights. I will not be in the taxi, but the driver will know where he has to take you.'

'And what if they don't let me go?' she quavered, suddenly fearful.

'They cannot stop you, Brenda. There will even be a policeman on the doorstep who can intervene if they do. Just tell them you have decided to leave and the way will be clear.'

☆

Craig's personal morality and his professional morality were at odds with one another. While his inner, Presbyterian conscience warned that what he was doing was not right, the incipient businessman in him proclaimed that his client's interests were paramount, or at least that his client would take the ultimate responsibility for whatever Craig did while under his instructions.

At present he was merely acting as a witness. If his client's English had improved by leaps and bounds in the weeks since his arrival in Scotland, understanding his wishes continued to be a major undertaking. 'Follow' might appear as 'fallow' or 'fellow'; 'cheque' had come out as both 'chuck' and 'tick'; and 'suspicious' was a word Felipe consistently failed to get his articulating organs round however much he huffed and puffed and spluttered.

This was Craig's second visit to the archbishop's palace. On neither occasion had its titular owner been present, and he felt rather like an adolescent invited to party in a house where the parents are on holiday. As he passed through the elaborate hallway, the thought of the accountancy examinations he would sit before the year was out comforted him. He wanted to be shut of this private detective business as quickly as he could. His increase in salary would help to pay for the transition.

Mick was still laid up in bed recovering from his shock, and Craig had expressly forbidden him to even consider involvement in the case of the pregnant virgins until he was back on his mental feet once more. He had taken the office paperwork in hand and had been amazed to discover the thriving state of his boss's finances. Craig's scrupulous nature did not stop him immediately awarding himself a subsidiary payment for all the extra responsibility he had assumed. That, too, consoled him as he pursued Felipe's wiggling backside down the corridors of the palace.

He had ignored Mick's instructions to raise the question of Euphemia MacFarrigle at his first meeting with the Basque priest. Craig felt that Mick continued to take an unbalanced view of her role in the troubles of the archdiocese. He had decided not to believe a word of Mick's tale of woe, although the reality of the appearing and disappearing tenement at 98 Otago Street was tucked away uncomfortably at the back of his mind. When he broached the subject of Euphemia with his employer, that would have to be raised, and it was a prospect Craig did not relish.

It was clear that Felipe distrusted the archbishop, who returned his suspicion with interest. The latter's farting attacks had mercifully abated during his sojourn on the health farm and he had lost no time in contacting the detective agency upon his return. Mick's suggestion that he should work with one party while Craig dealt with the other promised to be lucrative, but had its dangers and struck the younger partner as unprincipled, even if the idea of each paying the same firm to have the other followed had an attractive symmetry about it. They had shelved the difficulty by simply not answering the archbishop's message.

The palace was on three floors plus a basement, and their search had brought them almost to ground level. Felipe was no fool. He had chosen a day when the archbishop was celebrating an ordination, one of lamentably few where he was still summoned to officiate. That would keep him busy until late evening. It was Mrs Donnelly's afternoon off and Felipe had double locked the main entrance and fastened the snib on the kitchen door so that she could not get back in without him knowing. Accompanied by Craig, he was using a neat little contraption he had brought with him from Rome to pick every lock in the building.

He opened cupboard after cupboard, and Craig grew tired of peeping over his shoulder at dusty, moth-eaten vestments or heaped-up back issues of the *Archdiocesan News*. He had always considered Roman Catholicism to be basically a theatrical spectacle. What they discovered only served to reinforce his view. The props ranged from monstrances, cruets and chalices to life-size saints in attitudes of agony or prayer – it was not always easy to say which. There were cribs and crucifixes and candle snuffers, crowns of thorns and fairy light haloes, black and purple and crimson velvet curtains, spears with sponges and even a centurion's helmet. A whole room was given over to costume storage, and Felipe insisted they poke like ferrets into every corner.

Craig was sure his clothes would stink of incense when he got back home. He had no idea what Felipe was looking for. He did not enjoy being near the cleric. Early on in their first interview he had realized who Felipe reminded him of, and the likeness to Alfred Coutts gave him a sense of nausea. While assuming he could be in no danger from a man of the cloth, he preferred to keep the Jesuit in front of him. There was no way he would risk bending over without first making sure of that man's whereabouts.

By the time they reached the basement and penetrated Mrs Donnelly's domain he was aching with tiredness. The Jesuit was indefatigable; sniffing, burrowing and rummaging in every box and package they came upon. Craig was distinctly hungry but the smells of stale cabbage and stewed tea did little to tempt his palate. The place was not adequately lit. Felipe had produced a torch from his right pocket. At the end of a murky corridor they stopped in front of a huge wardrobe that looked as if it could have accommodated an entire rugby team. Fiddle as he might, Felipe could do nothing with the padlock on it. He disappeared, then came back with a jemmy he had noticed in the course of their perlustrations. Craig could not help admiring his thoroughness and perspicacity.

It took only the gentlest of efforts to prise the wardrobe open. Then a strange thing happened. As the high doors parted, a glistening white waterfall trickled forth, a rustling plastic shower as if a reservoir of milk had burst its dam. Emitting short, suppressed squeals of delight and surprise, Felipe spread the doors wider and wider still, so that more and more of the shimmering packages tumbled out with a magical susurration, as at the release of a great tension. Soon he and Craig were standing knee-deep in a sea of condoms.

☆

Daniel could not imagine what the uproar downstairs was about. It was highly unusual for his parents to receive visitors during the week, but when the doorbell rang half an hour earlier he felt no desire to find out who had called. A reproduction of a Dürer drawing was taped to the wall in front of him, and he was attempting, with little enough success, to copy it on to his sketch pad. Now his father's voice rose in anger while his mother moaned in the background in a way that set the hairs on the back of his neck tingling. He heard heavy steps climbing the stair and stuck the pencil behind his ear. The door of his room was thrown violently open.

'Would you mind coming downstairs, you little pervert?' shouted his father. 'Just come downstairs and listen to what Father Flynn has been telling us.'

The pad slipped from his knees to the floor. His cheeks were burning. It enraged him that this might be interpreted as an admission of guilt when it felt more like anger. He thought his father was about to hit him and clenched his fists. The man merely gestured towards the stairs with a weird grin, as if a special treat was in store. On the landing he met his sister's head peering nervously from her bedroom door.

'Get back in there!' growled his father. 'This filth is not for ears like yours!'

His mother was still whimpering. Fr Flynn's measured Irish tones urged calm. What on earth had brought the rector of his former school to the house? He was out of the place for good, and safe at the art school. Surely the man had no power to hurt him now.

The living coal effect gas fire was blazing. The curtains had not yet been drawn over the panorama window and the glass

139

doors giving on to the back lawn. Two boxers danced manically across the television screen. His father must have been watching the match when Fr Flynn arrived. His mother had evidently been correcting homework in the kitchen. Her face was twisted by shock and anger. Tears had smudged her make-up and her cheeks had a grey, ashen look. She glanced quickly at him when he entered the room, then buried her face in her hands.

'What are they going to say at school?' she moaned. 'What are they going to say?'

Mr Kane did not sit down but paused by the door, arms akimbo. He pointed to a jotter that had been tossed violently on to the carpet.

'Take a look at that!' he shouted. 'See if you can recognize your handiwork!'

Stunned, Daniel bent to pick up the jotter. He opened it at the first page and recognized Gerald's handwriting. 'I take the pillar as my symbol of despair,' he read. The words meant nothing to him. He raised his head and looked to Fr Flynn, hoping for enlightenment.

'The boy is dead,' he heard his mother's voice say. 'They found the body this morning.'

I knew it was Gerald, thought Daniel. What do I feel? What do I feel? The news was like a chunk of heavy quartz thrust into his hand. He turned it back and forth, watching how the crystals caught the light, wondering if it would explode. He could have sworn his hearing was affected. What the adults were saying came to him from far off, as if through a thick filter.

'What matters is that other boys should be protected from him. Until he can get treatment, of course.'

'You can't get treatment for that kind of thing, Father. It's congenital. The boy's been a no-goer from the start,' said Mr Kane. 'Second born. You know the kind of problems they cause.'

'Who has been told?' asked his wife. 'Has the news spread far? You have to realize about my work. The scandal must be contained in every way possible.'

'Have no fear, Mrs Kane. Catholic priests have faced martyr-dom rather than reveal the secrets of the confessional. Though the confessional has no claim on me here, I do not intend to broadcast this tragedy to the four winds. We are experts in discretion. What concerns me is the soul of the boy that died, and the soul of your son.'

'If it were up to me, I'd have him taken to court. After all, he's under age, isn't he? Is that a crime or isn't it?'

'How could you, George? Don't you see what that would do to the family? We'd have to leave the area, leave . . . the country.'

'Daniel,' asked Fr Flynn, 'when did you last see Gerald?'

His question was met with a stubborn silence.

'You are not in a particularly strong position, my boy,' smirked the priest. 'I think it would be in your interests to talk.'

'Enough of your impertinence,' shouted Mr Kane, raising his hand to strike.

'Lay one finger on me and you'll get more than you bargained for.'

'They're going to fight! They're going to fight! Stop them, Father!' howled Mrs Kane.

Daniel shifted round behind the sofa and sat down in the empty armchair by the fire. His father stood, hand still raised but curiously shrunken, then took his place meekly beside Mrs Kane and put his arm round her. Daniel found himself regretting he had not taken the opportunity to hit the man.

'Have you been to confession?' Fr Flynn went on. 'Are you persisting in a state of mortal sin? Do you have any idea of the danger to your immortal soul?'

'I'll never go to confession again, Father. It was you who killed him. All of you together.'

Everything fell into place: repentance, rejection, despair, suicide . . . Daniel was appalled to taste salt tears on his lips just at the moment when he needed all his strength. He covered his face with his hands. All the rigidity went out of his shoulders and he shook with sobbing.

'This is a dreadful thing for a Catholic family,' Fr Flynn was saying. 'But then, the best parents are sent the heaviest crosses. It's precisely when we think we are doing well that the devil gets the chance to put us to the test. And he has done a fine piece of work here, let me tell you.'

'He has to go,' said Mr Kane. 'I'm not sheltering any poofs in this house.'

'We certainly don't want him close to the other children,' agreed Mrs Kane.

'But perhaps these tears are tears of repentance,' murmured the priest.

Daniel shook his head violently, made a lunge for the jotter and banged the door behind him. A moment later he was in his room, the bed jammed across the door to keep pursuit at bay. But no one followed. He could hear agitated voices conferring in the sitting room below. He sat on the floor with his back to the bed, opened the jotter and began to read.

☆

Mother Genevieve, or Brenda, as she now thought of herself, prepared for the journey from St Pius XXVII's in a state oddly compounded of trance and practicality. She had a small stock of non-ecclesiastical garments for use on ecumenical occasions, or when it had been important to give a forward-looking image of the order she represented. She picked on a dusty blue pleated skirt, suddenly painfully conscious of the hairs on her lower legs and the imprisoned, mealy look of her calves. Then she pulled a creamy blouse of man-made fibre over her head, settling her ample bosom as comfortably as she could inside it. A blue cardigan and a pastel grey raincoat completed the outfit. She did not possess a hat.

Waiting for the taxi to arrive made her unbearably tense. A voice inside kept repeating that Cyril would inevitably let her down. He had made his visit in a moment of aberration. Once he was able to think things over more calmly he would realize that he could not possibly compromise himself by aiding a Catholic nun to escape her superiors' control, especially given the scandal that must have been caused by his wife deserting him. But sure enough, just before one o'clock, a taxi laboured clamorously up the steep and narrow driveway and tooted its horn outside the front door.

Fr Ryan emerged from his study as she rushed downstairs. She nearly careered into him and caught his glance of astonishment. His words were lost over her shoulder as she grabbed the front-door handle, swung it neatly open and shut it behind her with an air of irrevocability. The taxi driver revved his engine. A gust of wind loosened her hair. She could not think how long it was since she had walked down the street without some sort of covering on her head.

The driver wanted to tell her something but she ordered him to move off at once. A group of pilgrims had gathered where the drive met the main road. Brenda had a fantasy of them pulling her out and forcing her to make that dreadful statue perform once more, as she had done so often and so unwillingly during these last weeks. All they did, though, was to squint through the tinted glass of the windows. She gave a regal wave, just like the Queen. The taxi left parish ground and was swallowed up in the city traffic.

She saw everything with new eyes. It was like being reborn. Little boys were scurrying across the rubble of a demolished building. Unemployed fathers pushed prams down the pavement with one arm while the other cradled a baby. Women her own age and older struggled along laden with bursting plastic super-market bags that must torment their clenched fingers on the trek home. The people in the cars that pulled up alongside them at the lights were endlessly fascinating. There were plumbers and carpenters in low slung vans, usually in pairs; businessmen hugging the steering wheel like a loved one, the passenger seat piled high with catalogues and folders; women on their own, or with children strapped in special seats behind; and even a Presbyterian minister she vaguely recognized. She instinctively moved to the other side of the taxi at the sight of him.

Brenda kept reminding herself that she had regularly travelled from one part of the city to another in her life as a nun. But today she entered a new world. If Glasgow had not changed, then she had, and in the process her relationship to all these people. She would have liked to stop and tell each of them about what was happening to her. Instead she told the driver to pull up outside a chemist's. He waited while she spent part of her precious store of cash on lipstick, a powder puff, an underarm spray and, as an ultimate, unjustifiable touch of vanity, a depilatory cream she had no idea how to use.

Now she was informed that Central Station was their destination. In the back of the taxi she tucked her purchases away in her small holdall and opened the envelope the driver had given her. It contained an adult single ticket to Largs and a brief, hand-written note from Cyril. She was to catch the next train and he would meet her on the platform there. After careful deliberation he had written 'yours' rather than 'love' but had added two 'x's which nullified the effects of his caution.

The station was in the midst of an early afternoon lull when she boarded the train. Schoolchildren in posh uniforms could be seen here and there. Middle-class housewives laden with glossy bags from Fraser's or Arnott Simpson's were heading back to the southern suburbs. An inspector slammed the door of her dingy carriage, and the train lurched across the Clyde, past Eglinton Toll and a gap she remembered a gauntlet of serried tenements filling when she was a child.

Because she was determined not to think of Cyril, the miraculous statue kept returning to her mind. They threaded their way through Paisley and Johnstone, towns Glasgow had drawn into its web with the passing decades. Next came Lochwinnoch and Kilbirnie, their low stretches of water already dark beneath the autumnal Renfrewshire moors. She could find no adequate explanation for what had happened at St Pius XXVII's. Her old beliefs and way of praying were obsolete, and she was uncertain whether this new force was an emanation of the devil or whether a saner, more mischievous and playful deity had entered her life. Although she had difficulty acknowledging it, she did not doubt that the laughing madonna presided over the journey she was making today and would guide her safely to a harbour she had ached to reach in all these years of renunciation.

The reunion on the platform at Largs was not dramatic. Cyril had spruced himself up noticeably since their last meeting. He was wearing what looked like a new brown coat. He was cleanshaven and had combed his hair neatly. He gave her a quick peck on the cheek as if they were a husband and wife whom a brief business trip had separated. Then he put his arm round her shoulder and took her holdall in his free hand.

'Shall we walk?' he asked. 'It isn't far.'

She did not answer. As they approached the seafront, the sun peeked out timidly from behind the clouds. The pavements glinted with recently fallen rain. A beam caught the surface of the sea, turning it from grey to liquid gold. The shape of Arran on the horizon was familiar to her from family holidays.

The guesthouse he had booked them into was in a quiet street not far from the beach. Cyril had taken two rooms with a connecting door. One had a double bed, the other a single. The larger room had an *en suite* bathroom with a shower.

The single bed remained unused. Shortly after their arrival Cyril drew the curtains over the window on to the back garden. Brenda did not have words in which to talk to herself about what happened that afternoon. It was not all desperately serious. In fact, what stuck in her mind was the moment they both burst into helpless laughter and had to collapse on to the bed until they sobered up. Cyril had noticed her amusement and had asked her why.

'You remember the Church of Scotland woman, the one from the youth group network?' she asked. 'When we went for the Chinese meal and she insisted on saying grace? "Always thank Jesus before putting anything in your mouth." Wasn't that what she said?'

They got dressed afterwards and walked the streets in happy silence. Something had happened to Brenda's balance. The centre of gravity in her body had shifted. She was acutely aware of the soles of her feet making contact with the ground, of how her legs supported her, and the rest of her body was poised at each step, like an athlete's on the point of breaking into an exultant run.

Going to Nardini's for an ice cream was her idea. A gentle rain was falling, though Arran was still in sunshine. They gazed through the glass panes at the stupendous seascape while she toyed lusciously with her chocolate sundae. All at once there was a flash. A small man was kneeling on the floor in front of them holding a camera.

'Nick MacAfee from the *Evening Standard*,' he smiled affably, holding out his hand. 'Pleased to meet you, Mother Genevieve.'

☆

Alan's nightmare began between eleven and eleven thirty in the morning. A voice from deep inside him warned it would not end, but this did not stop him closing his eyes and pinching himself hard several times during the course of the day in a despairing effort to wake up. He had got off to an early start. He called in at his office in the BBC building and left a note for his producer before going to the Mitchell Library to do a bit of background research. He was on his way to Maryhill to interview a youth worker (the woman Brenda remembered, the one who always insisted on saying grace) when he heard the noise.

His immediate reaction was to ignore it, as he would telltale creakings from the bodywork of his car, or a stain in the cornice above the window. Like them, it betokened a problem he preferred not to face up to until it became absolutely necessary.

It came again and then again. He pulled up on the far side of the railway bridge beyond the library on Maryhill Road. Against his will, because he preferred to believe he was imagining things, he looked over his shoulder at the back seat. A small baby was lying there. The white knitted shawl it was wrapped in had fallen open to reveal the nappy in a plastic casing. The nappy must have been sodden because a tiny trickle of urine was leaking out on to the dark suede fabric of the car's upholstery. The baby's immense eyes caught his gaze and held it. It smiled.

Alan turned round and looked at the road ahead of him. Everything else was normal. The green embankment climbing to the canal, with the high-rise blocks beyond, gave no sign of anything untoward. Cars were swerving past on his right, and his own lights, which he had dutifully switched on, were flashing regularly. He was obsessively careful about locking his car whenever he left it. There was no way anyone could have got inside. What he was seeing was a mirage.

He started up the engine and drove on, turning right off the main road among some pleasant villas, in the direction of the youth worker's home. The baby started to cry. Its sobs grew louder and louder. Absolute panic seized him. He contemplated dumping the car and running. Then he remembered seeing a police station just before he turned off. They would be able to help him.

The officer in charge barely concealed the derision Alan's story inspired in him.

'If you left your car locked in both places, how could someone put a baby into it? And why would they want to? We get people in here who've lost their babies. You're the first to have been landed with one. Had a fight with the wife, is that it? Or a problem with the minder?'

Alan, who was beginning to tremble, went over the events of the morning once more.

'Look sir,' the officer said, 'there's no way you can park this baby on us. I'm quite happy to take your name and address and get in touch if anyone claims it. But this is a police station, not a day nursery.'

Alan was close to tears. He appealed to a trim young policewoman filling in forms further down the counter.

'But I swear it's not mine. I've never been near a baby. I don't know what to do with it.'

'Sergeant Connolly,' said the officer, 'would you mind going out and taking a look?'

She tutted, put down her pen, and followed Alan into the yard. The squawling could be heard quite a distance away through the closed windows of the car. Alan flicked his remote control and the little levers on the doors popped up. Sergeant Connolly opened the door, making consolatory noises, and bent over. This is it, thought Alan, her feminine instincts will get the better of her. I'll be shot of it. Instead she retreated in distaste and scowled reproachfully at him.

'You do realize you're breaking the law, sir? There's no way you can be allowed to transport an infant like that without a special seat. And the poor thing is in an appalling condition. It needs feeding and its nappy changed at once.'

'But I keep telling you, it's not mine! How can you expect me to have a special seat if I don't even have a baby?'

'Sorry, sir. As far as we are concerned you appear to be in charge of this infant. I recommend you make the chemist's on Maryhill Road your first stop and then go straight to a garage suppliers.'

She turned on her heel and went back into the station. The baby's cries were heartrending. Alan picked it up and hugged it close, partly to get it to stop and partly because it was expressing exactly what he felt. Comforting it was a way of soothing his own panic. The volume of the wailing decreased slightly and the baby's lips twitched expressively next to his shirt pocket. His grip put pressure on the nappy package and a foul-smelling green slime oozed forth, staining the shawl and his shirt.

The women in the chemist's glared at him as if he was a murderer. One of them produced a huge cardboard box of nappies and then got busy in the back shop making up a bottle. The other came round from behind the counter and tutted and hushed the baby but would not take hold of it. Alan thought if he could get it out of his arms he would make a dash for the car. But the woman was too sharp for him.

They showed him how to give the bottle.

'What's his name?' said one. It had not occurred to Alan to wonder what the baby's sex was. Now, for a reason unknown to himself, he simply answered: 'Hector.'

'Hector,' the woman behind the counter echoed approvingly. 'He'll grow up to be a fine, strapping lad. Now you just take him home, sir, and sort things out with your wife.'

He did not have enough ready cash to pay for nappies, bottle, baby food and various gadgets the women considered to be essential. As he wrote a cheque clumsily with one hand, the voice within him warned it was only the first of many.

He stopped the car at the next public telephone. After being fed, Hector had promptly fallen asleep. Alan considered leaving him but, on second thoughts, picked him up and took him with him. Was he going crazy? Could he be afraid someone would run off with Hector? Wasn't that exactly what he wanted?

'Jackie?' he asked. 'Is that you?'

She sounded irritated.

'Why are you calling me here?'

'Look, Jackie, something awful has happened. Can you get away from work?'

'No, I can't. What's going on?'

'It's too complicated to explain over the phone. Can I come to the office then?'

'No, you certainly can't. We've got an important client here and I have a meeting in five minutes. Ring me back this evening.'

The line went dead. Alan got back into the car and headed for Govan. Surely he could offload the baby on to his mother. After all, she had brought up three of her own, all of them boys.

☆

Daniel had been forbidden to leave the house until further notice. The interdict left him puzzled, marooned as he was in a no man's land between adolescence and adulthood. There had been no significant restrictions from his parents for him to disobey for such a long time that he reacted listlessly. If he got up and went, where would he go? The aching feeling in the pit of his stomach never abandoned him. He had hardly eaten since that first night and he lacked the strength to formulate a response.

All that changed on Wednesday morning. He got off to sleep about three o'clock. When he woke again at seven the funeral was uppermost in his mind. He could not allow them to commemorate Gerald's death while he, the most important person, was absent. After all, he was, or considered himself to be, responsible for it. His father would not speak to him, and the other children had been ordered to ignore him. His mother's evasive responses when challenged over breakfast aroused his suspicions. It must be today.

He waited till they had gone, then looked up Gerald's parish in the phone book. A woman answered from the priest's house. She could not have been more helpful. There was to be no funeral because of the unfortunate circumstances of the death. But a memorial service was planned for ten o'clock at St Ignatius'. Afterwards the coffin would be accompanied to a cemetery on the north side of the city by close family and friends.

Daniel's mother had engaged the mortice lock on the front door and removed the key to the kitchen. He had not thought to try the doors on the previous days. Now he found himself a prisoner. He stuffed the cash from the secret box under his bed into the pocket of his jerkin and went downstairs again. The security locks on the French doors to the garden meant he could not get out there. In the end he wrenched the kitchen window open and clambered awkwardly across the sink, knocking the plastic rack for the dishes and a couple of milk bottles to the floor in the process. He fell out on to the flowerbed, whether from haste or weakness he could not tell, dusted himself down and gazed triumphantly at the gaping window. Let burglars break in and take whatever they wished. He no longer had any reason to protect the place. He gave a bitter laugh.

It was a quarter to ten and he broke into a run. The avenue with its semi-detached villas and neat front gardens was so familiar. He had walked down this way to the station most weekday mornings for as long as he could remember, first to St Ignatius' and then to the art school. Now everything was changed. He half expected one of the neighbours to come out and challenge him. But the cars had disappeared from the short driveways. Almost all the houses were empty. Mrs Cunningham waved a duster from her sitting-room window. He returned the greeting only half consciously.

Just past the shopping centre he hailed a taxi. According to his calculations he had had twelve pounds in the box. That should cover the journey from Bishopbriggs to the city centre. There was no time to be lost. If he took a train he risked missing the service altogether.

As it was the heavy traffic delayed them considerably. The taxi driver took nearly seven pounds, and when Daniel got in sight of the church people were already coming out. Three black cars were drawn up in front. He halted his headlong career. His parents were among the mourners. They said something to Gerald's mother, then detached themselves from the group and disappeared around the corner. Evidently they were not going to the cemetery.

He was indignant to see how few people had attended. Gerald deserved much more than this! And they would be ashamed of the dead boy, condemning him, whereas Daniel was filled with admiration for his definitive gesture, for a courage he himself did not yet have. He watched in a daze until the last car filled up, then ran towards it. It was moving off when he tapped on the window. They pulled in and rolled it down. He did not recognize the faces.

'Have you got room for me?'

A tear-bedraggled woman regarded him distrustfully.

'Sorry. There's no room,' she said.

The window went up again and the car departed. Daniel turned and made for Renfrew Street. The first taxi he hailed stopped immediately.

'I've only got five pounds,' he said, 'and I need to get to the Bilsland cemetery. How far can you take me?'

'Pop in, my lad,' said the man.

He reached the gates with three pounds to spare. The cortège had drawn up along the path, hearses in front, two or three ordinary cars behind. Daniel slowed to a walk, not sure how to confront this situation. The ground was sodden and the grass squelched beneath his feet. He sighted the mourners over a rise and through some trees. There were two or three figures among them clothed entirely in black. The sight of dog collars hurt his eyes.

Everyone was concentrating on the burial, and he managed to sidle up without attracting attention. Peering over the shoulders of those in front he recognized Gerald's mother, supported by relatives. The black veil hanging from her hat prevented him seeing her face. A man next to her was making a speech. He took it this was Gerald's uncle. He had never met him but knew a few stories about him. The rector Fr Flynn was close by, flanked by two prefects from St Ignatius', their blazers rimmed with the distinctive gold.

Then Mr Bleeper came forward to the edge of the grave and began speaking. At first Daniel did not register what was happening. His eyes were riveted on the polished wood of the coffin with its bunches of chrysanthemums and red roses. It was poised on two planks, and the ropes were neatly coiled on either side, ready for lowering it into the earth. He could not get an idea out of his head, however inappropriate it was to the time and place. He kept thinking about his sperm inside Gerald's body, while Gerald's body was inside the coffin, soon to be below the earth. Gradually Mr Bleeper's voice was borne in upon him. He could make nothing of the words. All that mattered was that this man was making a speech over Gerald's body.

He let the saliva build up in his mouth, sucking his cheeks in to accumulate as much as possible, then shouldered his way to the front. People were too surprised to stop him. As he drew himself up in front of Mr Bleeper, the scholastic's voice trailed off into silence. Everyone was staring at them expectantly.

Daniel struck the man once, hard, across the cheek, with the back of his right hand and then, as he bowed his head, spat richly on to his habit. He glimpsed the foaming grey flecking the black fabric and heard Mr Bleeper's whimper of denial, as if the blow had been an accusation he wished to but could not confute.

Voices were raised and someone laid a hand on Daniel's shoulder. He shook it off and started to run. It was raining and the drops brought a refreshing coolness to his cheeks. After a couple of minutes he slowed down. No one was following him. There was no point in rushing. He had nowhere to go. He would have to return home at some point, but not now.

He was on the main road again, halfway down the hill, when a taxi came to a halt at the kerb just ahead of him. The door swung open and a primly dressed woman with curled spectacle frames leant out.

'Euphemia MacFarrigle,' she said. 'Delighted to make your acquaintance. Please get in.'

☆

The quickest route from Maryhill to Govan leads through Jordanhill and the Clyde Tunnel. But Alan was so preoccupied that he found himself in Sauchiehall Street before he knew it. Hector had woken up and was whimpering in a subdued fashion from the back seat. He drove right into the centre of town, parked near the Tron on a double yellow line and hurried into a large department store carrying the baby. All he had planned to do was get a dummy. The car seat could wait till later. But while he was inside, a beautifully designed little sling carrier in crimson corduroy caught his eye and he bought that too. He knew he was behaving in a contradictory fashion. If all went according to plan he would be rid of the baby within the hour. So why was he spending valuable money on all this paraphernalia?

Hector settled comfortably into the sling across his chest. Alan was able to rest his arms at last. This way he could check on all Hector's movements and had only to bend his head to catch a whiff of that delicious baby fragrance.

The worst had happened. A traffic warden was writing down the particulars of his car in her book. Alan came to a halt in front of her. She looked up with a frown, then glimpsed the baby and her expression changed.

'What a little sweetie!' she beamed. 'We've got our hands full today, haven't we, sir?'

She tore the page out, crushed it expressively into a little ball and tossed it into the gutter, then turned on her heels.

Alan was not prepared for the look of absolute horror he got from Mrs Donaldson when she opened the door. She was halfway through taking the curlers out of her hair. There was a towel over her shoulders, and she was brandishing a lilac-coloured plastic brush in one hand. He practically had to push his way in. When he shut the door her face crumpled and she burst into tears exactly like a child whose favourite toy has just been smashed.

'What's this?' she squealed. 'What's this? My first grandchild a bastard and you bring it into this house? How could you do this to me?'

She ran from him into the kitchen, slamming the door. At the sound of her voice Hector, too, had begun to cry. Alan stroked the huge, downy skull. It was warm to the touch of his chilled hand. He tried to open the kitchen door. To his astonishment he realized that his mother was gripping the handle on the other side. He had to put his shoulder to it to get in. She retreated behind the table, pulling chairs out from it to barricade herself in front of the sink.

'I don't want your bastard git in here!' she shouted. 'Take it away, do you hear me? Take it away!'

'But Mum,' protested Alan. 'It's not mine . . .' He was about to say 'I found it', but the words struck him as ridiculous.

Mrs Donaldson was beating her fists on the scrubbed surface of the table.

'All these years I have waited, wondering when I'd meet the girl, wondering who you would choose, hoping I'd like her, hoping you two would make a go of it. And now you do this to me!'

'Get a hold of yourself, woman,' said Alan, losing his patience. 'You don't understand. I'm not asking you to take the child in. I just want to leave him here for a couple of hours while I get things sorted out.'

'Oh no, my man, oh no.' His mother grinned sardonically and shook her head. 'Don't try and pull that one on me! That's how it always starts. "Just for an afternoon." "Only help me out now and again." Oh no. I've done my time, so I have, done my time with three of you little blighters, and if you think I want to start all over again, you've got another think coming!'

'It's not even my baby!' yelled Alan. 'Don't you understand? Somebody dumped it in the back seat of my car!'

Mrs Donaldson was not listening, totally occupied with her own train of thought.

'As if it wasn't enough to lose one son! Fraser's a good lad and a more loyal son than you will ever be. But don't imagine I have any illusions about his kind. What he's got between his legs will never serve to bring us honest grandchildren. And I pinned my hopes on you! You're a fine-looking man in a steady job, all the girls must fancy you. Now you've blown it all and let her land you with the child!'

Hector was bawling full tilt. Illumination struck Mrs Donaldson.

'A Catholic!' she screeched. 'The mother's a Catholic! All a man needs to do is look at one of those loose-living bitches and they get pregnant! That's what comes of these stupid religious programmes and mixing of creeds! How could you betray us like this? Have you forgotten that your father is a member of the Orange Lodge? What's its name, then?' she growled, with heavy irony. 'Brendan? Michael? Joseph?'

She had worked herself up into a fury. Her face was red and puffy and she kept baring her beautifully symmetrical, un-naturally white false teeth. Looking around her, she grabbed the sweeping brush and began to swing it in wide arcs, advancing menacingly towards Alan and the distraught baby. In one of her lunges she knocked the pulley, and the shadows of the drying sheets set the whole room dancing.

Clutching Hector in both arms, Alan allowed himself to be chased out of the house and on to the landing. As the door banged shut the large glass pane shook in its setting. The chain was put across with an air of finality.

☆

The strange lady took Daniel to an expensive Italian restaurant on Royal Exchange Square, and nibbled at a salad while he tucked into pasta, fish and a glorious pudding. She was prepared to indulge him in everything except his desire for wine. She was strictly teetotal, she informed him, and could not in conscience encourage him to develop a taste for the stuff while in her company.

'Why won't you drink?' he asked, wiping his lips with the napkin. The rich, oily sauce left a deep red stain on it.

'It's a condition I have. Too complicated to explain. Alcohol has a very peculiar effect on me which takes several days to wear off.'

She plagued him with questions about Gerald. Although he was unable to find out what her connection with him had been, she was evidently highly disturbed by the business of the suicide.

'Are you a Catholic?' asked Daniel. 'Do you think he'll go to hell?'

'Enough of that nonsense,' she answered sharply, tutting and shaking her head. 'What bothers me is the waste and the trouble I am likely to get into. I was too late, you see. If I had got there in time things would have been different.'

She was obsessed with the idea that Gerald had written, or wanted to write, poetry. Daniel insisted that all Gerald had ever written was his school homework. This was not the full truth and he grew ill at ease under Euphemia's penetrating gaze. She was not someone he found it easy to lie to. However, when he saw the size of the pudding he was being treated to, it was not fear but gratitude that prompted him to tell her about the jotter. Having started to talk about Gerald's despair he ran into difficulties with the reasons for it and was forced to a halt.

'Don't worry,' she said. 'I know all about you two and it doesn't bother me one bit. What was in the jotter?'

Alarmed, he asked her what she knew, and how, but she merely looked smug and patted her bulky handbag. She was holding it on her knees having just taken out her lipstick and powder puff to check on her appearance. Daniel found it incongruously vain in an ageing widow. She adjusted her hat.

'Other people may be uncomfortable about the two of you being poofs but I have to tell you I blow neither hot nor cold regarding such matters. I have more pressing concerns to think about. Do you write poetry yourself?'

Again that penetrating gaze.

'No, I'm at the art school. I draw.'

'That's not right at all,' she said, with a touch of irritation. Daniel took umbrage.

'I'm very sorry, I'm sure,' he said, 'but I can't transform myself into a genius overnight just to suit you.'

For a moment he thought she was going to get angry. He had the distinct impression that the pink wings adorning her spectacles quivered. Then the cloud passed from her face and she smiled.

'My place for coffee? Do you agree?'

Daniel reflected that he could very happily make a habit of going everywhere in taxis as they sped away from the river and up towards the city's West End. Euphemia had engaged their driver in a discussion about horse racing. She was apparently quite an expert and, although her views surprised the driver, he listened with attention and considerable respect. Daniel kept trying to put the two parts of the day together; waking up, breaking out of the house and seeing Gerald's coffin, then lunch and whatever came next with Euphemia. But they belonged to different worlds. It troubled him that the day of Gerald's burial should have such a festive air. He had left his grief behind at the graveyard. When would it pounce on him again?

Euphemia's flat was an odd but vaguely exciting place. The hall was dimly lit. The sitting room had a glorious view of the sky from a triple bay window. He did not take in the furnishings. He was very tired and flopped into an armchair.

'I have to go and change and make a few phone calls,' she said. 'Then I'll get coffee and we can have a longer chat. Why don't you read something to keep yourself occupied? This, for example.'

She took a book down from the shelves by the window and placed it on the table in front of him. It was poetry. The poor woman clearly had poetry on the brain. He nevertheless felt obliged to flick through it. There were rather attractive line drawings between the various sections. It was in two languages; English on the right, and what looked like German on the left. There were Biblical names in the titles, Latin and French expressions, a poem about Buddha and another about a panther.

His eye fell on the word 'Requiem', given a whole page to itself. A drawing opposite showed a young man in turn-of-the-century dress, who had closed the door of his house and was hurrying down the street with an air of distraction. Daniel turned over. The German meant nothing to him. He read the English opening:

> *Did I really never see you? You*
> *weigh my heart down like a task I can't*
> *get started on because it is so hard.*
> *Now let me try to put you into words,*
> *you who are dead now, dead because*
> *you wanted it so passionately. Did*
> *it bring you the relief that you expected*
> *or was no longer being alive*
> *far from the same as being dead?*

His hands gripped the book. His body had gone quite tense. His eyes sped down the page.

> *Why couldn't you have held out till the weight*
> *became unbearable? That's when it flips*
> *over. Being unadulterated*
> *is what makes it so heavy.*

The knot in his chest tightened so much he thought he would burst open. Another knot formed in his throat as if he had swallowed an apple whole.

> *You got it wrong. Until the end of time*
> *this is what must be said of you. And if*
> *a hero should come who's able to tear*
> *the meaning we take for the face of things*
> *off like a mask, revealing visages*
> *whose frenzied eyes have long gazed noiselessly*
> *at us through concealed holes, this is one face*
> *that will not change: you got it wrong.*

Not only his throat but the whole of his jaw was paralysed. He wanted to raise his shoulders high to free them from some burden and let air into his chest. His eyes were pricking.

> *If a woman had lightly placed her hand*
> *on the beginning of this rage, before*
> *it became violent, or you had met*
> *someone with business, intimate business,*

without a word, when you took your dumb way
to do the deed, or if the way had led
past an active workshop, one where men
were hammering, where day's a simple truth,
if there had been just enough room in your
filled gaze for the image of a struggling
beetle to enter there, illumination
would suddenly have let you read the writing . . .

Daniel was so absorbed that he did not notice the doorbell ringing, did not hear Euphemia's greeting or Cissie's answer as she entered and they both went into the kitchen to set the tray.

I know, you lay in front of it and ran
your fingers down the grooves, as one attempts
to make out the inscription on a grave.
Anything you found that burned you held
as light over these lines. The flame, however,
went out before you understood, perhaps
it was your breath, or else your trembling hand,
perhaps it went out of its own accord
as flames so often do. You never read
the message, and we are too far away,
there's too much pain for us to dare to read.

His eyes filled with tears and the letters swam into incomprehensibility. The knot in his chest burst. He breathed in deeply and gave a cry of absolute despair as Euphemia pushed the door open and came in with the coffee. A moment later Cissie's arms were around him. He smelled her perfume and felt her lips on his cheek as she cuddled him and murmured softly: 'Poor dear, my poor, poor dear.'

☆

Daphne McGlone and Marie Therese McLaughlin surveyed the crowd in the reception room on the first floor of the archbishop's palace. The great hanging chandeliers with their festoons of bulbs had been lit and the partitions that normally divided the space into two were folded back. Under each of the solemn mantelpieces a coal fire blazed which drew clusters of guests from the cocktail party, until the heat got too much for them and they moved off, yielding their places to other coteries.

Red and green streamers, golden stars and strings of cut-out angels enlivened the walls, and were reflected to infinity in the facing series of long mirrors which made the room look even bigger than it was. The light and heat were all the more festive because outside a chill but clear winter day had already waned.

At this time of year it was traditional for the archbishop to give a party for those employed in the archdiocesan administration. A selection of worthies from the parishes under his jurisdiction were also invited along. He normally welcomed his guests at the top of the stairs as they arrived, then gave a formal greeting that set the party on its way. No one had dared to comment on his failure to appear this year. The mystery provoked an undertow of excitement and apprehension that could clearly be detected in the babble of voices.

'I wonder why Cissie hasn't come?' pondered Daphne.

'She's certainly been behaving very oddly lately. She's missed two meetings of the sodality already,' observed Marie Therese.

'Sh-sh-sh!' hissed Daphne in alarm. 'You know we're not even supposed to mention that here!'

Passing by on his way to the window recess, Fraser Donaldson raised his glass and toasted the two ladies politely. He had caught sight of his younger brother Craig and was filled with a glow of tenderness at the thought that another member of the family might be on the point of converting.

'Hi there!' he said. 'Fancy meeting you at such a gathering! Planning to join the fold?'

'I'm here strictly on business,' was the surly answer.

All Craig's attempts to dissuade Mick McFall from coming had proved useless. His boss insisted he was back to normal, although you had only to look at his wandered face and shabby dress to realize he was no longer the full shilling. Mick had so far spent the party roaming from one side of the room to the other in search of the archbishop while Craig watched from a concerned distance.

'Doing some work for the archdiocese?' asked Fraser, trying to be jocular in spite of the rebuff. 'Are we at last going to find out the mysterious nature of this job of yours? Who's your employer?'

Craig nodded in the direction of a small, round figure, bald-headed and dressed entirely in black. Fraser's heart missed a beat.

He had already noticed the man, who inspired an emotion he found no name for. Although the shape was oddly familiar he could not for the life of him remember where they had met.

'Oh look, here's Sandra!' cried Daphne.

Sandra Luperini, a tight grip on her handbag, head bent so as to reveal the full curve of her furry pale peach hat, was advancing grimly towards them from the door.

'What's the matter?' asked Daphne.

'I've just been speaking to Mrs Donnelly,' said Sandra.

'That's who else is missing!' said Marie Therese triumphantly. 'I knew there was something strange about this year's party.'

'Lower your voice,' Sandra muttered through gritted teeth. Marie Therese felt peeved and pursed her lips, but Daphne leant forward obligingly to get the news.

'There is a danger of detection,' said Sandra.

'What?' cried Daphne, and looked around her in alarm. She caught the eye of her parish priest and nodded to him. Luckily he showed no inclination to join their group. He was thick in gossip with Mother Colette of the Holy Shroud. Just as well, thought Daphne. That woman could pick up a whiff of scandal at a distance of a mile.

'I have good news for you!' Fr Feenan, the archbishop's secretary, told Dr Quinn. 'That dreadful business of the virgins is working itself out! Mother Rodelinda has taken matters entirely in hand.'

'But what tactics is she using? The babies must have been born by now. I hope she got a doctor in. I decided to wash my hands of the whole affair, as Mother Genevieve's replacement is far too ruthless for my taste.'

'Not for nothing was she named O'Sharkey when still in the world,' said Fr Feenan. 'But she is a loyal servant of Mother Church. You must forgive the little pun,' he smiled. 'Even we clerics need the relief of a touch of humour from time to time.'

The double doors to the rear of the room opened and the archbishop was ushered in, hobbling on a walking stick. He had aged at least ten years since his ordeal in front of the television cameras. Several of the faithful rushed over and went down on their knees to kiss his ring.

'Mrs Donnelly was terribly upset,' explained Sandra. 'She was even worried someone might have noticed me calling on her. She's been forbidden to attend, you know. Confined to the kitchen and basement until further notice. And the archbishop's secretary has confiscated her keys.'

'Good Lord!' said Daphne. 'What on earth can she have been doing?'

'Perhaps that's why she cancelled our last meeting at such short notice,' said Marie Therese. 'It was most frustrating as I had a particularly large haul to bring in. I stuffed them into a biscuit tin and put it on the top shelf in the kitchen. But it's only a matter of time before they are found.'

There was the sound of breaking glass. Felipe had spotted Fraser at last and had lost no time in making himself known. At the sound of the Basque priest's voice Fraser went white as a sheet and dropped his drink. Felipe dusted him down obligingly, then grabbed him by the lapels and hauled him off in the direction of the gentlemen's toilet.

'The archbishop looks absolutely dreadful,' Bruce Marshall commented to Dr Quinn. He was Alan's immediate boss in the religious programmes division at the BBC. 'Still, after what he's been through I suppose it's hardly surprising.'

'Where's your sidekick?' asked Quinn, eager to change the subject. 'Alan Donaldson, isn't that his name? He never misses one of these dos.'

Marshall frowned.

'He should have been here half an hour ago. Normally he's a very reliable chap. It would take something quite out of the ordinary to keep him away. Mind you, recent events have been putting all of us under unusual strain.' He turned to Fr Feenan. 'Statue still laughing, then? Or has all that ground to a halt since Mother Genevieve got her man?'

'I believe there have been further occurrences,' said Fr Feenan in clipped tones. 'Huge crowds of the faithful still gather at the church each evening. We are currently drawing up plans for a Comic Grotto. It has the potential of raising considerable funds for the archdiocese. You ought to take an interest. It might do something to improve your viewing figures.'

'What happened to your film?' asked Quinn, taking the attack into the enemy camp. 'I understood you had our miracle on celluloid.'

'Most peculiar,' answered Marshall. 'That part of the film was burnt. Over exposed. Far too much light getting into the lens. It's totally unusable.'

'Hello, girls,' said Frances MacAweaney breezily, pushing her way into the circle. As usual, she was horridly overdressed. 'So tell me why yesterday's meeting was cancelled.'

'If you ask me,' hazarded Daphne, ignoring Frances, 'she's being held responsible for the farting. Everybody knows it was because of the food he was being fed.'

'No, it's to do with us,' said Sandra, with chilling emphasis. 'They are on to us.'

'Who?' The news took the wind completely out of Frances' sails.

'The church authorities. Maybe even the police.'

'But why would anyone want to call in the police?' asked Marie Therese. 'No one's been breaking the law!'

Fraser allowed himself to be steered like an automaton. Felipe took him into a cubicle, put the snib on the door and planted a succulent kiss on the astonished man's lips.

'Darling!' he enthused, and there were tears in his eyes. 'I thought I had list you for over!'

He was about to drop his trousers there and then. Fraser made feverish gestures of demur.

'Not here,' he said. 'Later.'

'Where?' implored Felipe. 'Tell me where?'

Mick had succeeded in drawing the archbishop to one side.

'So you can lead us to this woman? To Euphemia O'Farrell?' the priest asked.

'MacFarrigle, your Grace,' said Mick. 'I can. But it will need careful planning.'

'And you are sure she is behind it all?'

'Beyond any shadow of a doubt. I have been at the receiving end of her diabolical magic and, believe me, the archdiocese will have no peace till she is put a stop to.'

'A full-scale exorcism should do the trick.' The archbishop nodded, rubbing his bony hands together. 'Not something I have been involved in for many years now. But then, those are skills one does not lose. My heart is with you, my son. No earthly entity could possibly have caused me the pain and distress that have been my lot in these last months.'

'It's God's work we've been engaged in.' Daphne was indignant. 'The authorities ought to give us a special prize instead of being angry with us.'

'That's as may be, but Mrs Donnelly spoke of receiving stolen goods.'

There was a yelp of fear. Someone had tapped Frances on the shoulder and she nearly jumped out of her skin. It was Berenice McLaverty, determined to enter the circle, arm in arm with Mother Colette. Sandra wrinkled her nose in disgust. There had been long discussions about whether or not Berenice should be invited to join the sodality. Sandra had opposed the initiative, officially because Berenice was untrustworthy, but really because she came from Dennistoun and her presence would lower the tone of the proceedings.

'So what's the big secret, girls?' asked Berenice. 'Any more details about the elopement?'

'In actual fact,' Marie Therese said frostily, 'we were just comparing advent calendars.'

Fr Feenan was having a few words with Craig.

'We have decided to keep this matter strictly private. The inexplicable affair of the . . . er . . . rubber contraptions . . . the contraceptive items, not to mince my words. You do understand, don't you? We will be happy to raise your fee in consideration of your . . . professional discretion. Is my meaning clear?'

Craig's expression was non-committal.

'We feel that, while it may be appropriate to inform the police at some point, the moment has not yet arrived. You see, our poor archbishop's health is not of the best, and the additional shock of renewed publicity . . .'

'One just cannot understand,' said Mother Colette, who had spent several years in England and liked to ape southern idioms, 'how a respectable woman who has devoted her life to God can up and off like that.'

'Especially when she has played a major part in a miracle!' said Daphne. She envied Mother Genevieve all the media coverage and found it hard to believe that any man could offer an acceptable substitute.

'Miracle, my foot,' said Sandra. 'The whole business was set up if you ask me. Who ever heard of a madonna laughing?'

'Even she must have had fun sometimes,' reflected Frances. 'Did you see the photograph in the *Evening Standard*? I think he looks rather handsome.'

'That's the advantage of being a Protestant, isn't it?' said Daphne. 'You can up and off with somebody new when you want to, even if you are a clergyman.'

'No wonder she had problems running her convent,' commented Marie Therese. 'I shudder to think what those girls got up to while she was in charge.'

As Felipe returned from the toilet, with Fraser following close behind, he jogged Dr Quinn's elbow. Fraser hurried on but Felipe stopped to greet the consultant. Quinn had been avoiding him studiously all through the party. Now he felt obliged to enquire after his health.

'That problem you had . . . You haven't been back to see me about it. I take it it's cleared up?'

'Oh, yes,' said Felipe. Twisting his features in an enormous effort, he articulated slowly and with absolute precision, 'De-flow-ered', then lost control and added with a dazzling smile: 'Bless hims gun for God!'

☆

Brenda offered to go on her own in a taxi but Cyril insisted on taking her in his car. He was concerned about the reception she might get at St Pius XXVII's. The least they could do would be to refuse to let her uplift her things. There was a danger that the confrontation might develop into much more than the termination of a brief and uncomfortable lodging arrangement.

She had taken their sudden notoriety very badly. When the photograph of the two of them in Nardini's ice-cream parlour appeared next day under the headline 'Mother Genevieve's Other Miracle' it brought all her guilt and fears tumbling out. She was a fallen woman. She had betrayed her vocation. He was a tempter and had corrupted her against her will. The miracle had deranged her temporarily, she claimed, and she could not be held responsible for what had taken place in the guesthouse the previous afternoon.

Cyril was curiously unaffected. Sex was nothing new to him, but it had never been so good before. From the moment he took Brenda into his arms he was convinced of the basic rightness of their union. His peculiarity — asset or handicap, he was still unsure how to regard it — far from evoking derision or consternation had been welcomed and praised. Their encounter brought home to him how little depended on male prowess and how much on the ability and enthusiasm of the woman. Having at last found one that suited him he was determined to hold on to her. Her reaction struck him as both predictable and thoroughly natural given the circumstances. He did not doubt for a minute that loyalty and persistence would bring their own rewards, cementing their relationship even further than front-page coverage was able to do.

Once she stopped reviling him there came profuse tears and a physical *rapprochement* — a replay of that afternoon, shorter in time but infinitely more refined in execution. Cyril was fascinated by the changes that took place in her on an almost hourly basis. She lost her sexless pallor, her cheeks took on new contours, her skin smelled differently and her gaze grew more searching. When they went on a shopping expedition the next morning to buy her new clothes, she proved remarkably choosy, sensitive to colour, cut and fabric.

What was to become of them? They stayed in the guesthouse for a week, which they packed with discussions of possible new careers, places of residence and sources of income. Determined to resign from the active ministry, he was confident, given his academic background, that lecturing or tutoring work would be forthcoming wherever they might end up. Brenda was confused. She considered hotel management, business studies and counselling by turns without managing to take in the reality of embarking on a new professional life.

She had a bout of agoraphobia during the week. She insisted that people were turning in the street to look at them and spotted newspaper photographers round every corner. Although a spoof interview had been printed in the paper, the media were hungry for more. A woman from a rival publication called at the guesthouse while they were out and left a phone number, which they did not ring. Two days later someone called Donaldson from BBC religious programmes telephoned from Glasgow. He had a pleasant voice and a gentle manner that inspired confidence. He wanted either Brenda or both of them to come into the studios and talk in front of the camera about the miracle and the changes it had brought in their lives. She declined courteously. There was even a letter from *Cosmopolitan* with two free copies of the magazine enclosed. Brenda devoured them in bed at night and fantasized secretly about how she would prefer to be photographed, wishing that she had bought the daring stockings they had lingered over a few days before.

The weather was consistently fine, fresh and wintry, with only occasional rain. On walks along the beach beyond the town they had plenty of opportunity to admire the delicate blues and greys of the December light and the infinite shades of brown and green they elicited from moorland and ploughed fields. Now and again Brenda would talk about her life at St Bridget's. She could not bring herself to share the story of the pregnant virgins with Cyril. He knew she was holding something back but did not press her.

A storm broke on their last night. Neither of them slept. Cyril was adamant that they should stay together but felt it unwise to go to the house he and Amanda had shared. He arranged with an Episcopalian friend for them to have the loan of a flatlet in Partickhill, where they could enjoy whatever anonymity it proved possible to keep. The plan was to move south to Brighton before Christmas. The proximity of London would allow him to assess the chances of remunerative work in the new year. A colleague of Cyril's from training days would be happy to put them up. He had dropped out before becoming a fully fledged priest and now ran a singles bar.

When they reached the parish house at St Pius XXVII's Fr Ryan was not at home. The room Brenda had occupied was locked. He had stripped it of its contents and thrown them into an old suitcase tied round with string.

The housekeeper was wide-eyed and fearful, prompted by her nature to be kind to Brenda but shocked at the recent notoriety. As Brenda was about to go she asked her to hold on, then emerged shamefaced from the kitchen with a battered brown envelope. 'To Mother Genevieve' was printed on it in neat capitals.

'Where did this come from?' asked Brenda.

'I don't know,' said the housekeeper hurriedly. Then, unclasping her hands: 'That is, a woman brought it. Mrs Kerr was her name. I believe she is the cleaning lady at the convent where you used to—'

'And why didn't you give it to me?'

'Well, you see, it went to Father Ryan. And he threw it into the wastepaper basket without opening it. I found it when I was cleaning. Maybe I shouldn't have kept it. He won't be pleased at all if he finds out. But it didn't seem right! After all, letters should go to the people they are addressed to.'

'Thank you so much,' said Brenda quietly, and kissed the woman on the forehead. 'You have been an absolute darling.'

'Who's it from?' asked Cyril as she tore it open.

He was turning the car into the main road. She did not reply at once but peered at the single page, holding it up so that it caught the light of the streetlamps they passed beneath. She finished reading, gave a deep sigh, and sat back.

'I can't leave Glasgow,' she said. 'At any rate, not yet.'

'Why not?'

'It's from my girls. They are being kept prisoners against their will and have appealed to me for help. You and I are going to have to rescue them.'

☆

'Did you remember to bring the cucumbers, Cissie?' asked Derek.

'I've got the cucumbers if you've got the bananas.'

'Why do we need both?' asked Charmaine.

'Bananas are more like the real thing,' said Philip. 'Anyway, it's more fun. They get mushy and everyone can peel them and eat them at the end.'

The subway escalator had broken down and they were toiling their way up the tunnel towards Queen Street Station. Their destination was a pub near the High Street whose name Cissie had never grasped, something like the Highlander's Halt or the Tartan Trews. Preoccupied as she was with Daniel's grief, and the story of him and Gerald, she had had little time to prepare herself for her first episode of HIV awareness activism.

Cissie was not sure that Euphemia was the best person to leave someone as distraught as Daniel with. Euphemia could be gruff and unpredictable, and on occasion showed a surprising insensitivity to other people's feelings. Her reactions were refreshing and often stimulating, but never quite what you would expect. And there was an odd atmosphere in her flat, which attracted Cissie while unsettling her at the same time.

Charmaine turned round and, with characteristic effusion, gave Cissie a hug as they were about to cross the street.

'I think it's really great you're with us,' she said. 'We need an old fogie or two so as people learn to take us seriously.'

Only three weeks ago, Cissie reflected, a lesbian was like a being from outer space. And now here she was arm in arm with one while two others walked in front.

Charmaine's skull was cleanshaven except for a single, intricately plaited pigtail decorated with beads and tassels which curled down from the top of her head, tense as a whip. It had a bell on the end that tinkled gently when she shook her head or laughed. She had rings in her nostrils, two on each side, and loved sticking silver stars across her cheeks. It was all stuff Cissie used to disapprove of enormously. Now she felt safer going on this expedition with such an ebullient, chunkily physical companion. Charmaine would pick up very quickly if there was any trouble in store. And she had a tongue which could reduce the hardest of hard men to blushing silence. Cissie had heard her in action when a drunk disturbed them at the preparatory meeting. Just to listen to her howl abuse was a sex education in itself.

The other two lesbians could hardly have been more conventional. One of them had four children and both worked for the council. Their sober, spartan clothes made Cissie feel positively coquettish. Derek had insisted she dress exactly as she would to go to church and had agreed only with difficulty to let her leave her handbag at home.

'We want you to look as ordinary as possible,' he said. 'The message will get across infinitely better that way.'

Did she have a crush on him? He could not be more than in

his early thirties, so she was indeed old enough to be his mother. He was slim and dark, tall in that fragile way that made her want to protect him from the other boys. He dressed with excellent, unobtrusive taste, preferring yellow and khaki shades. It was a tough job that could not pay particularly well. She had only one explanation for his utter dedication to his work. She had not felt able to discuss this with him. Each time they met she scrutinized him anxiously for signs of illness, but found nothing to confirm her suspicions beyond his slender waist. And that might just be the effect of a careful diet. He neither drank nor smoked, and exercised each day.

'Why is this pub letting us do it?' asked Philip.

'They're not just letting us do it, they're giving a big donation into the bargain,' said Brian.

'The owner lost her brother earlier this year,' said Derek. 'He wasn't gay, but he had come off drugs a while ago. Unfortunately there was a lot of needle sharing. That's how he got the virus. He was married with three kids.'

'She owns several pubs, doesn't she, Derek?' chipped in Charmaine.

'Yes,' he answered. 'I suppose we could call this a trial run. Here we are.'

The place was crammed. They had to push their way between closely packed bodies to reach the bar.

'Free booze,' Brian whispered knowingly into Cissie's ear.

Nobody took any notice of them until Mrs Anderson, the proprietress, rang a ship's bell behind the bar. An expectant silence fell.

'OK, Derek. Do your stuff,' said Mrs Anderson.

Cissie held her breath. How did he manage to keep his voice so steady and calm? Mind you, no one was heckling, as she had feared they might. He stood with his back to the gantry. A small space had cleared in front of him. She watched his delicate hands move to illustrate an idea. It was all familiar to her. She had had to learn the main points herself, in the correct order. She panicked for a moment as she tried to remember exactly what the current wisdom was on oral sex.

At first she did not dare, but as Derek proceeded, and nothing happened, she looked around the circle of faces. They were ordinary Glasgow people. There were several family parties and an unusually large number of women. A group of teenagers in one corner had come from a nearby youth club. But the *habitués* were here, too: older men in cloth caps grasping their half-drunk pints; a businessman or two still wearing suits, who had not made it home for tea; and the local football team relaxing after a workout.

The moment had come.

'This is a condom,' said Derek, holding one up. He tore the package open and took it out. As he did so, according to instructions, the members of the team cheered and tossed condoms into the crowd like confetti at a wedding ceremony. There was jostling and laughter. The listeners entered into the spirit of the thing and vied with each other to catch one.

Now she and Charmaine moved into action. Each had to pick a team of five, including both men and women and as many different sorts of individual as they could find. Chairs were lined up facing one another. The atmosphere in the pub was electric. It was possibly the heat, or else excitement at the competition that was about to take place.

'This,' announced Brian, pointing to his right, 'is the banana eam. The other is the cucumber team. Hand out the fruit and vegetables, folks. Now, if you look carefully, Aileen will demonstrate the way to put a condom on. Then Cissie and Charmaine will get out the stopwatches and we can begin.'

It all struck her as remarkably easy. What were the chances of getting Sandra Luperini or Daphne McGlone involved? This was so much more fun than the sodality. And it didn't have that furtive, secret air about it.

Cissie only hoped things would go as smoothly when they got to the Safe Sex Quiz.

☆

Coming up the stairs to the second-floor landing, Jackie was alarmed to see a light on in her hall. She could not have left it on herself that morning. She never used the ceiling lights, rather the lamp by the phone.

She had called in at the supermarket on the way home. She put down the bags and her briefcase and rummaged in her shoulder bag for the keys. A number of thoughts flashed through her mind. Perhaps it was Alan. She did not like him using his key to get into the flat when she was out. He hardly ever did so, but if it was him, she would have to share the nice microwave Chinese dinner for one she had just bought. She was very hungry, and it was unfair. Then she remembered his phone call earlier in the day. After all the stress at work she was definitely not in an appropriate frame of mind to help him sort out his problems.

'Alan?' she enquired as she opened the door, then dropped the bags inside. It was hardly likely to be robbers at this time in the evening. The lights were on in the kitchen and the sitting room but nobody responded. Her nostrils picked up an unusual smell.

An opened carton of nappies was on the kitchen table. One of the bathroom towels had been spread on it. A saucepan had been used to boil milk and there were white blobs on the linoleum where it had spilled. For a reason she could not articulate she tiptoed into the sitting room. The gas fire was going full tilt. A half-empty plastic bottle was perched on top of a pile of glossy magazines on her coffee table. In front of it, on the sofa, sat Alan, eyes shut fast, with a small baby asleep on his chest, perched like a chimpanzee halfway up a tree.

'Good God!' she said.

Alan awoke with a start. The baby slid down. He caught it in the nick of time. It began to splutter, like an engine having difficulty igniting. Soon it would bawl. That was the strange smell. Jackie hated babies. All at once she saw red.

'What the hell are you doing here?' she shouted, so loudly it astonished even her. 'How dare you come in here and make use of my flat in this way?'

'But Jackie . . .' said Alan, patting the baby on its back. He already knew it was going to be useless.

'Don't try and explain! I don't even want to know. Do you think I so much as care who the mother is? Whoever you've been two-timing me with you can take your troubles there and dump them on her, do you hear? Get that brat out of this house!'

She had left the sitting room, still shouting, and made for the bedroom. She needed to do something physical to calm the rage that had invaded her. She took the single drawer assigned to

Alan from the chest and emptied its contents into an old holdall. Vests, underpants, socks . . . the lot. Next came his shirts, his bedside books and the framed photograph of him on her dressing table.

He was standing at the door with the baby, watching her, every now and then mumbling syllables that never quite got to being words.

'Don't speak,' she said. 'You'll only make it worse. This has been in the offing for a while and you've provided me with an excellent excuse for throwing you out!'

Her voice crescendoed and the last three words were spat into his face as she lugged the holdall from the room and dumped it on the landing. Alan offered no resistance. Still clutching the baby, he went and got the nappies from the kitchen, took a plastic bag with cartons of milk out of the fridge and added them to the growing pile outside the front door.

His compliance made her even angrier. It was insulting that he should let her end their relationship in this way without doing anything to dissuade her. If he had answered back she would have had material to build a scene on. As it was, the whole thing had an air of finality that almost unnerved her.

'There,' she said, once he, the baby and his belongings were all on the landing. She paused lamely with her hand on the doorknob, racking her brain for an especially pithy conclusive phrase. The baby had hushed but its eyes were wide open. Alan's, she now saw, were filled with tears. She tutted impatiently and slammed the door.

The light in the hall went out. Alan's cheeks were wet.

'Well, Hector,' he said in wavering tones, 'looks like it's just you and me from now on.'

FIVE

By eight o'clock Daniel was hungry again, so Euphemia sent out for a fish supper. The concept of having a fish supper delivered to your door was new to Daniel. He could not think of any shop in the neighbourhood that offered a service of this kind. Nevertheless the doorbell duly rang, and shortly afterwards he was presented with a deliciously flaky piece of haddock in batter flanked by crisp, dry chips, all set out neatly on a tray. True to her beliefs, Euphemia had no alcohol in the house but, as a special concession, a bottle of Beck's arrived along with the meal. She opened his beer and provided a glass and there was a generous dollop of tomato sauce at the side of his plate. Euphemia had no appetite herself and was content with a slice of white bread and a cup of tea.

Conversation was difficult. Daniel had calmed down before Cissie left, and immediately felt ashamed at having let his feelings get the better of him. There was a severity about Euphemia that did not encourage outpourings. He could not think what to say to her and she was equally nonplussed. When he offered to leave she looked startled, then informed him that he was expected to stay for the night.

'You can phone your parents tomorrow,' she told him. 'Let them stew for a bit.'

She tried asking more questions about Gerald but it just made him extremely upset, so she gave up, not without a sigh of frustration. Daniel understood that it was not really him she was concerned about. He decided he was there under false pretences, and this conviction, along with the guilt which was an important part of his feelings about Gerald, did little to help the evening pass more smoothly. They watched two soap operas on television. Euphemia was fascinated by the situations, commenting aloud again and again in a way that irritated him. In any case he associated soap operas with family evenings in

Bishopbriggs and did not take kindly to having to sit through them while he was away. When the second one ended she ordered him to have a bath. He was sent off to bed once he was dry.

An old carpet with a flowery pattern was not big enough to hide the dirty brown linoleum of the bedroom floor. There was a narrow window and the dark mahogany cupboard had a mirror on its central door. She gave him a pair of flannel pyjamas, with a soft belt he had to knot at the waist. They had blue and white stripes and were faded from much washing and ironing. He wondered if they had belonged to her husband. Euphemia's husband was a figure he did not find it easy to visualize.

He fell asleep at once, then woke towards midnight. As he had feared earlier in the day, all the pain of the burial started coming back. He wanted to give it physical expression but was afraid even to cry out in case he should disturb his host. If he had been at home he could at least have listened to his Walkman. Then an odd thing occurred.

The curtains on the window did not quite reach to the floor. Light from outside, presumably a streetlamp, penetrated between and under them, casting a distorted rectangle on to the wall next to the door. As Daniel watched, the points of light at the corners of the rectangle grew more brilliant. Then they came away from the wall and began to move around the room. At first their movements were entirely haphazard, but soon he realized that they were creating patterns like those of skilled dancers moving across a ballroom floor. Each point divided, then divided again until a whole company of pinpricks of light was travelling to and fro across the bedroom, forming figures that held for a moment, then dissolved, yielding their place to others. He'd seen something of the kind on computer screens that had been left idle. This was more exciting because it was three-dimensional. The phenomenon was accompanied by sounds, beginning as a low humming which broke up into different elements just like the dividing points of light. The harmonies they made reminded him of electronic music, and had a comforting, powerfully hypnotic effect. Before he knew it he was fast asleep again.

When he woke up it was daylight. His watch had stopped at ten to three though he guessed it must be after eight. He pulled his clothes on and made the bed, folded the pyjamas and laid them neatly on top of the quilt, then ventured into the hall. Euphemia, he supposed, was still asleep. He was unsure whether to enter the kitchen, which he suspected was the last door on the left, when a voice coming from the sitting room stopped him in his tracks. It was a high, whining voice. For a reason he could not explain, he felt sure it was not human. When Euphemia answered, then burst out laughing, he drew near the closed door to eavesdrop.

'Irresponsible, that's what I call it. It's all very well you being invested with high office but you have to show yourself equal to the task. How could you possibly leave me and my unit to face that without warning us?'

All Euphemia did was to laugh. This made the voice even angrier.

'Can you imagine what it was like? That great thing coming at us again and again in a confined space, like a live battering ram? And all of a sudden this flood of smoky white liquid with thousands of little creatures swimming desperately in it, competing to get there first? Not to mention all the juices before it arrived, sending us slithering up and down. It was impossible to get a grip anywhere. And when it all got under way we had to dart backwards and forwards for an hour and more, keeping to the sides to avoid being hit!'

'Put it all down to experience!'

'I certainly will not. You left us there deliberately for your own entertainment and nothing else. Our business is playing jokes on others, not having them played on us!'

Struck with remorse at his indiscretion, Daniel knocked and opened the door. The voice broke off. Euphemia was standing by the window. When he turned to the fireplace, for a split second the image of a creature resembling a faun was imprinted on his retina. It was about four feet high and furry from the waist down. There were tufts of dark hair at the tips of its pointed ears and it had a strikingly alive tail that rose in an elegant S-curve from between its buttocks.

Daniel blinked and it disappeared. All that remained was a majestic ginger tabby cat, rather larger than normal, which licked the back of one paw, rubbed its muzzle absent-mindedly, then stared lazily at him as if questioning his right to exist.

'Time for breakfast,' said Euphemia brusquely. 'Pay no attention to him. Sometimes he's more trouble than he's worth.' And she waltzed past, leading the way to the kitchen. The hem of her gorgeous patterned silk dressing gown fluttered behind her as she went.

When breakfast was over she instructed him to phone home.

'There'll be nobody there,' he protested.

'I think you'll find you're wrong,' she said, and left him to it.

To his surprise his mother answered. If she was worried about where he had spent the night, she did not say so. Her tones were businesslike although he detected the anxiety and tension behind them. He was not to return home. She had packed everything he would need for the time being into two suitcases. She would pick him up in the city centre at midday and drive him to Aunt Maeve's in Falkirk, where he was to stay until further notice.

'Who's Aunt Maeve?' Euphemia asked.

'Actually, she's a great aunt. Maeve McCooey, a sister of my mother's mother. We see her at Christmas time and usually hear from her at birthdays, but she's hardly close to the family.'

'They're sending you there to keep you out of harm's way.'

'Until they come up with something better, yes. What am I going to do for money? I have to get in and out to the art school.'

'There are plenty of trains. And they'll see you have everything you need. You won't have any cause to make trouble. In so far as they can they want to keep things resolutely normal. What's this woman like?'

'She's a spinster. I think she's quite well off. She works in hospital administration or the social work department, or something. She lives on her own in a big terraced house.'

'And is she religious?'

'I presume she is. I haven't the faintest idea.'

Daniel sniggered. It struck him as comical that Euphemia should worry about whether Aunt Maeve went to mass or not.

She looked at her watch.

'Well, you'd better be going. I'll phone for a taxi.'

She scribbled a number on the back of a supermarket receipt.

'This is so you can get in touch if you need me. Be sure to call before you come,' she added, with special emphasis.

'Why?'

'You might not find me in. Let's just say I'm not always at home to visitors.'

☆

'Keep singing, Fatima,' said Juliet.

'But I'm exhausted. I can't keep it up any longer.'

'You have to. Go back to "Mother of sinners, hope of the hopeless." I like that bit,' said Viviana.

'We need you to cover the noise. Anyway, we're nearly finished. Have you got a grip on it, Viviana?'

'They'll be amazed at us having turned so pious all of a sudden,' giggled Viviana.

'It's freezing in here,' said Fatima. 'Every night for the last three we've had the window open till past midnight. Can't you file faster?'

'Shut up and sing,' said Juliet. 'They're due in about twenty minutes.'

She worked away with an intensity that amazed even herself, given what they had been through in the last two months.

'Time's running out. We'll have to pull it.'

Juliet and Viviana set their feet against the lower bars and tugged. Fatima came up and peered over their shoulders.

'Refuge of sinners,' she moaned, 'ivory tower . . .'

With a gasp the other two broke the final spar. A neat rectangle came loose at the centre of the grid, leaving just enough space to put a head and shoulders through. Juliet stood back and surveyed her handiwork with pride.

'And they haven't noticed a thing,' she said.

'We're not out yet,' admonished Viviana.

'And what's going to happen to Mrs Kerr?' asked Fatima. 'Won't they find out she smuggled the file to us?'

Juliet hushed her. There was a wall about seven feet high at the bottom of the garden. A streetlamp in the lane shone straight on to the top of it, and she could see the end of a ladder hovering to and fro like the antennae of an insect.

'They're here.'

Brenda wondered if anyone had heard the engine, then realized she had heard nothing herself. The lane was a steep slope, and Cyril had switched the motor off at the top, allowing the minibus to edge down gradually until it stopped just outside the convent. He was worried that even the squeaking of brakes might attract unwanted attention. Brenda was checking that they had everything ready on the back seat. There were shawls for the mothers. They had brought three carry cots with abundant blankets, and she had made up bottles just before they set off. It was too much to ask for that the infants should remain asleep all through the escape – the warm milk would be useful in quieting them. Cyril was now mounting the first ladder awkwardly, with a second one over his shoulder, which he let down into the garden.

He called to Brenda. They had agreed that he would stay in the lane at the wheel of the minibus, respecting the sanctity of the place. She knew every nook and cranny in the wall and every corner of the garden. She was wearing jeans and trainers and was delighted at her own agility as she scrambled over. The place gave her a strangely proprietorial feeling, as if it were still her convent.

On solid earth again, she flashed the torch in the agreed signal. The window had been drawn wide up. A dark figure was struggling through. She got there just in time to catch Viviana as she fell out. Viviana got to her feet and they kissed decorously. Brenda pointed to the ladder at the bottom of the garden then turned to help Fatima.

'I'm stuck!' she wailed. 'I've changed my mind! I don't want to go! It's a sin!'

But with Juliet pushing vigorously from behind and Brenda pulling in front she had little choice. In the tussle the lower part of the iron grid, which was very old, came away from its socket in the crumbling stone sill and fell to the ground with a resounding clang. Brenda climbed through to help Juliet with the babies. Instead of waiting, Fatima careered down the garden, imagining the entire Catholic hierarchy on her heels.

The room was cold and dark. The only light came through the broken bars. Brenda could not see Juliet's face.

'My dear,' she asked, 'where are the children?'

To her astonishment Juliet burst into tears. Brenda hugged her. The feel and smell of the fabric of Juliet's habit were alien. It all belonged to another life. Brenda had come such a long way.

'What has happened? Tell me!'

Juliet was bent double with grief.

'They took them away from us! Two weeks ago!'

All at once she and Brenda were blinded. Mother Rodelinda had thrown the door open and switched on the overhead light.

'Just what I was waiting for!' she growled. 'Brenda MacCafferty back in town!'

Brenda drew herself up.

'Philomena O'Sharkey,' she said with dignity. 'Our paths have crossed once more.'

'You God forsaken daughter of Eve! Miserable whore and sinner, what new mischief have you come to wreak upon us? Give me back my girls! *Retro Satana!*'

The Mother Superior grabbed hold of Juliet but got a savage kick in the shins for her pains. Covered by Brenda, the young mother scampered to the window and made her bid for freedom.

'I'll get the police on to you! I should have known you couldn't keep your nose out of this mess once it was started!'

She had taken Brenda by the shoulders and was shaking her vigorously like a doll. Brenda was alarmed at the other woman's strength but her presence of mind did not fail her.

'Don't try and pull the wool over my eyes, Philomena! It's you who have to fear the police, not me! You wouldn't dare call them in after what you have subjected these girls to!'

It was developing into a full-scale hand to hand. Brenda hugged Mother Rodelinda tightly like a wrestler, thrusting her head into the crook of the other woman's neck in case she tried to bite.

'Where are the babies?' she hissed, squeezing hard. 'What have you done with the babies?'

But it was dangerous to hang on. Already other nuns were gathering at the door, uncertain whether to pitch in or not. Brenda lifted her right knee and jabbed it as energetically as she could into Mother Rodelinda's stomach. Her opponent sagged in her arms.

Almost before she knew it Brenda was out in the garden. She could hear Cyril revving the engine of the minibus. The ladder behind her fell to the ground as she turned at the top of the wall to look back. Lights were on all over the building and a nun was rushing to the door in the back wall, brandishing the key.

'Forget the ladders!' called Cyril. 'Jump in!'

Another pair of nuns appeared in the glare of the headlights at the end of the lane but jumped to one side as the minibus swerved round the corner. He drove straight through red traffic lights on to Great Western Road.

✩

Alan was getting a dressing-down from Bruce Marshall.

'I'm sorry, but your behaviour is totally unacceptable. Half the time you're not here when you're supposed to be. If it so happens that we're in luck, and you do turn up, you've got that bloody baby with you. The only way we could get you on camera yesterday was to persuade the production assistant to hold the little mite. And then you kept rushing over between takes to make sure he was OK. What on earth do you think you're playing at? And come to think of it, who's got him now?'

He had sat Alan down in the armchair before starting, and delivered his tirade walking up and down between the desk and the window. He paused, towering over Alan. Marshall was a big man.

'Your secretary.'

Marshall snorted.

'And you fell asleep during the team conference yesterday. Not once, but twice. I'm not a vain man, but when a team member starts snoring during a presentation it does get to me. If you would even come clean and tell us what this is all about! I take it the baby is yours?'

Silence.

'Look, Alan' – Marshall patted him on the shoulder in a comradely way – 'I know you were going out with that graphics woman Jackie. But it can't be hers because everyone knows she hasn't been pregnant. And the news on the West End grapevine is that she has chucked you anyway. Either you were two-timing her or you're carrying the can for another guy.'

He sat on the edge of his desk and tried softening his approach.

'Who's the mother, now? At least tell me that. She must be quite a girl for you to take on childminding on top of what is, theoretically at least, a full-time job.'

Alan shrugged hopelessly. 'And if I told you I'd no idea?'

'I wouldn't believe you.'

'Well don't then.'

Time to get hard, Marshall decided.

'You're here on a contract, my man, and at present you are breaking its terms. You don't have a job for life. I presume you're aware of that. And anywhere else you try to go they'll want to know from me how you made out here.'

Alan bit his lip resolutely. He was not going to be moved. In any case, there was nothing he could do. He had no concessions to make.

'I've decided to put you on half time. And half time means half pay. When you come in, no baby. Is that clear? Find yourself a crèche or something.'

Sullenly, avoiding eye contact, Alan got up and straightened his jacket.

'If that's how you want to play it—'

'That's how,' cut in Bruce. 'You certainly don't make things easy for yourself. Or for me. You can go.'

Once outside the office, Alan looked at his watch. He had no time to lose. This was the last day. His last chance. Marshall's secretary was fascinated by Hector. It didn't matter that he had dribbled all over the pile of letters she had typed that morning. She was reluctant to see him go. He was infinitely better company than her boss.

'Where are you off to?' she asked as Alan fitted him into the sling.

'The Copthorne Hotel. I'll explain later.'

'Or maybe not,' she said, as he disappeared into the lift.

Ten minutes later he was at the reception desk.

'I'll pass on your message,' the man behind it said. 'But I don't see why they should pay any more attention today than they did yesterday or the day before.'

'It's still worth trying,' said Alan good-humouredly, and took a seat.

He got ready to feed Hector. All this waiting around would

have been a lot more tedious if he hadn't had the baby with him. Suddenly he was conscious of being watched. He looked up and his eyes met those of an attractive, snazzily dressed young woman. He had noticed her on the previous days. Presumably she was staying there on business. She didn't look as if she came from Glasgow.

Alan was a good-looking man and used to finding women's eyes upon him. Now that he invariably had Hector with him he couldn't flirt in the usual nonchalant way. There was something in this woman's attitude that irked him: amusement, superiority, he could not tell which. He pretended to ignore her until Hector was sucking away contentedly, then looked up again. She had come over and was standing next to him.

'You're so New Age it's just not true,' she said in a London accent. 'But the baby's a real star.'

She settled her bag strap on her shoulder and sauntered off up the stairs. Alan wondered if Hector would inherit his obsession with women's legs, then had to remind himself that the baby was not his son and would inherit nothing, not even his good looks.

Five minutes later the phone at the desk rang. The receptionist called Alan over.

'Looks like you're in luck,' he whispered, pointing to the receiver.

'Hello?'

'You're Alan Donaldson, right? The guy who's been hanging round waiting to do an interview with Ceòl? This is Amy Sudbury, their manager. Can you come upstairs right now?'

'Me and the baby?'

'Yes, you and the baby,' the woman confirmed drily.

It was his break. The group had been furious about the last feature they had done. Now *New Musical Express* was pressing for material but the band would only agree if they had full control of what was printed and could choose the writer.

'You look as if you'd fit the bill,' she said, offering him a cigarette.

He refused. She lit her own and handed him a list of questions.

'Tomorrow morning at seven?'

'Fine,' he said and hesitated. 'What about payment?'

'We're worried about the content,' she said impatiently. 'Money's not an issue. Take whatever you can get the *NME* to give you. Here's the number to ring. Just give them my name. We've got the pics already.'

'So you managed to do business at last,' observed the man at the desk when he got down. 'Pity about the baby. He must really cramp your style.'

'Not at all,' said Alan. He kissed the top of Hector's head. 'In actual fact, he brings me luck.'

☆

Daniel had been staying with Maeve for over a week when she woke up with a start in the middle of the night. A woman's voice had been calling her in a dream. She had the impression that something was urgently wrong. She looked at the figures on her digital alarm clock. It was nearly four. The sense of danger had not left her.

She switched on the light, put on her dressing gown and went out on to the landing. The door of Daniel's room was open and the light in the hall at the bottom of the stairs was on. Her heart was beating faster than usual. Her senses were strained to breaking point. She padded softly downstairs in her slippers. A faint noise came from the kitchen. It might just have been him breathing.

When she went in, he was sitting at the other side of the table. The shards of a broken wine goblet were scattered across it. Both his sleeves were rolled up. He had stretched his left arm out on the table so as to expose the wrist. In his right he was holding a sharp dagger of crystal. He looked as if he had been sitting in that position for some time.

Maeve suddenly felt absolutely calm, the kind of calm that came over her on the very few occasions when she confronted violent situations in her work. He looked up and smiled.

'Sorry about the glass,' he said.

His hand slumped and the piece of crystal dropped on to the table. Maeve leant over and picked it up gingerly between thumb and forefinger. She ran the thumb of her other hand softly across his wrist, with its thin blue veins. It was like brushing the strings of a musical instrument. He had not hurt himself. She tossed the shard into the bucket then got a brush to sweep up the remaining fragments.

'I'll make some tea,' she said.

He sat there unmoving. In the silence the rushes of heat through the electric kettle were deafening, like waves breaking intermittently on shingle. Then it erupted, rattling its plastic lid until the cut-out switch was activated. Maeve did everything exactly as she normally would. She heated the pot, emptying it into the sink, then left the tea to brew and set cups, saucers and spoons, milk and sugar on the table. She filled the cups.

'Milk?' she asked.

He had not been there long enough for her to know how he preferred it.

'Milk and one sugar,' he said.

She stirred her own cup and put the cosy over the pot.

'It was a dream,' said Daniel. 'A dream about Gerald. Did they tell you about Gerald?'

'No,' said Maeve. 'They told me practically nothing.'

'He was in my year at school. We were lovers. I've been going to public toilets since I was twelve. He was innocent. He killed himself. If I hadn't touched him he wouldn't have died.'

There was a pause.

'So what about the dream?' said Maeve.

'I get it regularly. Not every night, but nearly. It's very simple, really.' He looked at her as if to apologize. 'He wants me there. Wants me with him. I suppose it's a sort of seduction. Only he's dead. So that's the only way I can get to him. The thing is' – his gaze met hers again – 'I can't do it.' Tears trembled in his eyes. 'I just can't do it.'

Another silence. Maeve got up.

'Wait here,' she told him. 'Don't move. There's something I want to show you.'

She came back carrying a cardboard box, with beautiful Paisley pattern paper on its sides and lid. It was done up with a ribbon. She put it down on the table and undid the ribbon, then took out four photographs and placed them in front of him. They were upside down for her but the right way up for him.

The first photograph showed two young women in a park.

Daniel could not tell the exact period. From their dress he would have said it was just after the war. It was not Glasgow. The weather in the photograph was very sunny. The two women looked happy. He realized the one on the right was Maeve.

In the next photograph they were in a boat, holding on to each other and laughing. The oar had slipped from the other woman's hand and Maeve was trying to retrieve it for her.

'What's her name?' he asked.

'Jocelyn,' said Maeve.

The other two were of Jocelyn. In one she was standing beside a white man in front of a hut. The people gathered round them presumably belonged to the tribe that had built the hut. The trees could have been palms, he was not sure. The last was a photograph of a painting. She was in a stiff pose and the likeness was not particularly good but still close enough for her to be identified.

'What happened?' he asked.

'I met her on holiday in Brighton. That was in nineteen sixty-one. I was twenty-five and she was twenty-eight. She was an anthropologist. She came from a very brainy family and had been to Cambridge. I moved down to England to be with her. Each year she went off on a field trip and wrote me letters. I missed her but I loved it too because of the letters. I've kept them all.'

She gestured towards the box. Daniel reached in and took out a necklace of strange, coloured pods and what might have been a comb, carved with intricate designs that resembled animals.

'In nineteen sixty-six she went to a Melanesian island. She got sick and died there. I wasn't supposed to go to the funeral because the family didn't know about me. But I did. I met the man she had been meant to marry. He couldn't understand why she kept putting him off. Then I came back to Scotland.'

'Has there been anyone else?'

She shook her head.

'Fancies, but nothing serious. I wouldn't have wanted anything else. Not appropriate for a woman in my position in Falkirk. And the kinds of thing that are available here don't hold much attraction for me, anyway. I nearly got married.' She laughed. 'But I stopped myself just in time.'

She put the objects and photographs back in the box and tied the ribbon again.

'More tea? And what about someone else for you?'

Daniel smiled.

'I wish I could be like you. It's so noble. I'm not made that way. There's someone after me.' His eyes twinkled. 'He's from my old school. His name's Colm. Nothing's really happened, more's the pity. I find myself wondering if it ever will.'

She waited. Clearly there was more to come.

'When I get the train each morning, there's a man I really like. He's older than me, thirty or so. Red hair and blue eyes. Lots of freckles. Slim, sensitive hands. He ought to be a pianist. Dressed in a dark suit and tie. It's too bourgeois for words.'

'And has anything happened?'

'I did my best, though there's not much you can do in twenty minutes on a crowded train. I tried to catch his eye, and he certainly noticed me. He's gay, no doubt about that. I followed him out of the station and down the street for a bit one morning. But I could see he was getting edgy so I gave up. Now he's stopped getting the train.'

Maeve drank the last of her tea. Things felt close to normal again. She leant across and touched Daniel's wrist with the tip of her index finger.

'We need help with this. I'll see what I can do.'

Daniel was suspicious.

'What sort of help do you mean?'

'Don't worry, it'll be confidential. And it won't come cheap. But that's not a problem. I'm happy to pay, at least for the time being.'

And so it was that, ten days later, Daniel rang a bell on the top floor of a close in Hyndland. A middle-aged man, small and rather hunched, with very thick spectacles, opened the door.

'Mister MacFarlane?' Daniel asked.

'That's me. Come in.'

Daniel was ushered upstairs to a warm attic room with a coombed roof. He had been afraid he might find the man sexually attractive but luckily he didn't.

'Where do you want to begin?' the man asked when they were

both settled in their armchairs. Daniel noticed a family of teddy bears gathered underneath the window.

'I'll begin with the toilets,' he said.

☆

'I wanted to have a word with you beforehand,' explained Fr Feenan. 'I'm most concerned about our archbishop. He hasn't been normal for several months now. And I have doubts about the wisdom of this latest exploit.'

Craig sat silent. Mick leant over and tapped his finger on the desk.

'Have no doubts, Father. Take it from me. She has to be confronted. You have no idea what she is like or what havoc she is capable of wreaking.'

Feenan turned to Craig.

'How many details about this incredible woman can you confirm? None of what I've heard so far fits together. I can't make sense of it.'

'The thing I can confirm is about the disappearing tenement,' said Craig, unwillingly but resolutely. 'One day it's there, one day it's not. And that's where she lives.'

They all got to their feet as the double doors opened and the archbishop shuffled in on his walking stick. His head was permanently bowed now and it was a notable effort for him to raise it and greet each of them in turn. He sat in a comfortable chair by the grand fireplace. The others arranged themselves around him.

'You've heard the latest?' he asked Fr Feenan, who nodded. 'So you will understand how urgent the situation has become.'

'Latest what?' asked Craig.

'The statue,' said the archbishop. 'It's started telling dirty jokes. One at two forty-five yesterday afternoon and another this morning at ten o'clock. There was a huge crowd.'

'Is there no end to this woman's powers and to her malice?' cried Mick, clutching his hands to his head.

'I'm still concerned about the position of the Jesuits,' Feenan insisted.

The archbishop merely tutted.

'Why won't you let me involve Gutierrez?'

'Don't be a fool!' rasped the archbishop. 'That man was sent to spy on me. He is intent on our destruction. I do not doubt for a moment that his orders are to get rid of me. And I will not let him do it, do you hear, I will not!'

The sick man half rose from his chair, eyes ablaze, then slumped back once more.

'He already has that business of the condoms on us. He will make ample use of it when the right time comes.'

'Did you know we had decided to sacrifice Mrs Donnelly?' Feenan asked Craig. 'The police are questioning her at this very moment. It was necessary to find a scapegoat. The affair could not be hushed up any longer. I, for one, cannot imagine that the items were stored there without at least her passive connivance.'

'Poor Mrs Donnelly!' moaned the archbishop. 'Why should she have to pay for MacFarrigle's crimes?'

'Let us fix a time and a date and make plans,' said Mick impatiently.

'We are waiting for Father Flynn,' said the archbishop.

'That is exactly what bothers me,' said Fr Feenan. 'One Jesuit is involved while the other is excluded. Have you forgotten the motto of the secular clergy? "Never trust a Jesuit." Do we really believe we can reveal to one what is concealed from another? Can it be possible that they are not collaborating? It is in their nature to work in tandem.'

A knock on the door introduced the headmaster of St Ignatius' and established a more formal atmosphere. With him was his deputy, Alphonsus MacAweaney, Frances' husband, a Latin master and an active leader of prayer groups throughout the city. Fr Flynn was businesslike and cut discussion to a minimum. He dealt directly with Mick and Fr Feenan, practically ignoring the archbishop, who sat rigid throughout, head bent, one arm extended to perch precariously on his walking stick.

'First of all, something has to be done about the statue. I have taken that in hand myself, naturally with the approval of his Grace. Secondly, I have decided to be present at the exorcism. Demonic activity on this scale is a rare occurrence in these latter days, and I do not wish to miss an opportunity to gather invaluable material. I will be accompanied by four school-masters and six prefects.'

'We are agreed that it would be unwise to involve females in this work,' said Mr MacAweaney. 'Susceptible as they are to the arts of the evil one. The prefects will carry thuribles and holy water. The schoolmasters will bear the sacred relics.'

'Splendid!' cried Mick, and clapped his hands.

The whole scenario was sending shivers down Craig's spine. 'Relics of what?' he butted in.

'The sacred relics of the Blessed Williamina MacLeod, virgin and traffic warden,' said Fr Feenan, joining his hands piously at the mention of her name. 'This month the entire diocese has been engaged in novenas for her canonization. She was born in Stornoway and brought up a member of the United Free Presbyterian Church. It was not until she settled in Glasgow in her early fifties that she converted. She is one of our greatest victories over the spirit of Calvin.'

'The Blessed Williamina donated her internal organs to charity,' said Mr MacAweaney. 'The remaining parts of her body were distributed among the faithful as relics. In these godless times the West of Scotland urgently requires a female saint to set alongside John Ogilvie. I firmly believe that Williamina is our strongest candidate.'

'That is yet another reason for putting a stop to Euphemia MacFarrigle,' said the archbishop. 'These dreadful events have seriously damaged our prestige in Rome. There will not be the slightest prospect of a canonization until we are seen to be fully back in control.'

'So when is it to be?' Mick asked eagerly.

'Father Flynn and I have drawn up detailed plans,' said Mr MacAweaney. 'Two days from now we will assemble for prayers at the university chaplaincy at ten o'clock in the evening. It is to be opened specially for the occasion. Everyone must wear dark clothes and observe the utmost discretion. Then we will proceed to Otago Street. His Grace will meet us in his limousine at the front door. Everything we need, including the relics, is to be stored in the boot. All that will remain will be for us to mount the stairs and confront the abomination.'

☆

'It's bitterly cold out there,' said Cissie, dusting the snowflakes off her coat before she let Cyril take it. 'We always get a spell of freezing weather in January.'

Brenda came out of the sitting room into the hall to meet her. She was carrying a baby. They looked at each other.

'You've changed,' said Cissie.

'So have you,' said Brenda. 'Such a lot of things have happened. Come in and sit down.'

The flat itself was bare and comfortless but warm. The litter of caring for small children scattered around the rooms made it less desolate. A young woman with close-cropped hair was nursing a second infant. She was introduced to Cissie as Juliet.

'So where are the others?' Cissie asked.

'This is Viviana's baby I'm holding,' said Brenda. 'She's through in the small bedroom getting some rest. And that one is Fatima's,' she added, pointing to the child in Juliet's arms.

'And what about yours?' Cissie asked Juliet.

The young woman said nothing, then burst into tears. She passed the baby to Cyril.

'I'm so sorry if I've spoken out of turn,' said Cissie.

'Don't worry, my dear. The situation is really quite complicated,' said Brenda. 'Why don't you go and make tea? Then I can fill you in.'

By the time Cissie brought things through, Juliet had stopped crying.

'Fatima's gone back to the convent,' she said. 'The little rat couldn't stand being away from Mother Rodelinda. She evidently enjoys being punished and can't wait for more. So her baby is going to be adopted.'

'Viviana is trying to decide what to do,' added Brenda. 'For the immediate future she's going to stay with her parents in Cheshire. To cope with leaving the convent and becoming a single mother at one and the same time is rather a tall order. Her parents have been very good about the whole affair. It will give her time to rest and recuperate and make plans.'

'But how did you find them?' asked Cissie.

'Oh, that was perfectly easy. Two babies were reported found in different parts of the city on exactly the same day last November. They had been taken into care. Viviana and

Fatima identified them at once and we were able to get them back.'

Cissie looked at Juliet but said nothing.

'That's the whole tragedy,' said Juliet. 'A man brought a third baby into Maryhill police station that very morning. They refused to help him and he took it away again without leaving a name or address.'

'The sergeant didn't even remember the make or registration number of his car,' said Brenda.

'I can tell you something,' put in Cyril, now that Fatima's baby was asleep, 'he's been given a very hard time by his superiors. That's not a mistake he'll make again in a hurry.'

'And how did Mother Rodelinda do it? When did she steal them?'

'That's the thing,' mused Cyril. 'It's hard to conceive how she could spirit them away and dump them in three different cars in far-flung parts of the city without having help or without anybody noticing. If you ask me, another agency has been at work.'

'And what do you plan to do?'

'We've tried everything,' said Juliet. 'Advertisements in the daily newspapers, the social work department, children's homes . . . It has all been absolutely useless. We're at our wit's end.'

'But I have one more idea,' said Brenda brightly. 'I've been thinking it over for the last few days and my mind is made up.'

She turned to Cyril.

'Where did we put the number of that man Donaldson from the BBC?'

☆

It was ten o'clock on Saturday night and Knight's Bar was chock-a-block. The circle Daniel was part of had to draw closer and closer together. The atmosphere in the pub had become stifling, although none of them was smoking. Canned music was blaring from all sides and you practically had to shout to make yourself heard or else put your mouth right up to the ear of the person you were speaking to.

Daniel didn't really mind. He found the conversation tedious. Most of Colm's friends were singers. The Christmas season was not long past and they were still comparing notes about carol services, complaining about unheated churches, bitching about different conductors and passing comments on what the front row of sopranos had been wearing.

He was getting more and more interested in landscapes, a development that did not encounter favour with his tutor at the art school. That afternoon in Falkirk he had been working up some outdoor sketches, adjusting and trying to balance the volumes of hills and clumps of trees. His mind kept wandering back to them. He could feel the pencil in his hand, and again and again lost the thread of the conversation he was meant to be taking part in.

It was good of Colm to take him out at weekends. His pocket money barely ran to one round of drinks and he was only able to stay on this late because Colm would put him up overnight. This was the fourth time running they had ended up in Knight's Bar on a Saturday. Daniel was not sure whether they were 'an item', as Colm's friends called it, or not. Colm lived with his mother and Daniel slept in a separate bedroom, except on one occasion when Mrs Harkins was away visiting her daughter-in-law in Surrey. Daniel had spent the evening on tenterhooks and breathed a sigh of relief when in the end Colm invited him to share his bed. But the older man lay absolutely rigid on his back and would not let Daniel cuddle him or even come close. All he got was the chastest of goodnight kisses and a pep talk. The gist of which was that Colm loved Daniel very much and was delighted to have him there, but that as a practising Catholic he could only acknowledge his homosexual feelings, not do anything about them. Having said this Colm turned his back and soon fell asleep. Daniel found the whole business all the more bizarre because he was absolutely sure Colm had a hard on. He lay awake for an hour or so trying to puzzle it out then, when he was sure Colm was sleeping soundly, jerked himself off as discreetly as he could. Otherwise he feared he would lie there awake all night.

'Why don't you come and sing with us at St Ignatius'?' asked one of the circle. 'If your speech is anything to go by you have a lovely voice and, after all, you are an old boy.'

Daniel sipped at his beer and looked sheepish. Hadn't the

man heard about Gerald and all the scandal? He turned to scan the bar and his eyes fell on an unusual but familiar figure ordering a drink. She was smart, in a rather haphazard way. She had a red cap and a long leather coat which hugged her slender hips becomingly. Boots and a string of fake pearls completed the outfit. When she got her gin and tonic and surveyed the crowd, he saw with a start that it was Euphemia, heavily made up and wearing garish lipstick but still looking about fifteen years younger. She smiled and beckoned him over.

Fraser was pouring his troubles out to Malcolm in another corner of the pub.

'Three times a night? How can you cope?'

'I can't. Don't you see how wasted away I am? I tell you, he's insatiable.'

'Thank God it's all clandestine and you don't get to see each other that often. Why don't you shop him?'

'I couldn't do that! I'd lose my job. And anyway, I'm not sure I want to.'

Fraser took a gulp of his vodka and lime and lowered his voice significantly. Malcolm had to press his face right up to him to hear.

'He's taking me to Rome.'

'What?'

'He says he's going back at the end of next month and wants me to be his secretary.'

'And that attracts you?'

'At least it'll get me out of this hellhole. My father has been making life a misery recently. He still goes on about me getting married. I don't know why my mother hasn't tipped him the word. She's definitely caught on.'

'If you go to Rome she'll think you're planning to become a priest. That'll go down a bomb. And can you face a lifetime of fucking?'

'He's sure to calm down sooner or later. I don't have any choice. I keep worrying about those terrible voices coming back. And the archbishop has been discredited. He won't stay in that job much longer and it was him that took me on. Whoever replaces him will want to make a clean sweep of things. I risk losing everything.'

'You risk ruining your health the other way, if you ask me.'

'Oh, we take precautions. After the first time, I insisted.'

'That's not what I meant. You're a wreck as it is. What are you going to look like after six more months of this regime?'

Euphemia bought Daniel another drink. He took it, feeling embarrassed that he had not been in touch with her.

'Things are going fine in Falkirk,' he said. 'I would have contacted you if I had needed to.'

She dismissed his apologies with a wave of her hand.

'Haven't you noticed who's got his eyes on you?' she asked.

Daniel looked perplexed.

'Just over there, by the cash register.'

As he turned round cautiously his eyes met those of the red-haired man from the train. He wasn't wearing a suit now, but a pale flannel shirt open at the neck. His padded jerkin was slung over his shoulder. The man held Daniel's eyes significantly, then turned back to his friends.

'Don't move,' said Euphemia. 'Wait here and let him come to you. I'm off to the powder room. Then I want to talk to Charmaine.'

She took her drink with her. Daniel stood stock still, not daring to turn his head. His heart was beating fast. Someone squeezed in at the bar between him and the person next to him. He moved back. It was the man.

'Care for another?' he asked, although Daniel's glass was full.

'I'll have a half.'

'Tom Jamieson,' said the man, staring at him hard, and holding out his hand. His sky blue eyes were bleary. He was evidently mildly sozzled.

'Daniel Kane,' he answered.

As they shook hands, the man gave a broad smile.

'Want to join me and my chums?' he asked, pointing over his shoulder with his thumb.

'Funny thing is, he has an inexhaustible supply of condoms,' Fraser was saying.

'Where can he get them from? I hardly see a priest going into the chemist's and buying them across the counter.'

'And he has the most hilarious stories about the Vatican. His

English is so bad I can't always be sure he means what he appears to be saying.' Fraser chuckled.

'Go on then, tell me,' said Malcolm, egging him on.

'It's absolutely blasphemous. But it's very funny. And the thing is I suspect it might be true.'

'Well?'

'You know about the third letter of the Madonna of Fatima?'

Malcolm reflected for a moment.

'I think I've forgotten. Fill me in.'

'Well, at the beginning of this century Our Lady appeared to some children on a hillside in Portugal. And she gave them three messages. The third is kept in an envelope and only the Pope gets to see it. It's supposed to foretell a huge catastrophe. But not according to Felipe.'

Fraser was laughing so much he had to stop. The people near to them glanced round, amused.

'Well, what does it say?' asked Malcolm, smiling but bewildered.

Tears were streaming down Fraser's cheeks.

' "Use a condom!" ' he spluttered.

The second conversation was not that much more interesting than the first. Tom was a lawyer, a junior partner in a city firm, and his friends were well-heeled professionals to a man, a little older than Colm's, and quite unconcerned about religion. Tom had recently bought a new flat and had moved back to his parents' home in Falkirk while alterations were being carried out. That was why he had been on the train. There was much talk of curtains and shades of paint. When Daniel announced he was at the art school, they began discussing, rather competitively, the paintings they had bought or were going to buy.

Daniel's mind drifted back to his drawings. All that mattered was that he was standing next to Tom, who kept very close and from time to time touched him, on the shoulder or the back of the neck or just above the waist. In no time at all they were calling for last orders. He had forgotten completely about Colm.

Tom turned to him. He was slightly taller and thoroughly merry by now.

'So who's taking you home tonight?' he asked.

'You are,' said Daniel.

'Congratulations,' said Bruce Marshall, wringing Alan's hand. 'This is an absolute coup. With the statue being smashed to pieces yesterday and the end of the miracle all over the papers today, we're going to have half of Scotland glued to their sets.'

'Don't mention it,' said Alan nervously. 'I honestly did very little. They offered it to me on a plate. And thanks for laying on the babysitter.'

He gestured towards a corner of the studio where a professional childminder in a pale blue uniform was playing with an entranced but sleepy Hector.

'It was the least I could do, old chap,' smiled Bruce, and patted him on the back. 'We need to talk about getting you in here full time again.'

No expense had been spared for what promised to be the highlight of the series. A panel of experts had been assembled, including a psychologist, a sexologist and a feminist. Representatives of the clergy and laity of Catholic and other denominations were among the carefully selected audience. A specialist in paranormal phenomena had even been rushed over from Edinburgh in a taxi. The contributors were arranged in a semicircle, with pride of place left in the middle for Brenda and Cyril. Two huge placards with blown-up photographs formed the backdrop. On one the laughing madonna on her pedestal towered above a seething mass of worshippers. The other showed the heap of shattered fragments vandals had reduced her to in the course of the previous night.

Alan gave the make-up girls an exceptionally hard time. Loss of sleep caused by Hector's colic had left dark circles beneath both eyes. He refused to leave his seat until he was satisfied that they had restored his looks to pristine condition. Next he painstakingly checked his schedule with the production secretary, annotating the running order on his clipboard.

He was to stand within the semicircle with his back to the cameras. A single cameraman concealed to one side would focus on his face. Moving to and fro he would direct the discussion, putting questions or giving his own views as he deemed fit. Bruce felt this new, dynamic format was more appropriate than an armchair discussion. Alan would either stir the flames of polemic or pour oil on troubled waters. It was the unpredictability that made programmes of this sort so exciting. And so nerve-racking.

The contributors were to sit patiently through the first ten minutes while Alan conducted an in-depth interview with the woman who had once been Mother Genevieve. She had insisted on having her newly acquired partner at her side throughout the transmission. Bruce had encouraged Alan to sideline him as much as possible. After all, Mother Genevieve had sparked the miracle off in the first place. Braithwaite was little more than an appendage.

The audience were hushed and the studio lights went down. All eyes turned to the green bulb on the panel beneath the producer's box. It flashed on.

'Welcome to tonight's edition of "Issues of Faith". We are privileged to have with us this evening the person at the centre of Scotland's biggest religious controversy of the decade. The woman in question, as I am sure you all know, is Mother Genevieve, formerly of Saint Bridget's Oratory in Glasgow's West End. She has recently reverted to her old name of Brenda MacCafferty and, if the latest newspaper reports are to be trusted, may soon be changing yet again when she marries her companion, Father Cyril Braithwaite, formerly of Saint Benedict Episcopalian Cathedral, also in Glasgow.

'Mother Genevieve, or shall I call you Brenda?, is there a connection between the miracle and your decision to marry?'

Brenda paused for a moment.

'Yes, I suppose there is.'

'Would you like to tell us about it?'

'I'm afraid I would find that rather difficult.'

This did not bode well. Beads of sweat broke out on Alan's forehead.

'Are you a believer in miracles?'

'Oh yes, I most definitely am.'

'And could you explain exactly what sort of a miracle took place at St Pius XXVII's?'

There was another pause. Brenda looked very hard into the camera.

'That isn't what I came here to talk about.'

Alan felt giddy. The blood was throbbing at his temples. He could see Bruce gesturing wildly to him from one side of the placards.

'I wanted to say something else,' she proceeded in a steady voice. 'And I hope that everyone in Glasgow and throughout central Scotland can hear me, because this is really important. On the second Monday in November three babies were taken from the convent I used to be in charge of. I don't know who took them or how. I don't even know who the fathers are, though I know the mothers. Two of the babies have been recovered. A man brought the third to a police station in Maryhill, but they turned him away. If any of you . . .'

There was a resounding crash. Her voice tailed off. The programme's presenter had fainted. His body was stretched out on the floor in full view of the cameras and at the centre of the semicircle of astonished and amused contributors.

☆

'Where's your assistant?' asked Fr Flynn.

Mick McFall shrugged.

'Perhaps he lost his nerve. He's always had problems coping with the supernatural. This isn't the first time he's chickened out.'

Fr Flynn curled his lip. They were about to cross University Avenue on the way from the chaplaincy to Otago Street. It was a fiercely cold night. Teachers and boys were wrapped up so tightly they could have been in swaddling clothes. Their breath rising in clouds around them added to the eeriness of the scene.

The limousine arrived as they rounded the corner. Fr Feenan dismounted and helped the archbishop out on to the pavement. Mick was relieved and a little surprised to discover that No. 98 was there. Evidently the recreants they were pursuing had opted for a confrontation. It would have been so easy for them to make the tenement vanish again. A shiver went down his spine. He would have preferred them to be cowardly. If they stood their ground they evidently thought they had a chance of winning.

The exorcists lined up in a matter of minutes. Fr Feenan went first, carrying a huge cross used only for the grandest of rituals in the cathedral. He was flanked by two tall prefects bearing giant candles. The archbishop came next, supported on either side by shivering and coughing altarboys in black copes and white surplices. He had a service book in a black leather pouch under his arm. After a great deal of footering, the other prefects had managed to ignite the incense in their thuribles. The smell was powerful and heady and gave the party a sorely needed boost of confidence. Everybody knew demons could not stand incense. The schoolmasters brought up the rear with the relics of Blessed Williamina. Alphonsus MacAweaney's quavering tenor voice rose in the school hymn as the procession moved off. A few of the boys joined in half-heartedly.

The vanguard came to a halt on the top landing. Mick hurried to the fore. He had undertaken to pick the lock if need be. The storm doors were folded back and the guttering light of the candles was reflected uncannily in the glass pane of the door. Only darkness was beyond. Mick rang the bell once. There was no answer. He tried again. Never one to waste an effort, he turned the handle. The door swung open. It had not even been locked. Such carelessness could only be a challenge.

Everyone fell silent when they shuffled into the hall. Panic seized Mick as he realized he was once more invading Euphemia's territory. He gripped the cameo of Blessed Williamina in his right coat pocket and the rosary beads in his left. The palms of his hands were sticky. There was a thin bar of light under the sitting-room door. He flung it open. Someone was sitting reading in front of a blazing fire. The armchair prevented him seeing whether it was Euphemia or not.

A middle-aged man, small and rather hunched, with very thick spectacles, rose and turned to face them.

'Edwin MacFarlane,' he said. 'Delighted to make your acquaintance, gentlemen. I won't trouble you to sit down. The police should be at the bottom of the stairs by now.'

☆

Fred didn't have to go in to the Orange Sun Café and had decided to spend the day in bed with the Sunday papers. Possessed by inexplicable enthusiasm, his lover had gone into the kitchen to tackle the week's washing-up. The skies beyond the window were like ragged cotton wool, stained varying shades of grey, with here and there a rift of light where the sun broke through. It had been drizzling gently since before midday.

He felt cold on his own under the duvet, and he needed to get up to find the colour section. Knowing his lover it would probably be in the toilet. He got up and, unable to locate a clean pair of underpants, simply pulled on his faded black jeans. Peering out across the wasteland in front of their tenement, he was puzzled to spot a huddle of coloured umbrellas. He called his lover.

'Those women are trying to light a fire,' he said incredulously, pointing his finger. 'Funny way to spend a wet Sunday afternoon.'

☆

'We should have brought some petrol,' Daphne McGlone was saying.

'Too dangerous. I was sure firelighters would do the trick,' muttered Sandra Luperini.

'It's crucial to destroy the evidence,' said Dorothy Gallaher.

'The problem is the rain. They just won't burn,' complained Frances MacAweaney, shivering from the cold.

Dorothy knelt on the muddy ground and blew hard on the struggling flames.

'What a horrible smell,' she said.

'It was good of Mrs Donnelly not to give us away,' said Marie Therese McLaughlin.

'Have you confessed yet?' asked Daphne.

'Confessed? What's going on? One minute we're doing God's work and the next we have to ask absolution for it!' said Sandra.

'I'm sad it's all over,' said Dorothy. 'It was so much fun. I feel there's nothing more to look forward to.'

'We'll think of something else,' said Daphne.

☆

'So you shopped the lot of them,' said Alan.

'What else was I to do?' asked Craig. 'I wasn't going to break the law, and I'd passed my accountancy entrance exams. Was I supposed to acquire a criminal record before I ditched the job?'

The two brothers were communing over a fraternal pint.

'You've nothing to be ashamed about. I find the whole business absolutely comical. What happened to them?'

'The schoolboys were released almost immediately, but they kept the rest in overnight for questioning. It was too much for the archbishop and Mick. The suggestion was that they could be referred to a psychiatrist and charges dropped. The archbishop has gone back into hospital. Things could be even nastier for Flynn, Feenan and the teachers.'

'And the Basque guy kept his hands clean?'

'They wouldn't let him in on it. There's something about him that makes my flesh creep.'

'I know what you mean,' said Alan, and took a gulp from his pint. 'Fraser's been seeing a lot of him recently.'

'It's worse than that,' said Craig. 'That priest is taking him back to Rome.'

'Well, I suppose it reduces the chances of Mum and Dad ever finding out,' said Alan. 'It would kill him, at any rate.'

There was a pregnant pause.

'Do you think it runs in the family? I mean, that our children . . .'

Alan looked at his brother and burst out laughing. The idea struck him as ridiculous.

'It's not like the flu, you know. You can't catch it that easily. And Fraser's not a bad guy. He's had a very hard time.'

'Talking of children, where's the baby?'

'He's at home. Mum's looking after him.'

Craig was astonished.

'But I thought she swore she'd never have anything to do with it!'

'She's come round. She still refuses to tell Dad or to have us in the house. But she's started visiting and she agreed to look after Hector this evening. Dad thinks she's at the Bingo. It means I can't stay out very late.'

He checked his watch. Craig looked at the bandage on his forehead.

'That was some gash you got when you fell over,' he commented.

Alan nodded but said nothing. He did not like to think of himself as the sort of person who faints.

'So you met the mother . . .' said Craig, feeding his brother a tentative line.

'Yes.'

'And what did you decide?'

'I refused to give it back.'

Craig, on the point of finishing his pint, put the glass down untouched. He was thunderstruck.

'Are you off your head? You were so desperate to get rid of the thing. You told me it wasn't even yours!'

The idea that his big brother had been lying to him really hurt.

'Look,' expostulated Alan, embarrassed and irritated at the same time, 'Hector's been with me for twelve weeks now. That's more time than he spent with his mother. Looking after a baby isn't like taking a friend's dog in while they go off on holiday. You get attached. I don't expect you to understand. I can't imagine what it would be like being without him. And he's brought me luck.'

'What did they pay you for the *NME* interview?'

'I won't tell you the exact figure, but it was as much as I could earn in four months at the BBC. Now Ceòl want me to do an article for a New York magazine and *New Musical Express* are so taken with me they've commissioned another two pieces.'

'What was she like?' asked Craig, his mind drifting back to Hector and his mother.

'Spunky. And pretty too. She cried when I refused to hand Hector over.'

Alan had cried too, before Juliet and Brenda came, at the prospect of giving the baby up. But he didn't tell Craig that.

'I asked her to move in. On a purely Platonic basis, of course.'

'You don't fancy her?'

'I don't know. It would feel strange, making love with Hector's mother.'

☆

Tom grabbed hold of Daniel.

'That's the third time you've woken up screaming,' he said.

'I know,' said Daniel.

'You don't need to apologize,' said Tom, drawing him in closer. 'Same dream?'

'I don't quite remember. Something about coffins and graves.'

'Gerald still there?'

'Of course he was,' Daniel answered sharply. 'Am I ever going to be free of this thing?'

They settled down to sleep again. The difference in height meant that if they lay facing the same way Daniel fitted neatly into the curve of Tom's body, and they could play at dribbling with their feet until they got tired.

'Ever thought of seeing anyone about it?' prompted Tom.

'I do,' said Daniel, and told him about the attic room with the coombed roof, the collection of teddy bears and Mr MacFarlane.

They were silent for a while.

'You know what?' said Tom. 'I think you should move in.'

Daniel grunted.

'It's frustrating seeing each other only at weekends. What's the point of you coming and going from Falkirk every day? You could get to the art school on foot from here.'

Daniel turned to face him.

'It would be against the law. I'm under age.'

Tom thought for a moment.

'It's not against the law for you to live here. Or for us to share a bed. Only for us to have sex together. And who's going to testify that we do that?'

'My parents?'

Tom laughed.

'That's the last thing they'd do. They're out to avoid scandal at all costs. We'd be OK. It'd just mean we'd have to be careful. Discreet.'

'And what about my stuff?'

'We could go and get it from your parents' house. I'm not worried about facing up to them. That would be it over and done with.'

Daniel pictured Tom's bright red Dyane with the roll-back roof parked at the front door while they loaded everything into the boot. He liked the idea.

'Think about it?'

'I will,' said Daniel, and snuggled closer.

He told Tom about Mr MacFarlane but not about the other dream. More than a dream it was a section of a bigger story. In part it had come to him, in part he had made it up. It lacked a beginning and an end. He wondered if he was supposed to invent these. He called it the Dream of the Bleeding Boy.

It happened in the past, in a metropolis in the south of Europe, maybe near the sea, with a very grand opera house. There was a huge foyer with a magnificent central staircase. Rows of boxes opened off the corridors at each level. The characters were a man and an adolescent. The man worked there as stage manager, or front of house, Daniel couldn't make up his mind which. He liked sex a lot and would often pick up other men during or after the show, and take them home. The boy was very beautiful but rather mysterious. They made love gently, came in each other's hands, then fell asleep. During the night the man woke up. The sheets were hot and sticky. He switched the light on. The boy was still asleep and he was bleeding, bleeding so profusely that he had stained the sheets of delicate white linen a brilliant red, as if he was painting them with his own blood. He could produce an endless flow without getting anaemic. His cheeks were as flushed as ever. The man woke the boy up and he was horrified when he saw what had happened. Apparently this wasn't the first time, although it might have been the first time someone else had been present. He pretended to go back to sleep but the next morning the boy was gone. After a couple of days the man gave his job up and set out in pursuit of the boy. That was where the story ended for the time being.

Daniel wept profusely when he told Mr MacFarlane about the dream. Mr MacFarlane held his hand and kept repeating: 'Yes, but he's alive, he's alive!'

☆

'I'm not ill. I'm burning through,' said Euphemia in exasperation.

This was just another of the very odd things she had taken to saying recently.

'But it's obviously a fever. Don't you think we ought to call a doctor?' asked Cissie.

Euphemia laughed derisively.

'I'd like to see what one of your doctors would make of me. He'd be totally out of his depth. It always gets like this when I stay longer than planned. The matter can't hold out. Too much strain. Touch me. I'm burning, amn't I?'

It was true. Her face reminded Cissie of those she had seen on an Italian bus at the height of summer, grey and puffy, rigid because the people were doing their best not to move in that burdensome heat.

'Cissie,' said Euphemia gravely, 'this is the last time we are going to meet. When it's all over I want you to get up and leave the flat. Don't take anything with you. Throw the key into running water. Water, do you hear me? It's most important. And do the same with anything I may have given you or you may have taken away from here. And never come back. Do not even set foot in this street. Do you promise?'

Cissie nodded in consternation.

'But what do you mean, "when it's all over"? What's going to happen? You're not going to die?'

'Die?' Euphemia was contemptuous. 'I don't even know the meaning of the word. Let's go into the sitting room. I want you to read to me.'

She took down a book from the shelf. Bound in fine red leather, it was delicately tooled and inlaid with designs in gold. She settled Cissie on the sofa, then sat in the armchair by the window, adopting her characteristic, very upright pose.

'Begin around the middle,' she commanded. 'Don't let the illustrations distract you.'

'*While the seventh, eighth and ninth orders patrol the outer battlements, vying in splendour with the precious stones adorning the walls of that great fortress, it is given to the tenth and eleventh to direct the winds and mould the clouds, to set the surface of the earthly waters trembling, to fill out the sails of ships and guide the tides—*'

'No, that won't do,' interrupted Euphemia. 'Try further on.'

'*Those of the second, third and fourth orders cannot take on visible form. So powerful is the light that burns within them that any material covering they might assume would be reduced to ashes in a matter of seconds. But it is given to the fifth and sixth to clothe themselves in matter of changeable aspect and to subsist in this condition for periods varying from as little as three or four hours to as much as a year, but rarely longer. While in material form their suffering is great, for they must constantly strive to contain their energy lest it destroy the envelope of matter and in so doing harm those mortals who . . .'*

For a while now Cissie had been conscious of strange noises coming from behind her shoulders. Her curiosity got the better of her and she broke off to look round. The postcards in Euphemia's collection were coming unstuck and fluttering to the ground. As each one fell, the angels on it struggled to free themselves and took form in the air of the room. The movement of their wings ruffled the remaining cards, shaking them down more quickly. The angels grew alarmingly in size as they emerged. They might have been hurtling towards Cissie from the bottom of a deep, dark cone, or magnified by a zoom lens whose focus span round with unbelievable rapidity. Now she knew the smell of angel's wings. It recalled at one moment orange blossoms in hot sun, at another almonds toasting gently beneath a grill. The soft plumes brushed her face and tickled her nostrils. She let go of the book and covered her eyes with her hands, so blinding was the brightness that emanated from them.

On that same trip to Italy she and Rob had spent several nights in a hilltop village. Their room gave on to the square at the summit of the hill. Every evening before sunset, swallows and swifts took part in a frantic race, swirling round beneath the eaves at headlong speed, driven by the sheer rushing exultation of flight. This was what the angels were now doing in Euphemia's sitting room. The circular movement grew faster and faster. Cissie took her hands away and saw that a space had cleared. The angels were rising far from her, getting smaller and smaller, and in their centre, lifted ever higher, soared the body of her friend. At last all she could see were her feet, like tiny pinpricks, as the chorus of angel voices faded, murmuring: 'Euphemia! Euphemia!'

☆

Alan had finally succeeded in getting Hector off to sleep. When he came back into the front room Juliet was kneeling by the gas fire. She had lit a cigarette.

'Is it a good idea for you to smoke?' he asked. 'I mean, the baby . . .'

'I don't normally,' she said. 'I'll stop soon. It's just to get me through a difficult period.'

He flopped into an armchair. He was worn out, physically and emotionally.

'You're so much better at it than me,' she said. 'I think I've lost the knack.'

'Don't worry. It'll come back. It's just that you've been separated for so long. Babies change very quickly.'

In the silence, against the purring of the fire, he could hear her drawing the smoke into her lungs. She looked at the cigarette, got up and stubbed it out.

'Time for bed,' she said.

'Go ahead,' said Alan. 'I'll pull out the divan.'

She stared at him in amazement.

'What do you mean?'

'I'm going to sleep in here.'

She sat down and brooded for a while.

'Don't you find me attractive?'

'Oh, no,' he said, 'quite the reverse. It's just that . . . We don't have to . . . I didn't assume . . .'

She laughed. 'It's a bit like the Holy Family, isn't it? I wonder if Mary and Joseph . . . ?'

He laughed, too. She came over and kissed him. The sweet, faintly rotten taste of tobacco on her lips aroused him. He put his arms around her. Her shoulders were very slim.

'After all,' she said, 'childbirth is the tough part. I've missed out on all the fun.'

☆

The airport bus sped along the motorway. Their luggage was safely stored in the boot but Felipe had insisted on keeping his briefcase with him. Now he nudged Fraser, and opened it ever so slightly. It was stuffed with condoms. Fraser felt nauseous.

Felipe snapped it shut and took a package from his pocket.

'For you,' he said tenderly.

When Fraser unwrapped it he found a bunch of gaudily painted flowers in plaster that appeared to have been broken off from a larger composition. Suddenly he realized.

'It's from the madonna!' he cried. 'You don't mean it was you who . . . ?'

Felipe shrugged and smiled.

'We had to,' he said. 'There was no udder wee.'

☆

It was a gloriously sunny afternoon in May. Daniel had parked Tom's car at the top of the slope leading down into Tighnabruaich, and taken up position with his sketchbook and watercolours in the centre of a field. The Kyles of Bute were stretched out before him, with Bute itself, Colintraive and the Cowal peninsula a succession of pale green ridges against the cloudless sky. In that light the contours were so sharp he could have sworn they had already been shaded in with a pencil. He was trying to mix a colour that would approximate to the green of a clump of Scots pines down at the water's edge.

He paused to look at the words written to one side and along the bottom of the page he was at work on. More and more now, as he painted, phrases and sentences would come into his head, and the only way to get rid of them was to jot them down next to his sketches in this way.

He read over what he had written that morning. It sounded like the beginning of a poem. Maybe Euphemia had been right after all.